"It's in my blood, Cece. I love this sport. But I can't stand by and let it endanger people's lives...."

"I know," she said, bending to kiss Blain's cheek. But the way it felt when her lips connected with his skin...well, it made her want to kiss something else.

No, she warned herself. She shouldn't. This wasn't a fantasy. This was a flesh-and-blood man.

"Blain, I don't think this is a good id—"

He pulled her to him, kissed her hard, and Cece settled onto his hard thighs as if she'd done it a million times before—and in her dreams, maybe she had. Only this was so much better than her fantasies.

pamela britton

dangerous CURVES

HQN™

ISBN 0-373-77035-9

DANGEROUS CURVES

Copyright © 2005 by Pamela Britton

This edition published by arrangement with Harlequin Books S.A.

® and TM are trademarks of the publisher. Trademarks indicated with ® are registered in the United States Patent and Trademark Office, the Canadian Trade Marks Office and in other countries.

www.HQNBooks.com

Printed in U.S.A.

Dedicated to Doug and Robin Richert,
two of NASCAR's finest.

Acknowledgments

I have to be honest in admitting that when I proposed writing a romantic suspense, I never realized the amount of research it would involve. The crime dramas on TV are nothing like real life, and so it's with much gratitude that I thank the following people for answering all my tedious law-enforcement questions.

Mark Kolla and the gang at Sean and Donna's wedding who graciously spent time helping me to straighten out my plot (in between drinking screwdrivers), and with a special thanks to my brother-in-law, Michael Mattocks, who never laughs at my silly ideas.

My pal in the FBI who asked not to be named (I could tell you, but then I'd have to kill you). *Thank you!* Thank you, thank you, thank you for answering all my questions about bombs, protective custody and what it's really like to be a female agent in an office full of men. You're an angel.

Lastly, as always, to my wonderful husband, a man who knows intuitively when I need to be left alone, and who's one heck of a plotting partner. I love you, Michael.

dangerous CURVES

CHAPTER ONE

SHE WAS FIVE FOOT SIX of spandex-wrapped, thigh-high-boots-wearing, bustier-clad woman. And she wasn't happy.

Shoving open the door of her boss's office, Cece Blackwell had to fight not to yell the words, "What do you mean I'm assigned the NASCAR case?"

The glare of fluorescent lights arched perfectly off her boss's prematurely bald head as he turned to face her, black brows—the color his hair should have been, if he'd had any—lifted above light gray eyes.

"I can't believe you'd do this to me," she added, placing her hands on her leather-clad waist, Cece so screaming mad she felt ready to lob her Carmen Miranda red earrings at him. Or maybe her matching bracelets. Yeah. They'd be easier to slip off.

"I won't do it," she huffed. "I won't." And darn if she didn't feel like stomping her feet like her neighbor's three-year-old daughter.

Bob's chubby-cheeked face remained blank. It was one thing she despised about him. No, envied, this ability he had to remain unruffled no matter what the circumstances. He was like one of those mimes you saw in the park, able to keep a straight face even as some dog doo-dooed on his leg. The talent was helped by the fact that he had wrinkle-free skin near impossible to glean the age of. Cece supposed Mother Nature had blessed him with such a complexion as a way of making up for the no hair thing.

But instead of addressing her concerns, Bob eyed her up and down. "You been working that organized crime ring?" he asked in his Bronx accent. "That's why you dressed like that?"

"You know I was," she said, referring to the rent-me-by-the-hour outfit she wore: rhinestone-studded black bustier, Band-Aid-wide leather skirt and the pièce de résistance, black thigh-high boots.

"The operative word being *was,* Bob," she gritted out between Screaming Red lips. "*Was* because they called me off the streets and told me I'd be working a new case, one that you know I have no desire to work. So tell me it isn't true, *Bob,* in which case I'll go change out of this hoochie wear, because if you tell me it *is* true, I quit."

"It's true," he said.

"I quit." She turned on a stiletto heel and jerked open the door.

"Cece, wait."

"Talk to the hand, Bob, 'cause the ears aren't listening."

"Damn it, Cece, you don't stop, you're fired."

She whirled to face him, hand falling off the handle. "I'm fired? *I'm* fired?" she raged, stabbing at herself with her finger, one of her fake press-on nails popping off and arcing through the hair like a boomerang. "You've got some nerve, you know that, Bob? You know about my past with the owner of that race team. You know every damn detail. And yet you're still assigning me this case? That'd be like—" she searched for the right words "—that'd be like me assigning you to work with your ex-wife." Bob winced. "I won't do it."

"You have to," he said, his face stern.

Her eyes narrowed. "No, I don't."

"This ain't no multiple choice, Cece. We need your expertise with explosives."

"Oh, yeah? Just like you needed my expertise working that organized crime ring? I've spent four weeks dressed like this. Four weeks and I'm this close to finding out the name of the guy who sold Mantos those explosives. You want me to walk away from that? I don't think so. Find someone else with the expertise."

"We want *you*."

Cece tottered over to Bob's desk, not caring that her breasts all but fell out as she leaned over the papers strewn on it. "Look, Bob, I've had a really bad day. Some man offered me a hundred bucks if I'd let him sniff my underwear. Another asked me to do a threesome. An evangelist talked my ear off for an hour because he was convinced he could save my soul. To say I'm in no mood for this would be an understatement. My feet hurt, I have a rub spot on the back of my knee and I'm convinced a bird pooped in my hair, only, see, I can't tell because makeup decided to turn my hair into their version of the Burning Bush, sans the flames, although there's so much hair spray in this mess—" she pointed at her teased and cemented blond hair "—I could give Michael Jackson a run for his money." She leaned even closer, her bonded hair not budging an inch. "Don't do this to me."

"It'd just be for a few days."

"This close to busting Mantos," she repeated, making tweezers out of her scarlet-red nails.

"Just think about it."

"Okay," she said straightening, looking up to the ceiling and tapping a red nail on her chin as if contemplating the color of a toupee for Bob. "Thought about it," she said, piercing him with a glare. "No."

Bob flung himself back in his chair, tossing a Snappy Lube pencil onto his desk. "You're impossible."

"Yeah, well, that's why we work so well together." She turned toward the door.

"I could force you."

"Don't bother," she called over her shoulder.

"I'm your boss," he added.

"Then act like it and tell upper management I said no."

A wolf whistle greeted her as she entered the

"bull pen," a maze of cubicles that housed the junior agents.

"Bite me," she said to no one in particular as she slammed Bob's office door with enough force to rattle the side window. She jabbed her spiked heels into the business-brown carpet as she stormed off to her office in another corner of the mostly glass highrise, the muted gray light that dribbled in mimicking the fog outside.

Damn Bob. Of all the dumb, fool things to ask her.

She jerked open the door of her office before slamming it closed. For a long second she just seethed as she stared out the window.

Blain Sanders. A name from the past. A man who'd been responsible for more humiliating teenage memories than she cared to admit. Even now she felt the sting of a blush as she recalled some of her more embarrassing moments—trying to get an afterschool job at the same place as he did, only to have him call her a stalker; slipping that ridiculous note that was supposed to be anonymous in his locker, only to have Billy Richards see her do it. And then, their senior year, she'd tried to get even with him by building a car that was faster than his. She'd succeeded at that, but then her dad died and her whole world had come crashing down.

Cece bent to grab some spare clothes from a filing cabinet drawer, trying to forget the memories, but like oil on top of water, they refused to be kept down; her dad's car accident, her brush with the law, her mom's death…some of the worst times of her life.

"Well, well, well. If it isn't Cecilia Blackwell."

She froze, her hands on some sweats, thinking maybe, just maybe, the voice had been part of a hair spray induced hallucination, because it was impossible for the day to get any worse then it already had.

Famous last words.

"I see you're dressing different."

But only one person called her by her full name like that, the syllables clipped like the snap of a 9 mm. She closed her eyes for a sec before opening them again to slowly turn and face the door.

Ten long years and a forgotten high school crush faced her.

Blain Sanders.

Terrific. Perfect timing.

"Well, well, well," she mimicked, "if it isn't the hometown hero." And she used her coolest I'm-an-FBI-agent-even-if-I'm-dressed-like-a-call-girl voice. She hadn't survived a year of coed training to blush when caught wearing next to nothing. Besides, he didn't seem to care, merely met her gaze directly.

"You're looking good," he said, and she knew he was being sarcastic 'cause there was no way, no how that Blain Sanders found her attractive.

"Gee, thanks," she answered, her mind screaming a different answer.

Get out.

Damn it. She'd fantasized about this moment, about meeting him again, but always in a chic black suit, black pumps and her hair pulled back in a smooth chignon. Instead she wore fishnet stockings—*fishnets,* for goodness' sake—next to no clothes and a head of hair big enough to be spotted by the Space Shuttle while he...*he* looked like he'd stepped from the pages of *People* magazine.

She eyed him up and down in an impartial I'm-no-longer-affected-by-him way. Rain-colored eyes still looked just as striking against a fringe of long, dark lashes. Strong jaw. Wide shoulders and a body that hadn't gained an ounce of fat in the ten years she'd gone up two sizes.

"Nice outfit," he said. It was the same voice as before, only...different. This voice dripped Southern like a jar of maple syrup, not surprising since he'd spent the last ten years of his life working the stock car circuit. Blain—California born and bred—had apparently adopted redneck ways.

"You always dress like that?"

What the heck do you think? she almost snapped. Instead she flicked her teased-and-shellacked hair and said, "Well, the dress code is pretty lax around here. I do what I can to be comfortable."

He lifted a brow. She placed her hands on her hips, giving him a stance à la Wonder Woman right down to the conical breasts.

"Of course I don't dress this way," she muttered. "I was doing an undercover gig on the East Side."

"The FBI lets you walk around that way?"

"Didn't someone tell you?" she snapped. "I'm not really FBI. Got the badge and gun out of a gumball machine. I was hoping for the Scooby-Doo necklace, but I guess it just wasn't my day."

His eyes darted to hers again. For half a heartbeat she thought she saw something drift through his silver gaze—interest, maybe—but she had to be seeing things. Blain Sanders. Mr. Celebrity. Mr. I Can Have Any Woman I Want. Mr. What's Your Name Again Sweetheart So I Can Sign Your Junior High Yearbook would *not* be noticing her. It used to drive her crazy when she'd had that huge crush on him because nothing, but nothing she'd said or did—and oh boy, had she done some things—ever made him remember her name, much less show interest in her.

Nah. Imagining things.

"If you're here to tell me you don't want me on the case," she said, "you're wasting your breath. I don't want it, either."

He crossed his arms in front of him, his pecs beneath his shirt bulging like those of a beach-bound muscle man. "Actually, I came here to tell you that it was me who wanted you *on* the case."

BLAIN WATCHED HER mouth gape in surprise, her startling green eyes grow wide. He'd forgotten the color of those eyes until that very moment; "antifreeze-green" he'd used to tease. She really did look ridiculous in that getup, or so he told himself because he did not, as a rule, find women in thigh-high boots attractive.

"Why the heck would you do that?" she snapped, the red hoop earrings she wore swinging with each jerk of her angry jaw, her boots squeaking as she shifted on her feet.

He shrugged, his eyes darting around the office. Wall of glass behind her, the California fog he didn't miss much creeping through the streets. Bachelor of Arts degree on the wall to his left. No pictures on the opposite one, to his right. Not even those "love your fellow co-worker" posters. Nothing but bare walls, a low shelf and a CD player behind her black-and-gray desk conspicuously devoid of files and clutter. Man, she didn't even have one of those little stuffed toys most women hung on their monitor. Typical Cece Blackwell. She was about as feminine as a case of motor oil.

"Hell-ooo," she reminded him of her presence. As if he could forget.

"You're the best person for the job," he stated.

"Well, you can just un-request me."

His eyes swung back to hers. "No," he surprised himself by saying—surprised, because during the whole trip from North Carolina he'd told himself he'd made a mistake in insisting she be assigned the case. He must be more shaken up over Randy's death than he'd thought, because requesting that Cece Blackwell work the case when all he had were some half-baked rumors about her success as an FBI agent was pure craziness. And yet here he was.

She'd changed, he thought, unable to stop himself from scanning her up and down. She looked like a woman. Granted, not the type of woman he'd be attracted to, but a woman nonetheless.

And that kind of perplexed him. She'd grown breasts since he'd last seen her.

"Excuse me, Blain, but I must have misunderstood you because I could have sworn you just said 'it was me who requested you,' which doesn't make any sense because that would mean you were willing to work with me, something I know from experience would be the last thing on earth *you'd* want to do. So let's go over this again. Did you or did you not just say that you requested me for this case?"

"I did."

She gave him a look, one he remembered from their youth. It usually meant a shovelful of sand or a sharp-tipped acorn was about to be thrown his way.

"Why in the heck would you do a stupid thing like that?"

"Like I said. You're the best."

"And just how do you know that?" she asked.

His gaze snapped up. "People back home talk."

She smirked, painted red lips compressing. "I haven't talked to anyone back home since my mom died."

"Not even Mr. Johnson?"

She closed her eyes, obviously recognizing the name. Mr. Johnson, ex-cop-turned-P.E.-teacher who had taken a shine to Cecilia Blackwell all through high school, especially when she'd chosen to pursue a career in law enforcement. He was also a big race fan, which was how Blain had kept up with Cece's life—though in an inadvertent way, because he wasn't interested in her.

He looked her up and down again.

Not interested at all.

"We talk on a regular basis," Blain admitted.

"I'm going to kill him," she said, and this time Blain eyed the column of her neck. Her skin looked soft there. Funny. The memories he'd carried of little Cecilia Blackwell were that of a grease-covered kid. One who'd had puppy love dangling from her stray dog eyes. Not the woman standing before him now. Taller. Long blond hair. Hourglass figure.

"Why? The old guy's proud of you. You're the only student of his that's gone any further than the local police department."

And Blain felt grudging respect for her. Most of their former classmates had never left town. Not so Cece. Like him, she'd struck out on her own. He admired that, no matter how much it irked him to admit it.

"Besides," he added, "who cares how I found out? What's important is that I know you'll be straight with me." He clenched his hands, trying to stifle emotions he didn't want her to see. "The president of our association refuses to postpone the next few races because we don't have proof that the wreck that killed my driver was no accident. All I have is a threatening letter that mentions a Cup race two weeks from now. Your bosses seem to think it's probably just a nutcase. NASCAR seems to think the same thing. I'm not so certain."

Blain had to look away for a second, hoping she didn't see how hard he fought for control at the memory of Randy.

Got a tire going bad.

They were the last words he'd said.

"I heard he was your driver," Cece said.

"He was." And his best friend. And his business partner.

"Sorry about your loss," she said, crossing her arms in front of her.

Not for Cece the show of sympathy most women would give him: the concerned touch, the sympathetic hug. No. She just tilted her head as she said, "But it still doesn't change the fact that this is a bad idea."

"I'm not going to beg." And he wouldn't, damn it. She *owed* him this.

"You don't have to. My answer is no."

He straightened and pulled out his trump card. "I'll tell your boss about the felony."

She paled beneath the makeup covering up the freckles he remembered. About the only thing still the same.

"What felony?" She tried to brazen it out.

"The one you got for stealing that car when you were seventeen. The one sealed now because you were a minor, but the one I'm sure you didn't tell the FBI about, since you were hired by them."

He found himself looking down at her, those wide green eyes. Pretty eyes, he'd always thought, despite the fact that he'd always teased her about them.

"Bastard."

He crossed his arms again and shrugged.

"You know damn well I didn't steal that car. Tommy Pritchert set me up to take the fall. I just happened to be driving the wrong car at the wrong time."

"Tell that to your boss."

She looked as if she wanted to throttle him. "You know well and good I can't do that."

"No. But I can."

And now she looked as if she wanted to bludgeon him.

"Did it ever occur to you that my successes as an FBI agent might be severely overrated?"

"Yeah." He took another step toward her. A hint of something tickled his nose. "You wearing perfume?" he asked in shock.

She tilted her head. "What of it?"

You build that car? he'd asked after she'd roared into the high school parking lot when they were seventeen.

What of it?

Same response. Same woman.

Or was it?

"Nothing," he answered—the same response he'd given her back then. "And even if Mr. Johnson *has* exaggerated, I remember the way you found out who'd keyed your car. You thought I'd done it, but instead you discovered that—"

"Rick Carpenter had done it," she finished.

"Yeah. My point being that the way you discovered who'd done it was pure genius."

"So let me get this straight," she said in a clipped voice, straightening, one hand held out, palm up. "You decided I'd be perfect for this case based on an idea I got off *Columbo?*"

"It worked. No one expected you to give a '69 Camaro away as bounty, but you did."

She shrugged. "I didn't give it away. I only let someone drive it for a week. The kid offered to buy it afterward and I let him. I'd beaten you enough times that I was through with it anyway."

Her words rankled—still, after all these years. Man, but she knew how to push his buttons. Even after he'd left the small town they'd grown up in he'd thought about the way she'd smoked his doors whenever they'd raced. Four championships and numerous awards later and he *still* couldn't believe she'd built a car that had beaten his. But he shouldn't let it rankle, he reminded himself. It was all the more reason to insist she work the case. No other agent this side of the Mississippi would have her knowledge of race cars. She was a pro. Plus an expert on explosives.

"Look, Cece, I don't know anybody else with the experience to solve this case. You're the closest thing to an ally that I've got and I need your help."

And for a second the wreck replayed in his mind again. Blain's knuckles ached, he clenched his fingers so hard. "I need your expertise. You'll give it to me, even if I have to blackmail you to do it."

She stared up at him, and he was surprised at how close he'd gotten. Age had changed her, he realized. Her cheekbones were more prominent. Lips fuller, her mouse-blond hair lighter, too.

"Fine," she snapped, her green eyes firing like spark plugs. "But don't blame me when it doesn't work out. You've no idea what it's like to work with someone you despise."

It was on the tip of his tongue to say he didn't despise her, but something made him hold back, something that made him feel uncomfortable and on edge at the same time.

But then, he always felt that way around Cece Blackwell.

CHAPTER TWO

THEY WERE SUPPOSED to meet at the San Francisco airport and fly to Las Vegas together for the Snappy Lube 500, a race Cece had heard about, but never seen live and in person. She'd been tempted to catch an earlier flight just so she could avoid him, but had decided that would be a cowardly thing to do—and she wasn't a coward.

Damn Bob.

And damn Blain for blackmailing her into this. It figured that her sworn enemy would have the wood on her.

She spun away from the window overlooking a bunch of jets, their engines revving with high-pitched whines. The smell of airplane fuel mixed oddly with pizza, the drone of flight attendants on the overhead speaker a constant buzz. On the landing strip a 747 braked, the roar of its reversed engines barely masked by the windows. To think, Blain Sanders usually flew around in his own jet. Must be nice.

"I should have resigned," she mumbled to herself.

Money was tight in the Blackwell household. Hell, she couldn't remember the last time she'd left town on a vacation. And yet here was Blain with his own jet, his own race team and countless other things Cece had only dreamed about.

Her overnight bag clocked her in the back as she turned again. She ignored the way the strap dug a furrow in her shoulder, just as she ignored the direction her thoughts had taken. A baby cried to her right. A teenaged couple fought over a wallet-sized CD player. And wherever she looked, race fans strolled or sat, all on their way to the track. They wore T-shirts, ball caps and jackets with team logos splashed across them. She spotted every sort of paraphernalia imaginable, from the ridiculous—tennis shoes with car numbers emblazoned on the sides—to the truly ridiculous—a suitcase shaped like a race car. Apparently a number of people, mostly men, didn't mind embarrassing themselves in public.

She'd taken only two steps when she saw who she was looking for: Blain-the-Blackmailer Sanders.

He strode toward their gate with the air of a man on a mission, or maybe someone who needed to relieve himself. Either way, he moved along at an impressive clip. He wore a tan leather jacket over a cream-colored turtleneck. His eyes scanned left and right, his big body parting the crowd like the prow of a ship. He reminded her of someone from Special Ops, not the owner of a race team. Women's eyes lingered. Men looked up, only to hastily look away. Blain seemed oblivious to it all.

Cece waited for him to spot her, but when his gaze slid over her and kept right on going, she stiffened. He didn't recognize her.

He stopped five feet away, his expression growing impatient. Checked his watch. Frowned. Looked up again.

Well, well, well. Granted, she wasn't in her hoochie-wear, but she didn't look *that* different. The face was the same even if the secondhand Ann Taylor suit—in basic black—and white cotton shirt were not. She'd pulled her hair back in a chignon, too, her face free of makeup. Okay, well, maybe not completely free. She'd dusted a bit of blush over her cheeks and a wisp of brown powder in the corner of her eyes, something one of her female co-workers had assured her would make them look bigger. All right, all right, and maybe she'd put mascara on, too. But that was it. Goodness knows she wasn't trying to impress Blain Sanders.

Speaking of which... "If you're looking for me," she called out, "I'm right here."

She watched him turn, watched his eyes zip right past her again, only to suddenly return with a snap. What ho? Did the lightbulb go on over his head?

It had.

He blinked, staring at her as if still disbelieving.

"What? You think I look better dressed as a prostitute?"

Someone walking by gave them a sharp glance—
a man, Cece noted. Race fan, she cataloged immediately. Midthirties. About five-eight. Beer gut his
most prominent feature.

You're not on the job, Cece. Chill out.

But she was always on the job, thanks to Mr.
Sanders here, and that irritated her all over again.

"Hey," the man said. "You're Blain Sanders."

Cece stiffened.

"You really are," the guy repeated.

The decibel level of his voice made Cece glance
around. Well, if they'd been trying to be inconspic-
uous, that plan had been shot to bits.

The man came forward, pudgy hand extended. "Mr.
Sanders," he said in a voice that sounded Bronxish.
"I'm your biggest fan." He pointed to his chest. "See?"

Oh, jeesh, the man had the pylon-orange Star Oil
logo emblazoned across his chest, the words Star Oil
Racing sprawled in fancy white script across the
shirt's black background.

"I can't believe it's really you."

"It's really me," Blain said, and was it her imagi-
nation or did his Southern voice sound anything but
hospitable?

"I mean, I've watched you for years. Even before you were with Star Oil. Since the time you
were with Mark Miller's team when you won your
first championship."

Oh, great. A bona fide groupie. Just what they
needed.

"I mean, this just makes my day."

Great, Cece silently said. *You go to Las Vegas with Blain. Have a terrific time.*

Blain's look clearly said *stay put.* That gave her pause. Had her expression been so transparent?

"Nice to meet you," Blain said taking the fan's hand.

The man grinned from ear to ear before looking her way, and Cece saw the moment he remembered that it was her prostitute comment that had drawn his attention in the first place.

She stiffened, about to set him straight, because it was obvious the guy thought her a working girl. Only a sudden thought came to mind, one of those thoughts she knew she should ignore, but she didn't because, jeesh, where Blain Sanders was concerned, you needed to get your licks in where you could.

"Blain darling," she drawled in a British accent. If she was going to be a prostitute, she was going to be a classy prostitute. "You said you'd get me a drink." She sidled up to him, placing her hand in his arm so she could walk her fingers up his biceps. "I'm thirsty," she pouted, looking up at him in what she hoped was a sultry fashion.

She saw his left eyelid twitch just before his light blue eyes narrowed.

Okay, so maybe this wasn't exactly professional. And maybe she shouldn't be such a cat, but she had a score or two to settle with the man, and some of that settling was going to happen right now.

"Don't make me wait," she added huskily.

"Oh, man. I'm sorry. You're busy," the man said. "Nice meeting you."

"Oh, no, don't go," Cece piped up before he could leave. "Blain adores having a chat with fans. At least I believe he does, but I'm afraid it's been a while since I last saw him. You know how it is." She smiled. "He's so busy he doesn't have time for a girl-friend." She glanced up at Blain. His eyes promised a slow death. "That's where I come in," she added, just out of spite. She turned back to the fan, bright-ening. "I say, would you like my card? I'm on call for Blain this week, but I could check my schedule for the next." She was proud of the way *schedule* came out. *Shhedual*. Very British.

The man apparently fell for it, at least judging by the way his mouth hung open. Blain made a noise, some sort of guttural growl. Very cavemanish.

Cece shifted her bag as if about to search through it.

"No, no," the man said, suddenly looking about as comfortable as a furrier at an animal-rights conven-tion.

She paused, eyes wide. "No? Oh, well. Too bad. We might have had a good time, you and I." She smiled mischievously, turning to Blain again and batting her eyelashes at him. "I'll just leave you two alone, then. Blain can, ah, catch up to me later."

The fan choked. Cece hooked a hand around the back of Blain's neck before he could move out of reach.

"Come here, darling, and give me a kiss."

Blain tried to draw back, his expression clearly warning *don't you dare*.

She smiled and silently answered, *Oh, I dare, Blain. I dare.*

Tell her boss about her felony, would he?

She tugged his head down, puckered her lips. He didn't go willingly, but he couldn't resist without causing a scene. She closed her eyes, realizing too late that she really didn't want to kiss him, either.

"Mmm, yummy," she purred just before their lips connected.

Wow.

She didn't know where that word came from, but touching lips with Blain was like dropping a bottle of nitro on the ground.

Blam.

Blain must have felt it, too, because his lips suddenly turned as hard as wheel hubs.

Cece jerked away, having the presence of mind to cover her confusion with a "Ta-ta," then turning on the heel of her black pump to saunter away, never mind that her nerves pinged an alarm at the way that kiss had made her feel...and the look of promised retribution in his eyes.

"Diet Coke," she said the moment she took a seat at the chrome and black vinyl bar not far away, tugging a bowl of Chex Mix in front of her. She'd been working too hard. That's why kissing him had felt so…well, odd. Working undercover made you forget things like what it's like to lay one on a sexy man.

Blain, sexy?

Well, yeah…sort of. Maybe.

She lobbed her thoughts away as she set her purse down next to the single-legged bar stool. It was a struggle to sit down while looking ladylike, but she managed, her reflection peeking out at her from between the necks of liquor bottles. Tightly drawn back ash-blond hair, glowing green eyes. She almost smiled at herself—almost, because from behind her suddenly appeared her nemesis. Blain.

Here we go.

"Don't you ever do that again," he drawled, and boy-oh-boy, did he look mad.

She swiveled, her legs brushing his. He glanced down, jerking back as if she'd said, "Boo."

"Don't do what, Blainy-poo?" she asked, tempted to run her foot up his shin just for kicks.

"You're not a prostitute, which is exactly what that man thought."

She kinda liked his accent, she decided, her eyes catching on his lips. They glistened from their kiss. She felt her gaze sharpen, disconcerted by the sudden lurch her stomach gave.

"What do you care what that guy thought?"

"I'm a celebrity and I don't like the possibility of some race fan getting on the Internet and telling people I'm into call girls."

She let out a quick "Oh, pul-leez" as her left leg

darted out involuntarily, almost as if it were determined to touch him of its own volition. His eyes followed the motion. She stopped. His eyes darted back up.

What was this? Was Blain Sanders looking at her legs? "A guy like that doesn't even own a computer." She swung her leg again. He glanced down.

He *was* looking at her legs.

"You might be surprised at how savvy race fans are. But that's not the point. The point is you shouldn't have kissed me," he said. Cece noticed that his eyes turned a deep, almost violet blue when angry.

She straightened as a new and unexpected discovery rolled through her. Blain Sanders was checking her out. He didn't want to check her out, she could tell, but he was definitely getting a fix on her.

She almost laughed because she would never, ever have thought the great man himself would stoop to eyeing *her* of all people.

"You're right. I shouldn't have."

But far from looking pleased at his small victory, he leaned toward her, and she could tell that she'd pushed him to the very edge of the short little pier he'd been standing on.

"Make sure it doesn't happen again," he snapped.

Oh, yeah? They would just have to see about that, Cece thought. Because there was one thing Mr. Blain Sanders didn't know. After her first year of college, when she'd realized men were looking at her in a way they'd never looked at her before, she'd used that knowledge to her advantage. Cece Blackwell had put herself through college working for Bimbos, a restaurant that prided itself more on the perkiness of its servers' breasts than on the freshness of its cuisine.

And the only thing she enjoyed more than McDonald's French fries was making men squirm, probably because most of her life men hadn't given her the time of day. Then she'd turned nineteen and voilà, sex goddess. It'd been darn disconcerting when the cutest guy on campus had asked her out. Who'd have thunk? But she'd never forgotten what it felt like to be the campus dog. So when she'd turned into Sleeping Beauty, she'd been smart enough to have fun with some Prince Charmings. Blain Sanders was no prince, but it'd be fun playing with him.

She'd make sure of it.

"IF ANYONE IN THE GARAGE asks how we know each other, just tell them we're old friends," Blain said as Cece Blackwell sat down next to him in one of the compact seats that filled the jet's interior. He looked over at her in time to see one side of her mouth tip up.

"What?" he asked.

"We were never friends," she said, her arm brushing his.

"Yeah, but we can't tell them the truth. NASCAR

doesn't want people to know an FBI agent is sniffing around."

"And why *did* you hate me so much?" she asked.

It took him a moment to follow her question, but not before he found himself asking, "Huh?"

"Why didn't you like me in school?"

He took his own seat, staring at her for a second as he replayed what she'd said, and then tried to frame his answer. "I didn't hate you," was all he could think of to say.

"Oh, you were never flat-out mean to me, but you didn't like me. That much was obvious." She reached beneath her to search for her seat belt. The movement opened up the shirt beneath her black jacket, giving him a glimpse of a white, frilly lace bra. Frilly? Since when?

"Look, Cecilia, I hardly knew you. How could I *hate* you?"

"Good point. But if that's true, why did you tell Jeff Mayer that he could do better than me when he and I started dating?"

What was she talking about…?

She lifted a brow as if trying to prod his memory. "We were at a convenience store and you saw me with him. I'd wandered off to another aisle and you must have thought I couldn't hear you, but I could." She tilted her head, a lock of blond hair slipping from behind her ear. "You told him the reason I lived in a double wide was because of the size of my ass."

He'd said *what?*

She smirked.

And then he remembered.

She lifted both brows this time, her expression turning to one of wry amusement. "It's coming back to you, isn't it?"

It felt like a welding torch had been lit near his face.

"So I'm sure you can understand why I thought you didn't like me."

She settled back in her seat. There wasn't much room between her and the seat in front of her, but she somehow managed to cross her legs, the look on her face a mix of smug and amused.

"Look," he said. "If I said something like that it was probably because I was sick and tired of you blabbing all over the school that your Camaro was faster than my Nova."

"It was."

"And because you told Gina Sellers that you wanted to ask me to the prom."

Her eyes widened.

"Yeah," he said. "I know about the crush you had. And so I was pretty certain that you weren't really interested in Jeff Mayer in any other way than getting closer to me."

Those green eyes of hers flickered with something. Humiliation? "You didn't know that for certain."

"Oh, yeah? Then why'd you dump him when I told him I didn't want him bringing you around?"

"I didn't dump him, he dumped *me*...because of *you*."

His body flicked back.

Her eyes narrowed. "You didn't know that, did you?"

And there was too much anger in her eyes for it not to be true. "He told me the opposite."

She leaned toward him, and the smell of her perfume hung between them for a second before a passing draft carried it away. It was a scent completely at odds with the image he'd carried around of her for years—acne medicine and car parts—not that he'd spent much time thinking about her. She smelled flowery. Almost feminine. Not like a tray of used motor oil.

"Look, Blain, I told you this was a really bad idea. You and I are like oil and water, always have been, always will. Why don't we just give this up right now?"

He stared across at her, at this new Cecilia Blackwell. Calm. Controlled. Not the pimple-faced girl he remembered. And though he'd never have admitted it to her when they were younger, he'd always admired the way she'd tackled challenges. Whenever she'd put her mind to something—souping up her Camaro, getting the best grades, whatever—she'd always been good at it. Always.

"No," he said, coming to an instant decision. "From what I hear, you're good at what you do. I want someone I can trust. You're it."

He thought she might say something else. Saw the word clearly in her eyes: *fool*. But she didn't say that. Instead she said, "Fine. Let's get down to business then, shall we?"

She leaned over and pulled out a brown partition folder from an overnight bag-type thing she'd stuffed under the seat in front of her. There was a yellow label on it that said Escrow File: 937 Orchard Road. Her old address from home, he recognized. How bizarre to remember that.

She straightened, the plane jerking back from the gate just as she did so. Her left breast brushed his right arm.

He felt scalded.

"Sorry," she murmured, hardly noticing.

He narrowed his eyes. No blush. No embarrassment. The Cece Blackwell he remembered would have had a hard time meeting his eyes.

This Cece glanced up at him boldly as she said, "I've put together a list of things I need to accomplish this weekend—learning the ins and outs of a race car garage, for one. Plus examining security, that sort of thing." Suddenly, a ray of light that shot out from around the terminal illuminated her face and eyes. It turned those eyes Caribbean green. He'd been there last year with a woman whose name he couldn't recall.

"When'd you have time to do that?" he asked.

"Last night," she said without looking up, her leg swinging again.

"In a hurry to get me out of your hair?"

"Eeyup," she responded as she opened the file, lifting her hand to the bridge of her nose, almost as if she were pushing up a pair of nonexistent glasses. When she realized what she'd done, she gave him a look.

"Contacts," she murmured.

He'd wondered what had happened to the glasses.

"According to what you told my superiors, you're suspicious about Randy Newell's death." She looked at him, her face serious. "If it's too hard to discuss the death of your friend, just let me know."

"Do it."

She turned back to the file. "Forensics is looking at the debris right now, but so far you're the only one who thinks something looked suspicious about the wreck."

He nodded, remembering yet again the way Randy's car had exploded. Just detonated. Fuel cell rupture. That's what they claimed. It happened. Rare, but it happened.

And Randy had been inside.

"I have to be honest. I don't see how someone could blow up a race car. They'd have to put the explosives inside the vehicle, but your tech inspection would've uncovered that. And what would be the motive? Terrorist act? If so, we'd have known by now. One thing about terrorists, they love to claim their work. And so if not that, maybe revenge? Revenge against who? You? Your driver?"

He felt her look over at him.

"Blain?"

He met her gaze, though he had to repeat her words in his head to remember what the question was.

"You all right?"

He told himself he was fine.

She grabbed his hand. "Blain?" she asked again.

He stared down at that hand. Her nails were short. No-nonsense. Not a lick of polish. Typical Cecilia.

"I'm fine," he said hoarsely, trying to focus on her, on the plane, on anything other than the sudden memory he had of Randy standing in the winner's circle after they'd won their first race together.

She tilted her head toward his, forcing his attention. "I lost my partner a few years back." She shook her head, still clasping Blain's hand, squeezing it gently before she released it. "I still think about him every day."

His breath hitched unexpectedly at the sadness in her eyes. She truly *did* seem to understand. "Actually," he said gruffly, suddenly uncomfortable with his feelings, "I just don't like flying."

She drew back, her pretty eyes widening. And then her lids narrowed, her lips compressing just before she said, "Liar."

He barked a laugh—just one little laugh—but it was the first since watching Randy's car fragment into a thousand pieces.

He opened his mouth, about to thank her, but a

voice came over the P.A. "Ladies and gentlemen, may I have your attention please. We need everyone to exit the plane. Immediately."

Blain looked up, wondering what the hell was going on.

"Bomb threat," Cece said, her eyes instantly and completely serious.

CHAPTER THREE

"IT WAS JUST a coincidence," Cece told Bob from the privacy of her Las Vegas hotel room via a Bureau cellphone. She and Blain were staying at the Rodeo, a western-themed resort meant to make someone think she was in the Wild West…or a B movie. Knotty pine furniture and a lodgepole pine bed filled the room. Various horses and cowboys galloping to save helpless calves were depicted in the prints hanging on the wall.

"I'm sure of it," she insisted. "Why would Blain's bad guys call in a bomb threat?"

"I agree it doesn't make a whole lot of sense," Bob said. "But we have to treat this as if it's not a coincidence."

Her hand tightened around the palm-size phone. "I know, I know, but I still think the whole thing is a wild-goose chase. If someone wanted to blow up a racetrack, or an airplane, why not just do it? Why tell someone you were going to do it beforehand?"

"That's what you're there to investigate."

"The letter about Blain's driver was probably sent

by some crackpot redneck mad at Blain for owning the car that beat his favorite driver," Cece muttered. "Not a real murderer."

"Look, Cece, it was a threat, and these days we have to take all threats seriously, including today's. I'll let you know what we find."

She inhaled, knowing he was right. They'd taken a lot of heat for 9/11. Didn't want to be caught with their pants down again. And, hell, these days a shopping list could get someone in trouble—if it had fertilizer and Clorox on it.

"When do you want me back?"

"As soon as you're done making your report."

The sooner the better, Cece thought. She didn't like the way being around Blain made her feel. For a second there on the plane she'd been overcome by memories of her old partner, of the look on his wife's face when she'd broken the news to her, and his kids' faces at the funeral....

"Got that, Cece?"

"Roger," she answered, stabbing the Off button without saying goodbye. This was no time to dwell on the past.

A knock sounded. Cece turned to the door. Blain. She'd told him to meet up with her the moment he'd settled into his room. Apparently that was now.

She crossed to the door, opening it.

"What'd he say?" Blain immediately asked, striding in without so much as a hello.

She shook her head, looking up and down the

hall before stepping back into her room and closing the door.

"He said he'll look into the threat," she summa-
rized.

Blain stopped in front of her one window, the Las
Vegas strip stretching out behind him. Blinking
lights flicked on and off, visible even in late morning. It was a warm day, despite it being early spring…
not that you'd guess it was spring by the mud-brown
mountains surrounding the city.

"Does he think it might be the same person who
sent me the letter?"

"Look, Blain, it's too early to tell. He's going to
have someone look into it. Meantime, I'm here to
check things out."

He didn't seem pleased. Well, she wasn't exactly
thrilled, either.

"Are you ready to leave?" he asked.

She nibbled on her lower lip, crossing her arms
in front of her. "I'll meet up with you later. I need to
change."

His eyes narrowed. She caught a look of suspi-
cion just before he asked, "Into what?"

She shrugged. "Something a little more racelike.
Remember, I'm not here in an official capacity.
Well, I am, but we don't want your fellow trackies
to know that."

"Trackies?" he asked with a lifted brow.

"What else should I call the people you work
with?"

"How about crew members?"

"Whatever," she said, lifting a hand in dismissal. "Just let me get changed. Unless you want me to show up in a business suit, toting an FBI badge."

He shook his head. "Just remember there's a dress code in the garage."

This time it was *her* brows that lifted.

He nodded. "No sleeveless shirts. No open-toed shoes. No bare legs."

She snapped her fingers in mock regret. "Damn. I guess that means I can't wear my thigh-highs."

His eyes narrowed further.

She rolled hers. "Relax, Blain. I promise not to embarrass you. I'll look the part. Just let me do my job."

AND SHE DID LOOK THE PART, judging by the raised brows she received from certain members of the male persuasion. As she walked toward the garage, she tried not to feel self-conscious. All those years at Bimbos and she still felt uncomfortable when gawked at—made her think she might have a piece of tissue trailing from her heel.

Perfect.

She'd decided on a chic yet revealing mode of dress—not for Blain's sake, although that might have been fun, but so she blended in better. And so she wore a black chemise covered by a black mesh, long-sleeved shirt, powder-blue jeans hugging her legs like giant tube socks, a black stripe of leather running down the side. Of course, tucked into her black half-boots was a .22 handgun. Still, she felt very sexy in an Annie Oakley kind of way.

Unfortunately, Nevada weather in the spring was like a woman who couldn't make up her mind, and so Cece damn near froze in the getup. Off in the distance what looked to be a thunderstorm was brewing, dark clouds gathering over the granite mountaintops. Terrific. And she'd forgotten a jacket.

A guard wearing a bright yellow coat eyed her up and down, the word *SECURITY* emblazoned across the front as if someone might mistake him for a race car. The obnoxious color wasn't very flattering to his Hispanic face, a face that lit up when he saw her.

"Good afternoon," he drawled flirtatiously as she paused near the entrance he "guarded." Yeah, right. The guy didn't even have a gun. "May I help you?" he added.

On a normal day Cece would give him one of her patented Death Star FBI agent looks. But this wasn't a normal day. Undercover. One of Blainy-poo's friends. So she smiled back, flicking her long blond hair over her shoulder à la Dallas Cowboys cheerleader.

"Good afternoon," she answered with a smile, flashing him the hot pass credential she'd picked up at a trailer outside the racetrack.

"Go right on in," he said, waving her by.

"Thank you," she drawled in a sexy alto she hadn't used since her days at Bimbos.

The Frankenstein heels of her boots sank into fresh tar as she headed toward the garage. Four white buildings were lined up like dominoes along the homestretch, the lesser mortals (i.e., race fans) kept out by the tall wrought-iron fence with giant don't-try-to-climb-this spikes at the top. The buildings were nice in a single-story, no-frills kind of way. Some cars were in their garage, others half out as if they'd stalled and come to a rolling halt. It wasn't race day, which really bummed her out. Yup. Her guilty little secret. She was a closet race car fan.

She paused midway between the fence and the garages and took it all in: the smell of burnt oil and high octane fuel. Compressors and air wrenches whirring in the distance. The *crack, crack, crack* of a motor idling. Crew members in their multicolor team shirts darting around.

Little darts of electricity lifted her skin into goose pimples. Dang. She'd always wondered what it was like on the inside.

She found Blain's car parked in a garage stall at the very end of the second building; the pylon-orange stars painted on the trunk lid were hard to miss. The front end of the vehicle was jacked up off the ground, and two men stood near the front, peering into the motor compartment as if a girlie flick played inside.

"Excuse me," she said, trying not to gawk as an ex-driver-turned-famous TV commentator walked past her, clipboard in hand, gray hair plastered in place like an elderly Ken doll.

A head peeked around the lifted hood, another from the other side, like two wide-eyed chickens peeking around a coop. She looked down as the sound of a creeper's wheels grinding against smooth concrete caught her attention. A pair of feet emerged from beneath the car—big feet in brown leather shoes. Legs. Black pants. Blain.

The thought was confirmed when a taut chest encased in a team orange, polo-style shirt turned into a tan face with angry eyes.

Uh-oh.

"Well, well, well." He glared up at her. "Look who decided to show up."

"Well, well, well," she drawled right back. "Blain Sanders at my feet. Just what I always wanted."

He frowned, rolling the creeper around so he could sit up. "You get lost on the way out here?" he asked, grabbing a red rag that lay nearby, then tossing it aside.

"No," she answered, smiling brightly, even though his question irritated the heck out of her.

"Get caught in traffic?"

"No," she repeated quickly. Okay, so she'd been primping. It wasn't often that she got to go undercover as a glamour girl. Usually she was playing the role of anything *but,* and she was woman enough to want to dress in cool clothes. "I just took my time."

He frowned again, his gaze scanning her up and down. And even though he sat at a lower elevation, he must have noticed how cold she was because she could have sworn his eyes caught on her less than soft nipples. She blushed, but darn it, it was cold standing here in the shadows. A stiff breeze blew between the garages, tossing dust and grit and empty wax cups around. "I thought team owners didn't work on cars."

"This team owner does," he grumbled, rising to his feet. "Especially when his crew chief is off running around and there's a problem."

She resisted the urge to step back. Blain was a big guy. *In a lot of places,* she found herself thinking before clamping down on *that* unprofessional and unwanted thought.

"Are you ready to give me a tour?"

He looked irritated. Really, really irritated. He glanced at the car, and the crew still gawking. He glared. The chicken heads ducked back behind the coop.

"In a minute," he said. "We're trying to figure out why the car doesn't start."

"Power?"

He shook his head.

"You sure?"

"Positive," he said, the one word managing to convey his utter disgust that she'd even attempt to diagnose the problem. Geez-oh-peets, if ever she needed a reminder of why she didn't like him, this was it. Funny, she'd forgotten how sexist he could be. That was why she'd taken great pleasure in waxing his doors when they'd been younger.

She glanced away, about to suggest something else, just to irk him. But the sight of a cord cocked at an odd angle as it sat atop the coil caught her attention, and despite herself, she squinted at it, because it sure didn't look like it was on right. It wasn't.

"Sooo," she drawled, "I suppose the fact that that thing over there," she pointed to a blue wire, "isn't on right has nothing to do with it?"

It took a moment for her comment to register, and when it did, Blain actually started, shoulders stiffening, head jerking up.

"Of course, maybe you guys invented a new type of coil wire that I've never heard of." She lifted a brow sarcastically. "Laser beam, maybe. Yeah, that must be it…lasers."

Blain's eyes narrowed.

Cece crossed her arms, feeling supremely smug as she stood there. Okay, it was luck that she'd just happened to glance at the coil, and luck that she'd chosen power as a possible diagnosis. But it was all she could do not to gloat as he looked in the direction she suggested, muffled an oath, then stormed over and popped the wire on right.

"Try it," he muttered, straightening.

A crew member shot her an "I'm impressed" look, then came around the hood of the car, reached in and flicked the starter switch.

Cece just about jumped out of her boots as the engine roared to life. She almost glanced down to make sure the things were still on her feet.

"Holy shlamoly," she cried, covering her ears.

Blain turned to her, shook his head, though she was positive he hadn't heard her. Nobody could possibly hear her. She was a mouth with no sound coming out of it.

"Cut it," he yelled over the cacophony, slicing his finger across his neck for added insurance.

Silence descended, silence so instant and so complete it was like walking outside after a rock concert.

"Thank you," she said, pulling her fingers out of her ears. "I'll send you the bill from my otorhinolaryngologist."

"Your *what?*" Blain asked, and did she detect a hint of curtness in his voice? Could he be a bit embarrassed? Just a tad?

One could only hope.

"Ear, nose and throat guy," she clarified.

The man that had started the car turned to her. "You just saved us a half hour of work."

She smiled brightly. "Yeah? Fancy that."

"Ee-yow," the other crew member cried. "Blain, where'd you find this girl? Gorgeous and she knows something about cars."

Gorgeous? Hardly. But she still blushed. Forever a dog in Cinderella's clothing. "Thanks," she said.

Blain glared at his crew again. They instantly went back to work.

"Wow. Impressive," she said as Blain walked toward her. "Can you make them jump through flaming hoops with that look, too? I hear Circus Circus down the road is looking for new acts."

His face didn't loosen up one bit as he said, "You know, you are without a doubt the most irritating, frustrating, exasperating woman of my acquaintance."

She smiled brightly, reached up and patted his smooth-shaven cheek. "Aw, gee, thanks." She spun away.

"Where are you going?"

"Problem solved, so that means I can go on my tour, right?"

He just looked at her, then shook his head. And could that be…was the sky falling…might that actually be a bit of a smile on his face?

"Thanks for the help," he said.

Her mouth fell open. An apology, too? From *him?*

"That was a good call," he added.

She studied him through narrow eyes, watching to see if his own eyes flicked to the right as he searched the creative side of his brain. It was a way to glean if a person was telling the truth, and she unashamedly used it now.

His eyes darted *left.* "I checked that cord when I first realized we had a problem. Obviously, I must not have pushed it back in all the way."

Ah, so this wasn't actually an apology per se. Rather, it was a saving of face.

"I see," she said, somehow disappointed. She turned away again, but he grabbed her arm this time, turning her back yet again. Gently, though.

"Wait," he said, lifting his hand, his face in profile as he stared at the ground and shook his head. "That came out wrong. I wasn't trying to make excuses. You were right. I was wrong. Good call."

He really was trying to act grateful. How...bizarre. She'd never had a kind word from the man.

"You're welcome," she said.

He nodded and it was then she realized that he hadn't let go of her arm. He must have realized it, too, because he suddenly released her like a hot exhaust manifold. She knew exactly how he felt because it seemed as if she'd been burned by one herself. She almost took a peek at her arm as she turned away yet again, Blain falling into step alongside.

"You know," she said—and she couldn't believe she was going to tell him this. She really couldn't. "I once tore apart a carburetor only to discover that I was out of gas the whole time."

"You did?"

She nodded, suddenly feeling as red as a Radio Flyer. Jeesh, why'd she tell him *that* embarrassing thing? "I was an hour on the side of that road. You wouldn't believe the number of guys that pulled over to help." She looked up at him, realizing as she did so that she'd tried to make him feel better. *Him.* Blain Sanders. The guy who had scarred her for life more times than she could count.

Had she lost her mind?

Thank God her cellphone rang then, because she needed a moment to tighten the screws in her head.

"Blackwell," she answered, forgetting for an instant that she was supposed to be a civvy and not a special agent.

It was Bob, and as usual, he was to the point. "Got a new suspect for you if this thing pans out."

"Oh?" she answered, turning away from Blain.

"It's Sanders."

CHAPTER FOUR

"IMPOSSIBLE."

It was the first word that came to Cece's mind, never mind that Blain's brows rose like twin drawbridges at her tone of voice. She lifted an index finger in the universal sign meaning *just one moment,* and turned away to try and find a quieter area. Quieter? Hah.

"Blain right there?" her boss asked when she told him to hold on a sec. At least she thought that's what he said. It sounded more like, "Brain dead?"

Yeah, she felt pretty brain dead at the moment. Here she was getting all excited about being in a stock car garage when what she should be doing was focusing on the job.

She walked to the end of the building, that ever-present cold wind poking rude fingers through her mesh shirt.

Note to self: no more cute shirts.

"Now what's this you say?" she said, crossing to the fence.

"Someone at the airport saw Sanders make a call on his cellphone just before you two boarded."

"So?"

"We looked into it. It was to the airline."

She tipped her head back for a second, a part of her noticing those storm clouds had gotten closer. "Oh, for goodness' sake, Bob. He could have called the airline for any number of reasons. Besides, he's the one that keeps insisting on an investigation. You told me yourself the president of the stock car association would rather this whole thing go away."

"Yeah, but he wouldn't be the first twisted mind to insist the Bureau investigate a crime he'd committed."

"*If* a crime was committed," she felt the need to say.

"One might have been."

"What do you know that I don't know?" she asked, instantly suspicious.

"Nothing, nothing. I'm just telling you to keep your eyes open."

Ridiculous. The whole thing was ridiculous. She would like to have told Bob all the various reasons why she doubted Blain Sanders was the perp, starting with the fact that he'd been the most disgusted with her when she'd been arrested all those years ago. "Boy Scout" didn't begin to describe Blain Sanders. But just then she saw the man of the hour himself round the corner of the building, waving her toward him.

"Will do," she said.

But when Cece stuffed her phone in her pocket,

she couldn't help but shake her head. Blain, a suspect. Hah! And, dang it, what was wrong with these jeans? They were too tight to get her damn cellphone back in her pocket.

Blain Sanders, stock car stalker. The thought of him as a bad guy was almost laughable. A man who refused to drag race on the street because it was illegal would not threaten to blow up a racetrack, much less kill his own driver.

"Trouble?" he asked as she joined up with him again.

"Nah. Just some office stuff."

The way his eyebrows arched like a cat's back made her think he didn't buy her excuse…not one bit, but that didn't stop her from saying, "You ready to go?"

He stared at her for half a heartbeat—long enough that she found herself thinking how odd it was to be here with him. After all the times she'd watched him on a giant TV, after all the times she'd fantasized about meeting up with him again.

Fantasize?

No. Not like that. Well, maybe once.

Or twice.

"Yeah. And we'll need to hurry if I'm going to show you around before the next practice."

She nodded, stepping up her pace alongside him. "Is your car all fixed?"

"Yeah. Thanks to you." But he didn't seem all that relieved.

"More troubles?"

He glanced at her in surprise. Cece glanced away, ostensibly to check out what was going on the garage, but more because she felt suddenly weird gazing at him. He looked so worried.

"Our lap times at this morning's practice weren't as good as they should be," he admitted.

"Yeah, but you practice again tomorrow."

"Yeah, but qualifying is today. If the weather holds."

Blain motioned toward the grandstands. Cece followed his gaze. She could see the leading edge of those giant, bubblelike clouds.

"We just can't catch a break. Ever since…"

His driver had died. He didn't need to complete the sentence. Cece could read the look in his eyes. Worried. Tense. Not like a suspect. Jeesh, she almost felt sorry for him.

Sympathy? For Blain Sanders? The man responsible for her one and only felony? Who'd given her such low self-esteem as a teenager that it'd taken a year of working at Bimbos before she'd started to think she might not be such an ugly duckling after all? Who'd blackmailed her into working this case? She must have bolts for brains.

They reached the rear of his car, but the moment they arrived, a white-coated racing official said, "Blain, I need to see you for a moment."

Blain motioned for her to stay put, then followed the guy into the garage. Secret, confidential meeting.

Must be important stuff. But that was okay because it gave her a moment to think.

Blain a suspect?

Not.

"You here with Blain?"

Cece jumped, turned.

And there he was. Lance Cooper. Blain's newly hired driver. Tall, handsome, and with such a warm smile on his face, it completely contradicted Cece's mental image of cocky race car drivers.

"Uh, yeah."

His smile grew wider, his white teeth startling against his tan face. Must be professionally bleached, Cece thought, even as she found herself wanting to return that grin.

"The crew told me he was with a woman," he said with a gleam in his light gray eyes. "One who fixed my car."

"That was me," she said, thinking that he seemed nice. 'Course, he was new to this particular level of racing so maybe it hadn't sunk in yet that he was a "big star."

"Thanks."

"My pleasure," she said, giving in to the temptation to smile. He reached out a hand to shake hers. Cece automatically took it, thinking his messy blond hair gave him an almost boyish look.

"How'd you figure out it was the coil wire?" he asked.

"Lucky guess," she answered, realizing there was

nothing boyish about the look that suddenly entered his eyes.

"Then lucky me." And the way he said the words…mmm mmm mmm, he was flirting.

She felt her cheeks heat. And then he crossed his arms, a brow lifting as a piratelike grin spread across his face. Naughty, naughty man. Not that she was attracted to him—no, no, no, something about his looks didn't quite appeal to her. Besides, he was Blain's driver, and she had a feeling if Blain saw her flirting—

"Don't you have an interview to do?" a disgruntled voice asked.

They both turned, and it was just as she'd thought. He looked peeved.

"Yeah, but they can wait," Lance answered.

Blain didn't say a word, just lifted a brow in a very analytical, Mr. Spock way, his meaning obvious.

"I'm going," his driver said.

When Cece met Blain's eyes it was to see him direct the same irritated gaze at her. "Follow me," he said.

Yes, sir, she silently answered, resisting the urge to salute. What was up with him? She had half a mind to drop her little bomb that he was considered a suspect, but then decided against it. She'd probably give him a heart attack right on the spot, and then she'd have to give him mouth-to-mouth.

Mmm.

Stop it, Cece.

He led her toward a row of big rigs parked around the perimeter of the garage. Her interest was piqued. The race car haulers. Cool. She'd always wanted to see what they looked like inside.

She didn't have time to examine them too closely, though, because his next words snapped at her like the sting of a rubber band.

"Lance Cooper is off-limits."

That made her stop. And it was almost biblical the way the world suddenly darkened, a puffy storm cloud obstructing the sun.

"What do you mean, off-limits?" she asked.

He crossed his own arms, leaning toward her a bit. "No romantic entanglements."

Unfortunately, that's what she thought he'd meant, and it really torqued her, too, because the man had no business saying who she could and could not get involved with. No say at all. Not that she was getting involved with anybody. No way.

"Look," she said. "I wasn't flirting with him, if that's what you think."

"You were smiling."

"So?"

"So, you're not here to cozy up to my driver," he said in a low voice, looking up for a second as a team member from a different crew came walking toward them. Without saying another word, Blain turned, heading toward his own hauler. With swift movements, he opened the dark-tinted glass door and stepped inside. Surprisingly warm air hit Cece in the face.

"Am I supposed to follow you, or is the lecture over?"

He stopped, and Cece didn't like that he towered above her. Not at all.

"I want to continue this conversation in the lounge."

"Ooo, the lounge," she said sotto voce, which only made him more angry, judging by the way his eyes narrowed.

Cece sighed. What a disaster. Not even one day together and already they were at each other's throats. Granted, she was provoking him a bit, but she wasn't doing it intentionally.

The moment she climbed the steps of the big rig and passed into the heated—yes, heated—interior, she came to an abrupt halt. "Whoa."

Sure, she'd seen the things on TV, but a thirty-inch screen in no way conveyed the enormity of what a hauler looked like on the inside. Fluorescent lights turned cabinets a blinding white. To her left a mini-kitchenette took up a good four feet.

"You coming?"

She hadn't even realized she'd stopped. Cece shook her head, somehow amused by it all. Most men couldn't keep their clothes in the hamper, but this place looked as spotless as the altar of a church. One of the bottom cabinets hadn't been closed all the way. Cece peeked inside. An engine block lay there. Jeesh. They built cabinets for their motor parts.

A second later Blain opened the door of the lounge. Cece hardly had time to notice the black leather couch, mirrors and natural wood cabinets lining the perimeter. She and Blain were practically nose-to-nose when he turned back to her, his eyes nearly the color of the blue flames that shot out of exhaust pipes.

"If you can give me one good reason why I shouldn't send you home, you better speak up."

One good reason? Only *one* good reason?

She almost lit into him. "Excuse me, but *you're* the reason I'm here."

He didn't look happy to be reminded of that. "I wanted you here to do some investigating, not flirt with drivers."

She stepped past him and sat down on the couch, her jean-clad rear sliding on the surface like a kid on a playground toy.

"Put a sock in it, Sanders."

Okay, not very professional. Not very polite, either, but the time for pleasantries was over. She lifted a hand, interrupting whatever it was he'd opened his mouth to say, probably something rude.

"All I did was talk to the guy."

"It was more than talking."

"No, it wasn't," she said.

"But I don't blame him for getting the wrong impression, dressed as you are."

What?

She drew herself up. "What bothers you more,

Sanders? That I look good in this outfit? Or that your driver thinks I do?"

Blain looked as if he'd swallowed a gallon of brake fluid.

"Go on," she said. "Admit it. I'm not what you expected and it's driving you nuts."

He crossed his arms again.

"I've changed. And you don't like the new me."

He met her gaze for long, long moments before saying, "This isn't working."

Cece met that gaze head-on. "You're right. It's not."

"I'll call your boss—"

"On a personal level," she interrupted, suddenly standing. There was no place for him to go, and so he was forced once again into close proximity with her. It was a tactic she'd learned at the academy. Invade a man's space and you'd get his attention, and maybe his respect.

"It's no secret we don't like each other," she said softly. "And it's no secret that I don't want to be here. But the fact of the matter is you were right to bring me on board. I'm the best person for the job. Don't let your personal feelings for me get in the way of what's right."

"What personal feelings?"

"The ones that make you dislike me."

"I don't dislike you," Blain said. "I…" He looked as if he didn't know what to say. "I'm just not confident in your abilities."

Hell of a time to realize that, she almost said aloud. Instead she said, "Okay, fine. Let's just get this out of the way then, shall we?"

"Get what out of the way?" he asked, the sleeves of his shirt stretching as he recrossed his arms, cords of muscles swelling as those arms flexed.

"Time to have it out. To lay it on the table."

He didn't say anything, just continued to give her that scrunched-brow glare men gave you when you irked them.

"You don't like me because I made a fool of myself by chasing you around when I was younger," she admitted. "You don't like me because I did some really stupid stuff back then, too. Stuff you still hold against me, obviously, or you wouldn't be so quick to get rid of me."

"Not true," he said, his blue eyes seeming darker all of sudden. Or maybe it was the fluorescent lights. Despite the half-a-million-dollar rig, one of them appeared to be on the fritz. The light click-click-clicked as it struggled to stay on.

"You still consider me a risk. With all the baggage still floating around in your head, it's a wonder you even mentioned my name to your stock car racing pals."

"I told you. I knew you'd play straight."

"What changed about that?"

This time it was his turn to straighten. "All right. Fine. Gloves off. The problem is you haven't changed. You're still the same Cece Blackwell. Outspoken. Unpredictable. Too much of a wild card."

And that was when the tiny cork holding her temper popped free.

"You don't know a damn thing, Blain Sanders."

And the jerk just stared down at her, not even flinching. She took a step toward him, a small step, but enough to remind him that she wasn't afraid of him, or any other man. "You just *think* you know who I am. Who I *was*," she corrected. "You don't have a clue about me. About how hard I struggled to finish high school while holding down a full-time job so I could help out my mom. About how hard I fought to be accepted by the popular kids in high school, you included."

She resisted the urge to stab her finger into his chest, but only by curling her hand into a fist.

"You were so full of yourself," she said. "So cocky and self-centered. I loved taking you down, even though a part of me did it because I wanted to get your attention, and because I needed to prove to myself that having more money than me didn't make you better."

"I didn't have more money than you."

"No, but your parents did."

His eyes narrowed and he started to shake his head.

"But you know what?" she said before he could say a word. "I did match up. My Camaro was the fastest damn car in high school, even though I had to scrimp and save for every part I put on that thing. And in the end, what did I have to do? Sell it to help my mom pay the mortgage."

His stony expression was suddenly tinged with surprise.

"That's right. I *had* to sell it. My Camaro. A car that was everything to me. The last thing I had of my dad's before he died. My last piece of *him*. And I had to sell it."

"Cece, I—"

"No. Let me finish."

But for a moment she couldn't go on, so overcome by a ridiculous, unbelievable stinging of tears that she had to inhale to stop from crying.

You beat him? her dad had asked.

I blew his doors off, Dad.

Good for you, Tiger.

She couldn't speak as the whole horrible time came rushing back to her again. Her dad's death. Her mom's financial spiral. That last terrible year of high school. And then her mom's death two years later. Jeesh, no wonder she'd been running with the wrong crowd. For a split second Cece felt the emotions coalesce within her: grief, humiliation, sadness. She tried to shove the feelings back inside, but like oil on hands, it was hard to wash them away.

"We were so damn broke," she found herself saying. "No life insurance. No money in the bank. Nothing. My mom and I tried as hard as we could to stay afloat, but life kept kicking us in the teeth. I swear that's why she died a few years later. She just gave up—the doctors called it a heart attack. I called it a broken heart. Not just because of her grief for my dad, but because of her grief at the human race. Nobody cared that she'd just lost her husband. Nobody cared that we'd sold everything we owned, *everything*—cars, furniture, jewelry—to make ends meet."

And this time it was she who crossed her arms, tipping her head back in the process, her stupid tears causing prisms in her eyes. "When she died I vowed never to put myself in that position. I have a job that I'm good at, money in the bank, and believe me, that's something that I'm proud of.

"So from where I stand, Blain Sanders, I'm more than competent to do a little investigating. Chances are this is nothing, anyway. But you're the one calling the shots, so if you want me to go home, I'll go."

She waited for him to say something, anything.

But he didn't.

"Fine. I'm outta here," she said, pushing past him and out the door. "Didn't want to come, anyway."

And the jerk let her go.

CHAPTER FIVE

HE SHOULD GO AFTER HER, Blain thought. Instead he heard the hollow thud of her footfalls on the center isle's rubber mat as she left the hauler.

She'd had tears in her eyes.

Blain had never, not ever, seen Cece Blackwell cry. Hell, a few days ago he'd have sworn she was incapable of doing such a thing.

Her mom had died? He hadn't heard about that.

Blain stood motionless for a few seconds more. In the end, his conscience made him move.

"Cece, wait," he said.

Fat drops of rain had started to come down, the asphalt dotted with Dalmatian spots. Cece was already near the garage, the overhang protecting her. He quickly caught up with her, and the damnedest thing was, she'd gotten control of herself. Her face looked frozen in anger as he stared down at her.

"Cece, wait."

She kept on going.

"I'm sorry," he called out.

Still moving.

He caught up, stepped around her, staying her with a hand when she would have darted by him. "I didn't know your mom had died."

She widened her eyes as if to ask, *Yeah, so?*

"I'm sorry."

At last she spoke. "Fine. Apology accepted."

She pushed past him.

"No, wait," he said, catching her arm. "Don't leave."

She glared.

"Please," he found himself saying, because the truth of the matter was, he *did* trust her to get the job done. She'd always been at the top of her class, even though he'd been shocked to learn just now that she'd held down a full-time job while doing it. How had she managed to do that? But he supposed it didn't matter. He had a bad feeling about Randy's death, and he was positive that if anyone could prove or disprove his theory, it was Cece. He didn't know why he felt that way, but he did.

"I *need* you."

She shivered, though she still glared.

"You cold?"

"No," she lied, shivering again.

"You are."

"No, I'm not."

He grabbed her hand, to find her fingers were like ice. "Jeesh, Cece, you *are* freezing. C'mon back inside the hauler. I'll get you a coat."

But she didn't move. He didn't, either. The rain

pinged atop the metal roof, but Blain was mesmerized by the expression in her eyes.

"You really want me to stay?" she asked, pulling her hand out of his grasp before tucking it beneath the crook of her arm.

"I do."

An air-ratchet went off in the distance, the high-pitched whir ending right as she asked, "Why?" and blinked away raindrops that clung to her lashes. "Give me the real reason you're so insistent I help you out."

He debated whether to tell her the truth, and decided he should. "Sonoma drags."

She looked puzzled. "The grudge matches?"

"It was the last time we raced. Do you remember?"

She nodded.

He shook his head a bit. "I thought you were anxious to beat me because it was *me* you were racing, but afterward, when you'd won, you got out of the car…and do you remember what you did?"

She shook her head.

"You didn't look at me—you looked up." Blain would never forget her face at that moment. Ecstatic, triumphant…and sad. "You whispered, 'This one's for you, Dad.' I saw it." And he'd been stunned. "I never forgot that day," he said. "It wasn't me you wanted to impress. You'd set your sights on winning that race in memory of your father."

Blain looked off, his gaze moving to the race-track. "I feel the same obligation to Randy. Every time I think about what happened, I vow to get to the

bottom of his wreck. You of all people should understand that kind of promise." He could tell from the
look on her face that she did. "Something's not right,
and I need your help to figure it out. Will you help
me?"

She shivered again. He thought she might refuse,
but then she said, "Fine" in a way that sounded almost resigned.

His shoulders slumped in relief. "Thanks, Cece."

"Yeah, well, don't thank me yet."

But he was grateful just the same. "C'mon," he
said, "let's get you into something warmer."

She took a deep breath, only to shiver again.
"Okay," she said through teeth that chattered.

By the time they made it back to the hauler they
were soaked, the droplets of rain so heavy they'd
turned the pavement a glistening ebony. Cece rubbed
her arms as she stood beneath the car lift that jutted
out over the back of the rig. Blain handed her a team
jacket a second later.

"Thanks," she said as she slipped the thing on.

And Blain, a man who'd never looked at Cece as
anything more than a means to an end suddenly saw
her in a much different light. She was a woman
who'd overcome tremendous odds to get where she
had. He realized now that she had depths he'd never
noticed before.

"You can keep it," he said, looking back at the garage, at anything but her. "You're going to need it by
the looks of things."

She followed his gaze as she zipped the jacket up. And suddenly it sounded as if someone had poured a wheelbarrow full of water on top of the hauler. It began to rain, *seriously* rain.

"Qualifying'll be postponed," he muttered.

"You think so?"

She had raindrops clinging to her blond hair and forehead, her tiny frame suddenly reminding him of high school. He had a memory of her getting out of the Camaro, of stalking up to him and challenging him to their first race. He'd accepted. She'd won. It still amazed him.

"Yeah," he said. "C'mon, let me grab a scanner so I can keep track of what's going on."

And that was how Blain Sanders found himself showing her around. And he had to admit, she impressed him. Not so much because she was a fast study—because she was—but because she knew a hell of a lot about stock car racing. More than she let on, he realized.

"So now you know what I do thirty-six weekends out of the year," he said as they halted beneath one of the track's massive grandstands, their breath puffing out like dragons.

"Forty," she said.

"Forty?"

"Well, sometimes it's more than that, right? Depends on if you qualify for the Bud races, or go to Japan."

He almost smiled. Yup. Just as he suspected. "How long have you been a fan?"

Rain dropped down the backs of the empty grandstands, well, not completely empty. A few diehard race fans sat beneath colorful tarps, hunched down, shivering and waiting in hopes the track got dry enough to run the practice, and then later, qualifying. It wasn't going to happen.

"What makes you think I'm a fan?" she asked, looking up at him out of a face turned gray by the storm's light.

"Cece, the way you talk is a dead giveaway. The average person doesn't know the difference between a Ford template and a Chevy template, but you did."

"I studied up," she said with a shrug.

The smell of stale beer, cigarettes and spilled food was familiar but for one thing: the scent of Cece carried to him on the same breeze.

"Bull," he said.

"All right," she said. "So I've been following the circuit for about five years now."

"Really?" He felt his left brow tug up.

She shrugged. "I didn't mean it to happen. One night I was out with some friends and I looked up and there you were." Cece remembered as if it was yesterday. "I nearly spat out a mouthful of beer."

She boldly met his gaze, daring him to mock her, but he didn't. Humph. And so she added, "At first I watched because it did my heart good to see you lose."

His gray eyes flickered and she held her breath, wondering why it was that she felt such an overwhelming need to provoke him. But when he didn't rise to the bait, she relented, giving him another burst of honesty. "But you didn't lose, at least not all the time, and by the time I realized you might have a shot at the year-end championship, I was hooked. I've been watching ever since."

He didn't say a word, and Cece didn't know what surprised her more, that he didn't say something snide, snooty or just plain rude, or the fact that he appeared to be—yes—it very definitely seemed like he was about to smile.

"That's why you looked giddy while I was showing you around."

She didn't take offense. "It's not every day someone gets to meet people she's only seen on TV."

His smile grew and Cece found herself thinking she liked it, not because it made him look more handsome—which it did—but because it put such warmth in his eyes, genuine warmth, as if he might be a really nice person.

You of all people should understand.... Cece swallowed past a lump in her throat.

"I remember when I first met Richard Petty. I'll never forget that day," he drawled in his Southern accent.

"So you know what I'm talking about."

He nodded, and a part of Cece could only think

how bizarre it was to be here with him, talking to him after wanting to hate him for so many years.

But then his expression turned curious. "Why didn't you tell me this earlier?"

She shrugged. "Truth be told, I didn't think you'd keep me around for longer than a few hours."

And that reminded Cece of what she'd been brought in to do—investigate, not make friends with Blain Sanders.

Who was currently a suspect.

She shook her head.

"What?" he asked.

"I need to get going," she answered. "I've still got a job to do."

She could tell the moment he remembered why it was they'd been brought together, too. The smile slid down his face like rain on a stormy day. And for a second she caught a glimpse of it, saw the unmistakable darkening of his eyes. Grief. He tried to hide it from her, but some things were impossible to conceal.

He'd lost a driver. Someone he'd known a long time. A friend. She knew all too well what that felt like.

"It was probably just an accident, Blain. I really doubt that letter you received is anything more than a worked-up fan."

"I hope you're right."

But he didn't believe her. So she said, "Think about it. Why send a threatening letter *after* you murder someone?" He winced at the term "murder," and Cece cursed herself. One of the things about working at the Bureau was how jaded you became using certain words. "Blain, if someone were really trying to go around scaring race fans, or killing drivers, they would have sent a note to the press, not to you."

He went silent for a second, his lips tightening. "You're not telling me anything I haven't heard already, Cece. It's just a crazy race fan. One who didn't like Randy and so he claimed to have killed him." He met her gaze. "But I don't believe it."

And that was why he couldn't be a suspect, Cece admitted—because killers didn't fight for justice. Crazy people didn't send themselves letters and then bring them to light. Supposing Blain was right—this whole thing really was a murder and some terrorist or crazed fan was out for blood—Blain had nothing to gain by going public. If he *was* a murderer, he'd have kept quiet. Nah. Supposing this wasn't a wild-goose chase, Blain was innocent.

"Well, if you're right, I don't see how someone could have done it. The garage is locked down tighter than Fort Knox."

"It is," he agreed, following her gaze to the infield, where the garage stood like a million-dollar industrial complex.

"I suppose it needs to be that way." She gave him a small smile. "To keep race fans out. Like me."

It worked. He didn't smile, but his expression

lightened in the way the sky slightly brightened just
before dawn. That was better.

What was better? she asked herself. Surely she
didn't care if Blain Sanders smiled?

Right?

Right?

"Yeah, fans like you," he said, and for a brief second he smiled. Cece felt triumphant—but then the
smile wafted away like so much smoke.

Triumphant?

"Look, I…" She gazed out over the grandstands,
at the cars in their stalls, the race crews milling
about, the security folks dragging some guy
away…. "What the—"

Blain followed her gaze. Just then some man
wearing a team uniform bent down to inspect his car.

"Oh, damn," Cece said, furious with herself that
she'd been so distracted by Blain that she hadn't
even noticed the commotion in the garage.

"Someone must have snuck in."

"Yeah," she said, turning to dash off. *But why?*

CHAPTER SIX

THEY RAN.

Cece kept ahead of him, though Blain managed to catch up to her from time to time. Their first stop was at the entrance to the infield tunnel, and it prompted Cece to reach for a badge Blain hadn't even known she was carrying. The woman who guarded the entrance waved Cece through. Frankly, she hardly paid any attention to either of them, despite the fact that they'd run up to her, were wet and obviously in a hurry.

"Cece, wait," Blain said as he moved to catch up.

But she didn't slow down. By the time they made it through the fluorescent-lit tunnel, Blain was feeling out of breath and grudgingly impressed with Cece's stamina.

"Which way?" she asked as they emerged into the rain again.

"This way," Blain said, turning toward the two-story VIP suites blocking the view from the pit road. There was an opening near the end of the building, and Blain wiped the rain from his face as they entered the garage.

Cece stopped abruptly. Blain looked toward where the security personnel had been a few moments before. Gone. He inhaled deeply, his heart pounding to the point that he could see his shirt move in rhythm to the beat.

"Took him away," Cece said, sounding far less out of breath than Blain.

They had. A lone security guard stood talking to Jeff Burks, crew chief of the number twenty-one car.

"We can go talk to Jeff," Blain said, setting off again.

But Cece didn't follow. He stopped, turned. Her hair had collected drops of rain like blades of grass, the team jacket she wore darker on the shoulders. Her chest barely rose and fell.

"You coming?" he asked.

"No."

His puzzled eyes must have asked the question he didn't.

"I shouldn't reveal my presence here," she answered.

He looked as confused as he felt because she said, "I know I ran down here like I was, but in hindsight, announcing the fact that I'm an FBI agent might not be such a good idea."

"Why not?"

"Because my boss doesn't want people to know I'm here. And because this is still just an investigation. If I go around questioning people, it'll raise flags."

"So raise them."

She reached out and touched Blain's arm. He hadn't put on a jacket, so it was bare and wet, and her palm was so warm it startled him.

"I was told to keep a low profile, Blain. Flashing my badge around is not low profile."

He gazed at her in frustration.

"Look," she said. "I sincerely doubt a bad guy would tinker with a race car in full view of race fans and television cameras."

Blain turned back to where said bad guy had stood. Jeff laughed at something the security guard had just said and it made Blain irritated with the whole situation all over again. Man, this uncertainty drove him nuts.

"They took the guy into custody, Blain. I'll get someone to call security and ask what all it was about, but not right now. I'd rather be more subtle."

"Fine," he said, glancing back at Jeff and the security guard. They were walking away, the crew apparently satisfied that all was well.

"I'll call my office and fill them in on what just happened."

He nodded.

She touched him again. "It's not that I don't believe you, Blain. I just don't want to answer the inevitable questions that'll be raised if word gets out that an FBI agent is snooping around the racetrack."

And as much as he wanted her to do the exact opposite of what she suggested, Blain found himself saying, "Fine."

She released his arm. "It's probably nothing."

He wiped a hand over his face, rain dripping off the edge of his palm. It probably was.

Damn, but he wished he could believe that.

"Let me make some calls and we'll find out for sure."

AND SHE'D BEEN RIGHT. Turned out some overzealous race fan had wanted to stuff a good luck sock into the frame of the car.

A sock.

Ridiculous, but not unheard of, and as Blain returned to his hotel room later that night, he found himself grateful that Cece had kept her head, that she'd been the calmer of the two, and that she'd been subtle in her handling of the situation. She'd impressed him. And she'd also made him think that maybe, just maybe, the feds were right. This was all a wild-goose chase.

He hoped so, he thought as he knocked on her hotel room door.

"Hey," she said in a tired voice after the door swung wide.

"Here's the information you wanted."

"Thanks." She took the papers from him as she leaned against the door frame. She looked beat. Exhausted. As if she'd worked nonstop since coming back to the hotel.

She probably had.

"Did you find out anything more about that guy?"

She nodded. "Nothing more than a race fan, complete with car-tire coffee table at home."

Blain's shoulders loosened. Maybe it was time to let it go. Maybe he *had* been overreacting.

"You finished working?"

She shook her head. "Looks like it'll be a long night. I want to get this wrapped up by tomorrow."

So she could leave. Head back to San Francisco.

He wished she didn't have to go.

"Have you had anything to eat?" he asked.

"No. And I don't really feel like going out to grab a bite, either."

"There are other ways to get a bite than going out," he said, pushing on her door so he could enter.

"What are you doing?" she asked after stepping aside.

"You need nourishment," he said, sparing the room hardly a glance as he went to her nightstand and picked up the phone. "You're no good to the investigation if you drop dead from starvation."

He didn't even hear her approach. Didn't even feel her behind him until her arm brushed his own, the white T-shirt she wore transferring static to the hair on his arms.

"Don't," she said, grabbing the phone from his hand. Green eyes that looked a hell of a lot different than they had in high school peered up at him without an ounce of hostility. Beautiful eyes, he admitted to himself. Unusual and striking with their gold and silver flecks, flecks that matched her loose hair.

"I'm fine. Really," she said, hanging up the phone. "I'll eat something later on. Right now I need to concentrate on my files, and this list of names." She held up the papers he'd given her.

Disappointment flickered through him.

"Hey," she said, her eyes brightening. "I heard they ran qualifying. Who won the pole?"

And he felt like a kid all of a sudden, boasting to the cute girl next door as he said, "We did."

She smiled up at him. Not that fake, sexy smile she'd used on him at the airport. Not the false smile she'd given him any number of times since, but a genuine, happy-for-him smile.

She was happy for him.

Why did that surprise Blain so damn much?

"That's wonderful," she said, her eyes sparkling with excitement. "You must be thrilled."

He *was* thrilled. And you know what? It felt good to share the information with her. Yeah, they might have started out on the wrong foot, but in the past twenty-four hours he'd developed a whole new respect for Cecilia Blackwell. She hadn't tossed his concerns aside. Hadn't treated his worries like they were nothing. So far she'd acted with absolute professionalism—well, aside from that incident at the airport, but overall, yeah, she'd done a good job. He respected her for that.

"Yeah, well, I wish you'd stick around for at least the Busch race tomorrow night." And he really did.

"Too much stuff to do this weekend."

He scanned her face, noted yet again how pretty she looked without makeup, how much she'd changed, how if she were any other woman, he'd...

He'd what?

Want to date her, he realized. Beauty, brains and a NASCAR fan—a guy could do a lot worse.

"I should get back to work," she said, looking suddenly uncomfortable.

Had she read in his eyes some of what he'd been thinking?

"What time do you leave tomorrow?"

"Late morning."

He didn't know what to say after that. "Then I guess this is goodbye, since I have to be at out the track early."

"I guess so," she said, looking anywhere but his eyes. "Good luck tomorrow and Sunday."

"Thanks." Damn it. He didn't want her to leave. He wanted to spend more time with her. To find out what she'd been up to in recent years. Who her favorite driver was. What kind of ice cream she liked.

What?

He stepped back. "Have a safe flight."

"Thanks," she said again. "You, too."

But as he turned away, he couldn't help but feel regret. His hand even lingered on the door for a moment, then quickly, before he changed his mind, he left her room.

"Bye," he heard as the door closed.

Yeah, bye.

Damn it.

CHAPTER SEVEN

CECE MAY HAVE HOPED for a clean getaway, but apparently that wasn't on the cards. A phone call from her boss had her speeding to the racetrack when she couldn't get through to Blain. Apparently the man didn't like being interrupted on race day, so he turned off his cellphone. Track officials were no help. Nor was anybody at his shop. Thus Cece found herself fighting race fans on their way to the Busch race. Returning to the track made her feel…anxious. Yeah, anxious.

She'd spent the whole night analyzing her feelings for Blain. Scratch that. She'd spent the whole night replaying the look on his face when he'd said goodbye. She could have sworn she'd seen regret in his eyes, regret she felt, too. And now here she was, about to face him again, and instead of concern over the news she had to impart, what she felt instead was anxiety that she was about to see him again.

She parked in the infield again, only today she was wearing regular jeans and a comfy off-white sweater that, perversely enough, was too warm, since today there were no thunderclouds in the distance. Thus she was overheated, out of sorts and not in a good mood when she finally tracked down Blain in his Cup car hauler, not the Busch car garage where she'd spent the last half hour looking for him.

"Cece," he said when he spotted her outside the sliding glass doors.

Cece almost didn't recognize him. He wore a different shirt—this one for a different sponsor—the blue polo shirt making his eyes all the more striking.

And there went her heart.

Thump, thump, thump, just as it used to do when they were kids. When he'd been out of her reach and she'd wished he wasn't, and now, oddly…he wasn't.

"Changed your mind, did you?" he asked with a huge grin.

"No," she said, suddenly feeling strange. Okay, so she probably wasn't looking forward to telling him her news. That was to be expected. But she had a feeling her sudden tension had to do more with seeing him face-to-face again than any official business.

Maybe, but that didn't make it any easier.

"I've been trying to get ahold of you all morning," she said, suddenly wanting to get this over with.

He looked wary, his smile dimming a few watts. "What's up?" he asked.

She took a deep breath, wishing she'd never gotten involved with this stupid investigation in the first place. But there was no sense in sugarcoating things.

And so she let out the breath and said, "Forensics came back with a preliminary report on the wreck that killed your friend."

"On a Saturday?"

"They work round the clock."

"And?"

Damn it, why did she hate doing this so much? "They found evidence of nitrates."

His mouth hung open, the smile completely gone now. "Explosives?"

She nodded, quickly and sharply. "It's nothing for certain yet, Blain. Just a chemical swipe that came back positive. They still have to run things through the computer, but I thought you should know."

The crowd roared. Blain looked off to the infield. Two paratroopers were in the air, red and blue streamers trailing behind the lower one, an American flag trailing behind the upper one.

Yeah, the American dream. Chasing killers. *Whoopdedoo.*

"Damn," he said. "I guess that means they're canceling the race."

She shook her head. "They're not. My boss has been on the phone with Daytona all morning. Until we come back with something positive, they won't do a thing."

"A chemical swipe isn't positive?"

She shook her head again. "No, it's not. The positive swab might have resulted from racing fuel mixing with some unknown compound. We won't know anything for certain for another day or two."

"But you're worried."

His perceptiveness surprised her. "I am. I watched the tapes last night. Maybe if I didn't know a lot about racing I might dismiss what happened as an accident, but you're right. The sequence of events is off. It looks like Randy's car exploded *before* he hit the wall."

Blain looked at the ground, and for a second Cece could see the grief in his eyes.

"Blain, I'm so sorry."

She had no idea why she'd said that—nor why she'd missed her plane, hopped in a car and driven all the way out to the track on a race day, just to tell him face-to-face. She could have waited until after the race, or this evening when he went back to his hotel.

"Yeah, well, I'm sorry, too," he said, over the noise of the crowd. Driver introductions were almost over, boos and hisses mixing with wild applause, creating a cacophony of noise that was almost indescribable.

"What are you going to do?" she asked.

"Don't know," he answered.

"You going to tell your driver?"

"On race day? I may as well pull him from the race if I do that."

"So you're going to race today, then."

"What do you think I should do?"

Stupid, how gratified it made her feel to be asked her opinion. "I think you should be concerned."

He nodded, looking grim.

"But I also think this is a different league, and thus not a target." Busch racing wasn't in the same echelon as the Cup tour, even if the cars did look the same. "It seems more likely that tomorrow's race would be the target, not today's. Besides, the note referred to the Cup car circuit, not this one."

"Lance is a Cup driver, too."

"Yeah, but not today."

"And what about tomorrow? What do I do then? We're trying to win a championship. Hell, we're trying to hold on to our sponsor. Star Oil doesn't like that a no-name kid is driving *their* car. We need a win to soothe their ruffled feathers, and to battle the negative image of a dead driver being associated with their logo."

"Stupid," Cece said.

"But fact."

Damned if you do, damned if you don't, Cece thought. "It's a no-win situation."

He crossed his arms, tension lines bracketing his mouth. "Yeah, it is."

"Let Lance race," Cece said on impulse, touching his arm, feeling the soft hairs that were in such contrast to his hard muscles. "I don't see any reason to think Busch cars will come under attack, too. Tomorrow...well, tomorrow might be a different story."

"You think so?"

"It's a gut feeling, but it's the best I can offer right now."

He stared into the distance for a moment, seeking answers to hard questions. When his eyes returned to Cece's face he still didn't say anything immediately. "All right. We'll race."

She hoped she wouldn't come to regret her words.

"On one condition."

She wondered what that could be.

"You stay."

"Stay?" she said in shock. "I can't stay. I need to get back."

He looked out over the homestretch, at the thousands of fans that sat in the stadium, and his face filled with such an expression of uncertainty, she couldn't look away.

"Yeah, but I'd really like it if you hung around."

He glanced back at her, that handsome, chiseled face that she used to fantasize about right in front of her. But it wasn't his nearness that caused her stomach to pitch, caused her to inhale a bit, to stare into blue, blue eyes. It was his words, and the sincerity she heard in them. She told herself not to be weak. Not to give in. So he wanted her around. It wasn't personal.

It sure *felt* personal.

The crowd roared.

To her right, another famous car owner nodded to Blain as he passed. A generator hummed. Cece looked toward the sound, her eyes nearly blinded by the white big rig that housed the "brains" of a major network.

He wanted her to stay.

"Okay," she said, but for one long moment, she wanted to be a race fan, not an FBI agent. Wanted to do this under different circumstances—not for the FBI, but for her own personal pleasure.

"You don't look all that enthusiastic," Blain said.

She opened her mouth, ready to feed him a pithy excuse; instead she found herself saying, "I wish I was here under different circumstances."

He straightened away from her, his eyes holding hers in one of those long, thoughtful glances that made her see things in his gaze she'd never seen before. Doubt. Resignation. Uncertainty.

"Me, too, Cece," he said. "Me, too. But c'mon. Maybe we can pretend everything's normal."

BUT IT WASN'T AS EASY as all that.

Not only was Cece battling concerns that a killer might be on the loose—Blain's crew suddenly all suspects—but she didn't like how nervous she felt at the prospect of being on pit road. During a race.

"Just make sure you stay outside the pit stall," Blain said, his blue headset off one ear so he could listen to her and his crew members at the same time. "When we come in for a stop, stay out of the way."

She had stared killers in the eye, looked down the

barrel of a nine-millimeter, but suddenly she felt as tense as a rookie on her first bust.

She nodded, tempted to wipe her suddenly sweaty hands on her black jeans. They passed through a chain-link fence that separated the garages from pit road, a swarm of humanity immediately enveloping them. Cece went on guard. Lord, it was like a rock concert, only more colorful, yellow-shirted crew mixing with spectators, family members and network personalities. Between bodies she could spy the race cars, a few crew chiefs squatting down by their driver's window, some drivers just sitting in their car alone, staring straight ahead. Busch racing wasn't the same level as Cup racing, but a lot of the same drivers drove both kinds of cars. So while there weren't as many people in the stands, she imagined most of the rest looked and felt the same as the big leagues.

Chaos. Crowds. Confusion. The perfect cover for a killer.

She tried not to think about that, or to lose Blain as they wormed their way among crew members and TV personalities. More than one person caught Blain's arm, wishing him luck, slapping him on the shoulder or the rear as he passed by. It all seemed surreal.

"Sit over here," he said when they found his stall. Someone had set up a bright red tent opposite Blain's pit. Stacks of tires were piled beneath the canopy, the black rubber turned a deep purple by the red, radiant light. Opposite them was a matching red toolbox as big as a car, which housed wrenches of every size and shape. On top of the whole thing sat a chair, a TV and an umbrella to cover it all.

"You'll know when we're about to pit," he said, "because everyone'll start moving around. Just stay back."

Got it. Stay back.

"I'll check in with you from time to time." But instead of turning away, he held her gaze. "Thanks for staying, Cece."

She nodded, struck by this stranger who stared down at her. Gone was Blain the Jerk. In his place was Blain the Nice Guy—Blain who tipped one side of his mouth up in an odd sort of smile before turning away from her, stepping into the stream of people and entering his pit. One of the crew members caught her eye, the man's mouth obstructed by his microphone. He winked. Cece nodded back at him, wondering…was he their perpetrator? Was there really a crackpot out there trying to knock off drivers? If so, was he here today?

A look at Blain confirmed he might be thinking the same thing. Sure, this was race day, but she had no doubt some of the tension in his eyes had little to do with competition.

A TV crew came up to him. To her surprise, a reporter shoved a microphone in his face. Somehow amid all the pandemonium she'd managed to forget that he was famous. They filmed him first, then a man Cece assumed must be the Busch car crew chief.

Another suspect?

Damn it, this drove her crazy. She was seeing bad guys everywhere.

That's what you're trained to do, Cece. So just do it.

She was a federal agent, a protector. It was her job to keep people safe. And if forensics' initial findings proved true, she'd make darn sure she did exactly that. She had to...for Blain.

CHAPTER EIGHT

"ROLLING," Lance said, his voice sounding tense, even to Blain's ears. They were all on edge. Race day, tense under normal circumstances, had reached new levels since Randy's death, even for his Busch team.

Blain barely heard the escalation in crowd noise as the cars took off. He glanced back at Cece. She stared at the group of cars, a hand lifted to shield her eyes. Her face looked as tense as his own, her concern for him evident every time their eyes met. Just when she'd become a confidante and a friend he had no idea, and yet somehow, she had. Not surprising, he thought, given that she was the only one in the garage who knew what he did: that someone might have tried to kill Randy.

Acid hit his stomach like peroxide on an open wound. He felt like calling Lance back. Felt like going to the nearest official and asking him to call off the race. But Cece was right; they didn't know anything for certain yet, and after all, the killer's note hadn't threatened this league.

Still…

The cars picked up speed, the sound like the roar of a hundred tornadoes. Angry whines that reached beneath his earphones and vibrated his chest cavity. Race day. Usually excitement filled him, but today that thrill was gone.

He motioned to Cece. She mouthed the word, "Me?" as she pointed to herself, blond brows lifted, and despite the tension, despite the acid in his gut, Blain found himself smiling. Cece, his fearless FBI agent, looked reluctant to enter the maw of his pit stall. But just like the Cece of old, he watched her straighten her shoulders and look both ways before crossing though the stream of owners and TV crews that moved up and down pit road. She came up alongside him and he handed her a pair of spare headphones that hung from a toolbox.

"Here," he yelled, because by now they'd be lucky to hear a DC-10 take off. The roar of the fans—nearly fifty thousand of them—drowned out all sound but that of the cars themselves.

She tugged them awkwardly over her ears and he flipped her mike down, pressing the button on the side of his own headphones. "If you need to talk, just press here and speak."

"Ah, thanks, honey," came Lance's familiar voice, his words syrupy-sweet. "But I'm not in the mood for sweet talk right now. Maybe later."

Cece's met Blain's gaze in shock.

He rolled his eyes and shook his head. Lance

thought himself a comedian. Turning to the track, Blain tried to find his car, the thunder of engines telling him the pack was on the back stretch. The smell of burnt rubber filled the air.

"Lance, cut the chatter. We're on the air." By that he meant people listening in.

But his new driver didn't appear to care. "Ah, honey, you're always spoiling my fun."

He met his crew chief's eyes. Mike Johnson had been in the business as long as Blain, but they were both a little baffled by Lance's stand-up comedy routine on race day.

"Hey, was it sexy Cece you gave a headset to?" Lance asked, obviously in a conversational mood.

Blain didn't answer.

"Because if it was, I have a little song for her—"

"No," his crew chief said. "Don't—"

Too late. Lance belted out the words to "Are You Lonesome Tonight?" as he swerved his car back and forth to warm the tires.

And then, to Blain's shock, Cece pressed her mike and interrupted him midstream. "Lance, there's a pack of dogs following you."

Which made every member of his Busch team laugh. Blain included, and it felt nice to forget, even if it was just for a second, that there was a killer on the loose.

"Ah, honey," Lance said, "they're just following the Big Dog." And then he howled like a wolf, causing everyone with headsets to clutch at their ears.

Blain rolled his eyes. Cece met his gaze and smiled.

And Blain felt like the sun came out, even though it was already shining brightly in the sky. And he was glad that she was there in the pit with them. Glad she was on his side. Glad she was trying to lighten his mood a bit.

"That's enough, Lance," Blain said. "Keep it up and you'll find yourself in the dog*house*."

"As long as Cece's in there with me."

"Now there's an offer the lady can't refuse," Blain's crew chief said. "A date in a doghouse."

"Believe me." Blain heard Cece's voice though the headset. "I've had worse."

Which prompted Lance to say, "Does that mean we're on, honey?"

"Only if I suddenly turn into a poodle."

"Mmm, doggie style—"

"Lance!" Blain cut him off sternly. The last thing they needed was a fine from the track officials.

His driver seemed to understand, because he went quiet, or maybe that was because they'd been ordered to line up. A few minutes later, Blain heard Lance say, "Houston, we have liftoff," and the Corvette pace car ducked off the track.

The race was on.

Blain's tension returned with a vengeance. He and his crew chief turned to the TV monitor mounted on the side of his toolbox. Lance expertly kept his tenth place starting position.

"Feels a little loose," Lance said.

"Bad?" came his crew chief's voice.

"Nah," Lance said. "I've felt looser. Usually women, but the car's okay."

Which elicited a few more wry shakes of the head.

"One-track mind," Mike said.

"That's why Mr. Sanders hired me," Lance replied. "My mind's always on a track of some sort."

Actually, he'd hired Lance because he'd seen promise in the kid's driving, promise that he hoped would come to full bloom under his crew chief's tutelage. That seemed to be proving true, judging by the way Lance drove today. Smooth, steady and yet with just an edge of recklessness. No question, Lance Cooper had what it took to be great.

Out of the corner of his eye Blain caught movement. One of his crew members came forward and talked to Cece. With hand gestures and the occasional shout, he did what Blain should have done— helped Cece become queen of the toolbox. He watched as her lithe frame climbed aboard the little seat anchored to the top. Usually he sat there, but it was safer for Cece to be out of the way. Plus, it gave her a better view in case…

But he didn't want to think about that, and so he didn't. Instead he concentrated on the race. That was all there was left to do: watch the action. A few seconds of madness when Lance made a pit stop, punctuated by long stretches of cars going round and round. And as the laps added up, Blain's tension eased. They ran good, at least until lap eighty-nine, when a bad pit stop put Lance ten spots down.

"And I was having sooo much fun," Lance quipped as he moved his car into position. Not for this kid the temper tantrums that so many drivers engaged in. Blain liked that about him.

"Clear," came the spotter's voice, indicating Lance could move into one of the two racing lanes.

Cece must have realized something was wrong by the look on Blain's face. She leaned down and asked, "What happened?"

"Bad pit stop," he answered. She nodded and straightened back up, but not before shooting him a look of disappointment. She liked this, he thought.

The cars picked up speed when the yellow light went out. The crowd roared, his crew stared at the television monitor. Someone tried to pass Lance going three wide into the turn two.

"Uh-oh," Lance said.

Blain jerked upright.

"Oh, shit," they heard next.

He turned toward the TV. Cece bolted upright, too, only she stood, hand shielding her eyes as she looked toward turn two. The TV monitor showed the wreck perfectly.

"Left, left, left," came the spotter's voice as suddenly spinning cars sent up a plume of dark gray smoke.

But there was no place for Lance to go. Blain

could see that. A car hit the wall, slid down the track. Lance T-boned him.

What came next happened so fast it would take several replays to figure it out, but suddenly Lance's car went airborne, despite the safety flaps. Metal flew off his car, smoke filled the air. Blain just watched as slowly, ever so slowly, his car came to a stop on the infield grass. Only it didn't look like a car anymore.

"Lance?" his crew chief asked.

Blain turned to his pit crew. They were standing on the pit wall, trying to get a view of the wreck. Mike stood in the center, his hand never leaving his headphones.

"Lance," he said again. "You okay, buddy?"

"I'm all right," Lance said slowly, much to the relief of everyone in the pit, and probably a few million people at home. "But I'm thinking I just blew my chances to impress Cece with my driving skills."

CHAPTER NINE

CECE WOULD NEVER FORGET the look on Blain's face for as long as she lived. His eyes weren't filled with disappointment, they were guarded, worried… afraid.

She'd watched him stare at the TV monitor as he watched the network's replay over and over. She'd climbed down and done the same thing, too. They weren't looking to see who'd caused the accident, they were looking to ensure that it actually *was* an accident, and the whole time they did, Cece wanted to lay a hand on his shoulder in comfort. She knew that every time he watched his car spin out of control he was reliving the loss of his driver, and worrying that Lance might have been a second victim.

In the end, it looked to be just that, a wreck. But Blain stormed out of his pit as if it were much more.

"Blain," she called out as he headed toward his Cup car hauler. "Blain!" she called again. He ignored her, Cece growing more and more frustrated as she followed him from the pits.

"Blain, darn it," she said, finally seizing his hand

by the open glass door at the back of the hauler. The chrome panels on either side gave her a perfect view of the way his face had hardened, of the way his eyes closed for a second before he turned to face her.

"Not here," he said, tugging his hand from her grasp.

She felt the loss of contact in a way that surprised her. Disappointment was *her* emotion now, and the sadness of a bystander who didn't know what to do, because she knew how he felt—she'd felt some of the same emotions when she'd seen Lance wreck.

Blain climbed the steps into the big rig. The place was deserted, most of Blain's Cup crew off doing other things.

"Blain, you're scaring me," Cece said the minute the door to his lounge closed.

He ignored her, pulling out a stool she hadn't noticed before tucked beneath a cabinet. When he opened the cabinet doors, a computer was exposed.

"What are you doing?" she asked, watching as he booted it up.

"Sending Barry Bidwell an e-mail."

Barry Bidwell, the head of NASCAR. "About what?" she asked, even though she knew.

"He needs to cancel tomorrow's race."

She'd known the words were coming, yet she still felt her stomach drop.

"Blain, he won't do that. My boss already talked to him. Until we have concrete evidence…"

"What more evidence do they need?" Blain

asked, turning toward her. He stood, flicking his stool toward the table in the center of the small room. It flew beneath it and crashed into the black couch on the other side. "All he has to do is watch the replay. Randy's car explodes. It just erupts. There's no rhyme or reason, it just does. Anyone who knows anything about racing would know it wasn't a faulty fuel tank."

"We don't know that for certain."

"The killer sent a note—"

She stepped toward him. The veins in his neck were swollen, his skin flush with fast-moving blood. "The note was received after the accident."

"It was mailed before the accident."

"We don't know that."

"It had to have been."

"Blain," she said, resting a hand on his arm, all the while asking herself why she kept touching him. "Calm down. There's still a chance Randy's death was nothing more than a string of coincidences."

"Coincidence!" he all but yelled, and she could feel him flinch beneath her hand. "You said yourself they've found evidence of nitrates."

"But that doesn't mean explosives. That's one of many possibilities."

"But *you* think it does."

She stiffened, her hand dropping to her side. She couldn't deny it.

"We can't risk it, Cece," he said, his voice low and calm. "If there's a chance, even a hint that some crazy person might be out to blow up a racetrack or a driver, then the race needs to be stopped."

Without realizing it, she began to slowly shake her head. "It won't happen, Blain. You know it and I know it. If it turns out the threat is valid, then all that'll happen is extra security measures. The show will go on, just as it has whenever other popular events have been threatened."

He didn't say anything, but she could tell when her words finally penetrated. The Federal Government put a brave face on things. A year ago a direct threat had been harbored against the Super Bowl. They'd had good cause to think it might be terrorists. But all they'd been told to do was alert the media and to step up security. Nobody, not the American public, football fans or the media, had been aware of just how serious a threat it'd been.

Blain turned and slowly sat down on the couch. She told herself to stand there. No, that wasn't right. She'd been trained to stand still while a victim assimilated facts. But for some reason she couldn't disconnect from Blain, and so she found herself going to him, squatting down in front of him. To her shock, she saw his eyes were rimmed with red. Blain Sanders, the jock, the celebrity, her high school nemesis, moved to tears.

"Blain," she said softly, taking his hand.

He didn't pull away.

"I don't know if I can do it, Cece."

And she knew how much that admission must

have cost him, even as a part of her took note of the nickname.

"I don't know if I can send Lance out again knowing he might—"

Be killed.

He didn't need to say the words. She gently squeezed his hand. "Lance takes that risk every day."

"Yeah, but not like this."

And it ate Blain up. She stared at him and marveled at a side of him she'd never seen. A softer side. Vulnerable. More human. He cared—genuinely cared—about his driver, and the shift from thinking of Blain as a self-centered jerk to a kind and caring human being stirred things she'd rather weren't disturbed.

"Blain, I have a feeling that even if you tell Lance what's going on, he'll still want to race. It's in his blood."

Their gazes connected and Cece was rocked by how poleaxed she felt when their eyes met.

"It's in my blood, too, Cece. I love this sport. I'd do anything to stay in it. But I can't stand by and let it endanger people's lives."

"I know," she said. She slowly rose to her feet, bending down to kiss him on the top of his head, an intimate, womanly gesture that took her by surprise. Only as she did, his head turned a bit and she ended by kissing his cheek, and the way it felt when her lips connected with his flesh…well, it made her want to kiss something else. She saw the desire that instantly flared in his own eyes, desire she'd caught a glimpse of last night.

No, she warned herself. She shouldn't. But something crackled in the air between them, something instant and undeniable, and before she could think better of it, she'd kissed a little closer to his mouth. Cece could feel him tense. She drew back a bit. His breath drifted over her, and the intimacy of inhaling the scent of him, when for so many years she'd fantasized...

"Cece," he said.

She stood still. This wasn't a fantasy. This was a flesh-and-blood man.

He reached up and tugged her head down to his own.

"Blain, I don't think this is a good id—"

He kissed her, pulled her to him, Cece settling on his hard thighs as if she'd done it a million times before—and in her dreams, maybe she had. Only this was so much better than her fantasies.

Then all thought fled. She opened her mouth, her heart thudding so loudly it whitewashed all other sound. And though she didn't want it, though she didn't expect it, excitement lit pinpoints of electricity through her body; it made her limbs shake, made her bite back a moan.

Kissing him was nothing like her fantasies. It was better than a fantasy. When he increased the pressure of his lips, she followed his lead and opened her mouth, and that was when it all erupted, when her body and her mind began to realize that this was an attraction unlike any she'd felt before.

She pulled away out of self-preservation, because she couldn't, just couldn't, deal with the reality of kissing Blain Sanders.

"That was a mistake," she said, pushing herself off him, a part of her mind scrambled beyond repair.

"Cece, that was—"

"A mistake," she repeated, shocked at what kissing him had done to her insides. Not to mention her unprofessional behavior in letting him—

"Look," she said, trying to get control of the situation. Control. That was good. When feeling pole-axed one should always appear in control. "Obviously we're both a little stressed. The race. Lance's wreck. It's only natural that we should gravitate toward each other."

You've never gravitated to a witness before.

"I don't think we should read too much into this…" *mind-blowing kiss,* she mentally finished. Toe-curling, breast-tingling, thigh-burning kiss.

Holy smoke.

"Cece, that wasn't—"

"Professional." She cut him off. She had to cut him off because she couldn't handle this right now— whatever *this* was. "You're right, and I'm sorry. I accept all the blame."

"Like hell you will."

She stiffened, not liking the sudden challenge she saw in his eyes. She'd seen that look on masculine faces before, though usually it was on a gun range. But it always meant confrontation.

"Okay then, fine," she said in a rush, because she was starting to feel a bit panicked. "It's all your fault. You shouldn't have kissed me. I'd slap your face if I didn't need to call in to the office." She glanced at the digital clock on the wall. "Wow, look at the time. I need to get going." And she was already backing toward the door. That alone should have alerted her to the seriousness of her reaction. Cece never, ever backed away from anything. "I'll check in with you when I get to San Francisco."

She spun away.

"Cece, wait—"

But she ignored him, the calm, cool FBI agent completely gone as, for the first time in her life, a woman emerged to take her place—a woman who suddenly felt about seventeen years old.

BLAIN FOLLOWED HER to the end of the hauler, but without making a scene, there wasn't a whole lot he could do.

She'd looked panicked.

It was a new expression for Cece's face. Never, not once when they'd been teenagers, nor anytime since, had he seen such a look. If their kiss hadn't already thrown him, her reaction to it certainly would have.

"Trouble with the new girlfriend?" his Cup car crew chief, Allen, said from behind him.

Girlfriend? That's what his crew thought?

Yeah. He supposed they did. Blain never brought women to a race—no time to baby-sit—but his gut twisted like spun rubber at the prospect of telling Allen Cece's true purpose.

A purpose that had just been complicated by that kiss.

"No trouble," he muttered.

"Well, if there is, I'm next in line to date her."

Lance's words had Blain turning toward the driver. He'd come up between the haulers, a beige butterfly bandage on his head. A look toward Cece revealed she'd made it almost to the end of the garage. It was now or never to go after her. Blain decided he'd leave her be...for now.

He shook his head, looked back at Lance. "They release you from the care center already?"

"Yup. I'm A-okay."

"Kinda hard to injure a head that already has nothing in it," said another one of his crew members. His white-and-orange team shirt was too big for his small frame, which made him look even more boyish when he grinned widely.

"This from a man who thought geometry had something to do with volcanoes."

"I told you," the dark-haired jackman said, "I just got geology and geometry confused."

"And he thinks I'm the one with a faulty head," Lance said, his eyes moving back to Cece. At least that's what it looked like. Blain followed his gaze. Sure enough, it could only be Cece he was staring at because the Cup garage was mostly deserted. Only Cece could hold Lance's eye.

Blain's hackles rose and he found himself saying, "She's not your type."

Lance glanced back at him, lifting a brow as he said, "Hell, by the looks of things, she's not your type, either."

Lance crossed his arms in front of him, and Blain found it ironic that the man wore a white T-shirt with Sanders Racing scrawled across the left pocket, and yet he appeared to be challenging Blain over a woman. Unbelievable.

"Cece's an old friend," Blain said. "I'm not interested in her romantically."

Hah! You are, too, buddy.

"I don't want to see her hurt," Blain said. "We've all seen how you treat women around here."

"Gentlemen, gentlemen," his crew chief said. "You do realize you sound an awful lot like you're fighting over a girl?"

Blain ordered his shoulders to relax. Damn it. When had this thing gotten so out of control? When had his *life* gotten out of control?

His cellphone beeped.

Blain looked down, recognizing the number on the display as the home office for NASCAR.

This couldn't be good.

IT WASN'T.

Blain stared around the plush conference room, various PR people, vice presidents and racing officials staring back at him from one of Phoenix International Raceway's conference rooms.

"It's not a gag order," Barry Bidwell, president of the stock car racing association, said. "We just don't want any wild rumors started."

"Rumors, Barry?" Blain asked.

"Yeah, rumors."

Blain had known the man since Blain was seventeen—a wet-behind-the-ears West Coast kid who had racing his blood. Back then he'd been Mr. Bidwell, and back then racing hadn't been a billion-dollar industry. Which was why, Blain suspected, they'd flown in to see him today. Wouldn't do to start a panic.

"The thing is, Blain, the FBI doesn't even know if the letter we received is connected to Randy's death."

Blain just stared at him. The man had gotten heavy in recent years. The fat of good living clung to his jowls and neck. Thinning black hair looked to have been recently plugged near the front, his suit the kind Barry wouldn't have been caught dead in twenty years ago. Hell, twenty years ago Barry couldn't have afforded the thing. Back then he'd been a smooth-talking Southerner with a vision of what stock car racing could be. The only thing that remained of that man was the accent.

"And we don't even know for sure that Randy's death was murder," Rick Vanhausen, the association's PR guy, said.

Blain smirked a moment before saying, "Don't hand me that crap, Rick. All you're doing is delaying the inevitable. You know it wasn't an accident. Cars don't explode *before* they hit a wall. You know it and I know it."

"All we're doing is asking you to keep quiet. Not indefinitely," Barry added quickly, raising his pudgy hands, "just for a few more days."

"And you couldn't do that over the phone?"

"We didn't think you'd listen over the phone."

And they'd have been right. In Blain's present mood he'd have likely hung up on them. Damn it.

"And because we wanted to tell you face-to-face that we think it'd be a bad idea if you pulled out of tomorrow's race."

"What?" Blain asked, shocked that they would say such a thing. Whether he raced or not was his choice, not theirs.

"Look, we know what you're thinking," Barry said with a glance at Rick. "We know you're probably scared. Worried about your new driver. But you can't respond by running."

Running?

"We don't want you pulling out."

"You can't tell me what to do."

"We control your licenses, Blain. It'd be a shame to lose them all simply because you don't want to cooperate."

"What?"

"Don't," Barry warned, holding up a hand.

"Don't say things that might make the situation worse."

"Like what? Calling you all a bunch of assholes? You are." Bastards. They couldn't do this. They couldn't. He wouldn't let him.

"Just cooperate with us, Blain. Keep quiet about this—and that includes telling your driver. If word leaks out about what's going on, we'll hold you responsible."

"Go ahead," Blain said, the anger that had been seeping through a tiny gasket of control finally blowing. "And while you're at it, why don't you fine me, too?"

"We will." Barry smiled. "By the time we're done, you'd be lucky to have ten cents in the bank." But then his face softened. "Blain, I hate to play hardball, but we really don't have any choice. We need your cooperation, and we'll do anything to get it."

And as he looked from Rick to Barry, Blain began to shake his head. "You know, I'm beginning to think the killer sent me that letter because they knew you guys would sit on it. Don't go breaking the almighty racing bank. Don't go scaring off fans. Don't go worrying the drivers and teams."

"That's not why we're putting a lid on this," Rick said.

"Bullshit," Blain said, standing up. "You forget, boys, I've been around this business a long, long time. And that's the problem with the association nowadays. It's turned into a business. A frickin' money-making machine. The last thing you want is for that money to stop pouring in."

Voices erupted around the room, Blain too upset to care.

"If you don't like it, Blain, you don't have to play."

Barry's voice boomed out, deep and unmistakable, as was the unspoken threat: keep quiet or you won't be allowed to race. Oh, yeah, the good ol' boys were good at putting a chokehold on things. They could keep someone out of racing with the snap of their fingers. They'd been doing it to women for years, despite their public ERA attitude.

"Are you threatening me?" Blain asked.

Mr. Bidwell looked as unfazed as an elephant confronted by a lamb. "No," he drawled. "I'm merely pointing out the possibilities. We need your cooperation. If you can't give it, I suggest you go home. Indefinitely."

"You know I can't do that."

"Then work with us, Blain. It'll only be for a few days."

But, see, that was the problem. Somehow Blain doubted that. They would keep the lid on this for as long as they could. He knew it. The unspoken question they were asking was for Blain to do that, too. That's why they'd flown out from Daytona now. It wasn't because they were trying to play nice. It was because they wanted him to understand just how serious they were.

"Fine," Blain said, furious, disgusted and, yeah, disillusioned. "I'll keep quiet. For now."

He left the last words hanging.

"Well, now, Blain," Barry said. "We appreciate that," he said in a cool, almost affable Southern drawl.

Bite me hovered on Blain's lips. Instead he moved away from the table, doing his best not to break the conference room's glass door as he exited.

"You think he'll do it?" Rick Vanhausen said after the door had closed.

"He'll do it," Barry replied. "He doesn't have a choice."

CHAPTER TEN

BLAIN HADN'T CALLED.

Cece thought about it the whole way into work that Monday, the BART train filled to capacity as it zoomed up the Bay Area peninsula.

She'd waited for the phone to ring all Saturday night, and when that failed, all Sunday morning.

But he hadn't called.

That bothered her. And that was bad. Very bad. She'd kissed him, and not only was it completely against the FBI's code of ethics, it was dangerous. You couldn't concentrate on an investigation if you were lusting after the case's primary contact.

Jeesh, what a mess.

"I was hoping you'd come in today," Bob said when she arrived at the office, her feet slipping to a halt as she passed his open door.

"Can't keep away," she said sarcastically. Technically she could have taken the day off after having to work all weekend, but she wanted to finish writing up some notes, then hand the case over to someone else.

Yeah, that's right, she was quitting the case.

But the look on Bob's face told her that might be harder than she thought.

"Come on in," he said.

Cece knew it was coming. Their forensics department worked around the clock. It wouldn't take them long to verify their preliminary findings.

Sure enough, Bob said without preamble, "Turns out your friend was right. His driver's death wasn't an accident."

If Cece hadn't been sitting down already, she would have then.

"Ballistics indicates the load was put in the frame of the race car near the back end. That's why nobody saw it."

The frame. Made sense. After what she'd learned this weekend, it would be the only place a crew and tech inspection wouldn't poke around. But she felt her muscles tense as the implications sank in.

"It's an inside job," she mused aloud. Unbelievable. After all her comments about it being a wild-goose chase, turned out Blain was right all along.

Bad. Very bad.

"From the report you filed—good work, by the way," Bob mumbled, "that means only someone at the shop could have placed the explosives."

"Who?" Cece found herself wondering, the faces of different team members floating through her mind. Was one of them out for blood? A terrorist? A serial killer?

"Why?" she asked aloud. "Aside from the terrorist angle, I can't imagine an insider targeting a driver. The people in this industry are loyal to the sport."

"A grudge, maybe?"

She leaned back. She knew crew members moved around a lot. Was it possible someone secretly had it out for Blain and his team? But then she began to shake her head. "The letter Blain received. It threatens to detonate another bomb at a racetrack. That doesn't seem personal."

"Maybe that's just a diversion," Bob said. "The point is that the investigation is at a whole new level now. When can you leave for North Carolina?"

"North Carolina?" Cece said instantly.

"We need you there ASAP."

"Can't someone from the Charlotte Bureau take over?"

"Negative."

Cece tried not to panic. The last thing she wanted was to see Blain Sanders again.

"I just don't think Mr. Sanders and I work well together."

"That's not what Sanders tells me."

He'd spoken to Blain? When?

She felt color enter her cheeks. "He was probably just being nice."

But Bob was shaking his head. "I need you, Cece. Sanders told me you were great this weekend. Topnotch. He also made it perfectly clear that he still wants you on the case."

"But, Bob—"

"No ifs, ands, or buts, Cece. Look, I know you don't like the man, but obviously you're able to put that aside. That's what a good agent's supposed to do. You're needed in North Carolina, and you'll leave today."

IT WASN'T HARD to get places when one worked for the FBI. Private jets were available to whisk agents wherever they wanted. Turned out a couple of West Coast agents were headed east the next day and so Cece was able to hitch a ride on a flight to Charlotte, her cast-iron stomach suddenly corroding on the inside. What would she say to Blain? What was she going to do when she saw him?

Ask him why he hadn't called.

No, she told herself. She wouldn't do that. What she needed to do was act like a mature adult. Meet Blain somewhere and tell him she wanted off the case. Frankly, he was the only one who could get her removed, because as long as he kept insisting she hang around, she'd be stuck.

So when the plane touched down, she was glad they were meeting in just a few hours. She'd taken the coward's way out and asked someone in her office to call and make arrangements for a rendezvous in the Best Western's lobby. But that didn't stop her hands from shaking when she arrived. Nor as she unpacked a half hour later, the hotel room just like a thousand others she'd stayed in. Queen-size bed jutting out from the middle of the wall, generic prints above it, nightstands to left and right. The only thing different was the color, a sort of avocado-green that brought to mind the seventies.

Someone knocked.

She wasn't expecting anyone other than the maid with some extra towels, so she didn't even think twice about opening the door, other than using her standard FBI caution.

"Hello, Cece."

She found herself standing there for a full three seconds before saying, "Blain," in shock, her heart taking on the rhythm of the mambo. "I—" *don't know what to say* "—wasn't expecting you."

"I was here early, thought I'd come up."

"How'd you get my room number?"

"Your boss."

She'd kill him. Of course, Bob didn't know her breathing would go all haywire just seeing Blain standing there, and that she'd feel half-dressed in her pink halter top and black slacks, wishing for the matching jacket still in her closet. Nor that she'd find herself wishing for her radio and her badge and for her hair to be up—all the things she suddenly real-ized were part of her day-to-day armor.

Blain stripped that away with a glance.

"Mind if I come in?"

Yes. Yes, she did mind. A lot.

"Actually, why don't I meet you downstairs?"

"Your boss told me Randy was murdered."

She'd assumed Blain had been told, and against her better judgment, she found herself looking for signs of how well he'd taken it.

Not good.

It was there in the tension on his brow, the way his pupils were slightly dilated. In the way those eyes kept shifting around, his hands in the pockets of his dark gray slacks as he looked anywhere but at her.

She stepped back from the door.

"C'mon in."

Damn it, Cece—have you no control?

Apparently not, she admitted as she watched him walk into her room, that sweet, masculine odor of his making her realize yet again that she had feelings for this man she likely shouldn't have.

"It was quite a shock," he said, turning to her near the bed. "In spite of your warning."

"I'm sorry, Blain," she said as the door closed behind him with a prison-cell click that made Cece's heart take off like a jet.

"I've had days to think about this," he said. "But I still can't believe someone killed him." And when he finally met her gaze, there were a million unanswered questions in his eyes. "Why?"

"I don't know," she replied honestly, crossing her arms in front of her, for the first time having to push away emotion to concentrate on her job. "But I promise you, we'll find them."

Which was the perfect opening for her to tell him

that it wasn't *her* who would *find* anything. That she wanted off the case. That he had to tell her boss that…only she hesitated. And it was then that she realized she didn't want to leave. Suddenly, resigning seemed like such a cowardly thing to do in light of Blain's obvious need. But then she took stock of the way her heart pounded in his presence, of the way she couldn't seem to stop herself from noticing how tired he looked, how sad…upset. And how she wanted to reach out and touch him.

"Blain, look, I have something I need to tell you."

He stiffened a bit, his chin lifting as if he was bracing for even worse news.

"I want off the case."

"No," he said quickly, simply.

"Yes," she said equally quickly.

"You can't."

She tightened her arms across the front of her, another thing her training told her was a defense mechanism. "Don't try and pull that blackmail shit on me, Blain Sanders, because I know you better now and I don't believe for a second that you'd go so far as to destroy my career."

He stared down at her, his eyes like those of a frightened child asking for help.

"Don't quit on me, Ceec."

And despite what she told herself not to feel, she still noticed the pull, the tug of sympathy.

Damn it.

"I really don't have a choice, Blain. But I can still

keep an eye on things from San Francisco. I just can't be involved with the actual investigation."

"Why not?"

Because I've got the hots for you. Because that can lead to trouble. Because once upon a time I was preoccupied while on the job and it got my partner killed.

She'd never allow that to happen again.

"I just think it's for the best."

He stared at her for a second longer, his eyes blinking once before he said, "Fine."

Fine?

"I was getting tired of keeping my hands off you, anyway."

He wh—

What?

"This way we can pick up where we left off in Las Vegas."

Oh, no—

"Blain, I don't think—"

He closed the distance between them. She moved away. At least she did so in her mind. In reality she stood rooted to the spot.

And that was when he kissed her.

And, damn it, she kissed him back, arched into him so quickly that her breasts bumped his chest, the connection sending instant heat to the aroused parts of her body. When he tipped his head and increased the pressure of his mouth, she opened for him, the hot, sweet taste of him sending her blood pumping even more.

She realized she wasn't going to stop him, real-ized she wanted him. If she were honest, she could admit to wanting him for years.

She'd resigned from the case. He'd made his in-terest known. Now she could take him up on the offer, even as a part of her wondered if this was just a way for him to forget about Randy's death.

So she touched him, moved her hand between them and stroked the length of him. He moaned, and she marveled for a moment that this was the same man who'd all but shunned her as a teen. Now *she* had the upper hand—no pun intended. She didn't hesitate to use it, either. She touched him again. He pushed into her. She got tired of the barricade be-tween them so she pushed her hand down his pants, frustrated by the cotton briefs he wore, but then he began to caress her breasts and so she decided she could wait a bit, even encouraged him to touch her some more by leaning into him.

She pulled her mouth away. "Take your pants off."

He didn't need any more urging, stepping out of his shoes a second later, his pants dropping from his waist. She got her first glimpse of a taut stomach last seen during teenage years.

His briefs came next.

He wanted her.

Blain Sanders wanted her.

"Your turn," he said as he pulled his cotton polo over his head.

A one-night stand. Sexual therapy. Whatever they would later call it, the time for fun and games was over. She could end it all now. Instead she pulled her shirt out of her waistband.

She liked the way his eyes stayed with her as she unbuttoned her top. And after she had slipped her arms out of the cotton sleeves, she liked the way he watched her undo her bra. The way he seemed to grow more erect as she stepped out of her shoes, then began to undo her pants. She felt the moisture begin to build between her legs and she slowly slid the fabric down. He looked momentarily surprised when he saw the gun strapped to her calf.

"Protection," she said.

"Not the kind of protection I had in mind."

She smiled a bit, though her fingers trembled as she removed the weapon. She flicked her hair behind her and went to him, and the moment she did, he touched her breasts.

The intimacy of him stroking her flesh made her burn all over again. He didn't move, didn't lean toward her, just touched her. His fingers felt almost raspy, the tips tracing lazy circles around her nipples so that they tightened and tightened. Just two fingers, that was all he used, but they teased her until she felt ready to jerk him toward her, to pull him on top of her, to let him thrust into her over and over and over again.

Cece tried to lead him to the bed, admitting that she'd dreamed about the moment for too long to wait, but he took control and pulled her toward the bathroom—though what he intended to do in there, she had no idea.

She soon found out. He opened the glass shower door, reaching in to turn on a spray of water. Ahh.

He turned back to her and Cece liked the way his eyes roamed over her. He could have been touching her with a sex toy and her reaction would have been no less heated. She would have taken him in hand except he leaned down and kissed her again, his tongue filling her mouth, hot flesh meeting hot flesh so that Cece found herself tilting her head, opening for him and kissing him back in a way that made it clear how ready she was to do whatever he wanted. Whatever. Mist from the shower covered them, cold at first. Cece's nipples grew taut. He must have felt it because he bent down and suckled one, and man, she had to smother a groan, her head falling back so that her hair nearly touched the small of her back. The shower spray grew hot and so did Cece, especially when Blain released her nipple and began to kiss her in other spots. Like the side of her ribs.

She gasped.

The curve of her belly.

She moaned.

The apex of her thighs.

She wanted, oh, how she wanted, to open for him, to allow him intimate access. Instead she guided him up, her gaze no doubt as glassy as his own when she said, "Later," then reached in to adjust the water temperature.

She wanted it cool, not hot—they both burned already. But Blain didn't give her time to get it just right. He came up against her, shoving her hair aside so he could suckle her neck, taking her beneath the cool stream of water so that they both gasped. Then she felt his hand slip between her legs, the slickness there made even more fluid by the cascading water. She touched him back. Their mouths met, water dripping down their faces to blend with their kiss, and when he stroked her, she stroked him back, her shoulders coming into contact with the cold tiles, hair growing wet and heavy on the ends. She hardly noticed. His finger, it'd found the spot…that sweet spot that made her spread her legs, made her wish he would bend his knees, push himself inside of her.

"Cece," he growled.

She realized that she'd guided him to her opening, that she was encouraging him to enter her, but he took control yet again, turning her before she could say a word. His erection found her rear crevice, and she wondered…but, no, he let his erection rest there as he reached around and found the spot again.

Her turn to gasp, her turn to take control as she reached behind her and spread herself so that her cheeks fully sheltered him. He groaned, then groaned again, squatting a bit so that he could rub himself fully along her valley. Cece pressed into him. They were both panting now, sexual excitement building inside Cece to the point that she never wanted it to end. She wanted to hover on the brink of her orgasm, wanted to revel in his harsh breaths, in the way his hard cock glided up and down her valley. If she bent over, he could enter her from the rear....

His finger found her entrance again. He pushed inside of her.

Cece climaxed.

She didn't mean to. Damn it. She didn't want to, but she lost herself to the knee-buckling shock of her orgasm. Blain's own breaths sounded harsh. He groaned and Cece knew he was coming, too, could feel his muscles spasm just before he went rigid behind her.

His hand slid out of her. She noticed then that his other hand lay flat against the wall to her right. His tan arm flexed as his elbow bent, as if he momentarily lost strength.

Water cooled their bodies. Maybe a little too cool. Blain slowly straightened. Cece did too. He turned her, his hands coming around to slide down the small of her back. And though she'd just been satiated, though she'd just had one of the best orgasms of her life, she wanted him to pick her up, to thrust himself inside of her.

He looked into her eyes. "That was..."

Her cell phone.

He looked toward the bathroom door.

Her cell phone rang on.

"Do you think you should get that?"

Not when I've got something better to do. But the professional in her couldn't quite bring herself to say that.

"Yeah," she said.

CHAPTER ELEVEN

"BLACKWELL," Cece answered, a towel the size of a dishrag clutched in front of her, which made her wonder why she even bothered since it was a bit like covering a nude painting with a Band-Aid.

"Agent Blackwell, this is Agent Ashton from the Charlotte Bureau."

All thoughts of coitus—or almost-coitus—fled as Cece felt her spine go vertical.

"Good morning, er—" she peeked out the window "—afternoon," she quickly corrected.

"Good afternoon," the man said in a drawl that rivaled Blain's. "Thought you might like to come down and give us your thoughts on the Newell murder."

Murder. The word had the cooling effect of an Arctic breeze.

"What time?" she said.

"Around four, which should give us some time to finish searching Sanders's shop."

"Fine," Cece said, wrapping the conversation up as Blain came into the room. He had a full-size towel, and a lot less to cover up. Cece clutched the dishrag to her chest once she'd hung up, feeling the unmistakable burn of post-coitus embarrassment.

"Um." *Um?* "That was the Charlotte office. They want me to come down later today."

He nodded. Cece glanced longingly at the beige-and-brown bedspread to her left. Maybe Blain wouldn't notice if she jerked the thing from the bed.

"Will they tell you if they turned up anything from my shop today?"

"Probably not," she said, deciding to act professional, despite the fact that her hair hung over one shoulder, wet, cold drips sliding down her breasts. "Once I tell them I'm off the investigation."

"Why are you clutching that towel like that?"

Because I'm suddenly horribly embarrassed, she wanted to tell him.

"I'm cold," she lied.

He reached for the towel around his waist as if he was going to whip it off and hand it to her.

"No," she quickly said. "Let me, ah, get my own towel."

She could tell he recognized her embarrassment. And why wouldn't he? He probably had a lot more experience with this sort of thing than she did. Between his fame and good looks, no doubt he had babes coming out of his ears.

Why had she let this happen?

When she came back, she felt about as professional as it was possible to be with a bath towel wrapped around one's middle.

He'd gotten dressed.

Thanks for the quickie, babe. I feel better about Randy already. Gotta dash now.

"Look," he said, "I should probably get back to the shop and talk to the investigators."

He *was* leaving. Damn it. The words heaped humiliation on top of the embarrassment like one too many tires atop a retread heap.

"Okay, sure," she said. "I'll let you know if I hear anything." Like a moan of pleasure. Or a grunt of satisfaction. Or flesh pounding into flesh…

Stop it!

She was a mature, sexually active adult. This sort of thing was old hat for her. Well, not old hat, but she was used to awkward goodbyes, and it was definitely time for him to say goodbye.

"I'll catch up to you later," she said.

Where? In another shower? a voice inside her head asked.

"When?" he demanded.

"Later," she said with a wave. She took a deep breath of damp Blain—not a good idea. "Thanks. I had a great time."

He blinked down at her, his face going a bit slack before he said, "Er, you're welcome?"

She smiled brightly, and when he didn't move, grabbed his hand and tugged him to the door. "I'll be in touch," she said.

"Cece—"

"Shh. Don't say a word," she said, touching his mouth with her hand. "I know. It was good for me, too." She stood up on tiptoe and kissed his cheek. "Drive carefully." She opened the door, gently but firmly shoving him out of it. He resisted, but a couple across the hall came to her rescue. Blain saw them, too, glanced back at her bath towel, and quickly stepped away from the door.

She shoved it closed in his face.

And that was that. She'd quit the case. All done. *Done Blain Sanders.*

She rested her head against the door and groaned. The head-resting became head-banging as she chastised herself for her moment of weakness.

Technically, they hadn't actually "done" it. Close enough.

And he'd let her, though she had a feeling it was only because he'd needed to forget about his friend for a while. But just the thought of that made the embarrassment increase tenfold. Great. A therapy fuck.

WHAT THE HELL had just happened?

Blain stared at Cece's hotel room door as if he could will the thing back open.

"Say, aren't you—"

"Blain Sanders," Blain finished numbly, his gaze dropping to the handle.

"That's what I thought," the guy said, holding out his hand.

Blain turned, taking the guy's hand, but his smile was automatic, the handshake routine.

"Good luck this weekend."

Yeah. Sure. "Thanks," Blain said, looking back to Cece's door.

He'd been used.

He kept staring at it, remembering the cool way she'd dismissed him. It made him feel...damn it, *used.* That was all there was to it.

He knocked.

No answer.

"Cece," he said, knocking again.

Still no answer. Was she ignoring him? Taking a shower? On the phone?

The elevator doors opened down the hall. An older couple got out. Blain nodded to them, wondering what the hell to do. He could stand around like an idiot and keep on knocking, but he had a feeling she wouldn't open the door.

He shook his head and turned away. But when he stepped outside the Best Western a few minutes later, he paused. Maybe he should go upstairs and try talking to her again because, damn it, he didn't like being used. He would go back.

WHEN CECE HEARD the second knock, she almost didn't answer it.

Blain. Again.

Who else could it be? Well, maybe her long-lost towels. Towels that she could really use now that the shower incident was over, she thought, pulling on her clothes.

Jeesh. What a mess.

"I'm coming, I'm coming," she said as the knock sounded again.

And she had to admit, her heart started pounding when she opened up the door.

It wasn't Blain. It was flowers. Cece could barely speak for a second, so surprised was she.

"Uh, you Cecilia Blackwell?"

"I am," she found herself saying.

Flowers.

From Blain. Be still my heart.

No, Cece. It's over. Right. *Right?*

"Miss Blackwell?" the guy said again, holding the things out.

"Oh, yeah, sure."

Flowers, she thought, the scent of them filling her nose. Roses, lilies and various other blossoms emitting a heavenly smell.

"Might want to put them in some water."

"Thanks," Cece said, handing the guy a buck from her pocket while juggling the vase.

And when the door closed she found herself thinking, geez, what the heck was she supposed to do now? Not only was Blain a damn nice guy, but he was the type to send a girl flowers.

She hadn't been sent flowers in years.

She set them down on one of the bed stands, staring at the things. What the heck did she do now? Call him? He hadn't called her the other day. She never had asked him why. It might have sounded too needy.

Tick, tick, tick, tick.

The sound penetrated the stillness of the room. Cece looked around, wondering if the bathroom light was on a timer or something. But the sound didn't come from the bathroom...it came from the nightstand. She approached, looking at the clock near the vase. Digital. Was it in the drawer?

It was when she leaned down that she realized where the sound was coming from.

The vase.

But no sooner had she ID'd the sound than she thought *no way.* That'd be ridiculous. Nobody used old-fashioned timers for bombs anymore.

Still, she peeked gingerly between the stems.

A brick of C4 sat beneath chopped-off stems.

"Holy shit," she said aloud, jumping back. And then she ran out of her hotel room and to the nearest fire alarm as if tongues of flame were at her heels. Because maybe in a couple of seconds there would be.

THEY EVACUATED THE HOTEL. By the time the bomb squad arrived, Cece had calmed down. To her shock, Blain had shown up spouting something about coming back to talk to her. She'd been too busy to spend much time with him, though he'd looked a bit panicked.

Now she sat in the conference room of the FBI's Charlotte Bureau, one Agent Henry Ashton sitting across from her.

"You certain you didn't tell someone at the race-track you were with the FBI?"

Someone had sent her a bomb. Or was it meant for Blain? Too hard to tell at the moment.

"Hell, Agent Ashton, who would I tell?"

Ashton frowned, glancing down at his papers. "It says here that Las Vegas Motor Speedway Security took someone away. Maybe you spoke to them?"

Had their suspect seen her rushing through the tunnel with Blain? Maybe overheard them?

Jeesh. She didn't know.

Agent Ashton sensed her self-doubt, Cece could tell. "Look," she said. "I don't know if someone overheard me or not. I doubt it. I'm a seasoned agent. I don't make mistakes."

Except when you're distracted.

Except when you want to be kissed.

Except when you have the hots for a case's lead contact.

Oh, jeesh.

She put a hand to her forehead.

"You don't look very convinced," Ashton said.

"I'm just jet-lagged."

"Is that why you didn't find it odd to be receiving flowers when you'd only just arrived?"

"No." *Not when I'd just booted a guy out of my hotel room after bopping his salami.*

What a mess.

Agent Ashton just continued to watch her. He had beady eyes. She hated men with beady eyes.

"Obviously, Agent Blackwell, you're a target. You *and* Mr. Sanders, since we can't be certain the killer didn't know he wasn't in the hotel room, too. He was there prior to the incident, was he not?"

The sly way his little rat eyes narrowed when he said it made Cece sit up. "He was," she admitted.

"And that confuses me. I thought you were set to meet him in the hotel lobby."

"He arrived early," she said, trying to sound as coolly professional as she could, given that she'd just had a light-duty explosive sent to her room.

"I see," Ashton said, and his weasel eyes glowed as if he were about to steal a giant egg from a nest.

"Mr. Sanders was in a hurry to discuss the latest details of the case."

"Ah," Ashton added in a tone of voice that made it clear he understood, which made Cece wonder if he'd had agents already tailing Blain, agents who might have been listening in….

Ah, crap. So that was why they weren't pointing the finger at Blain anymore. He was being watched. Closely watched, it would appear.

"And so given the fact that you and Blain were…together—" Cece was almost positive she didn't imagine the pause before the word "—we can't rule out the possibility that he might be a target, too."

"I understand," she said, suddenly overcome by a bad, bad feeling.

"Agent Blackwell, I have to be honest with you. I don't understand why Mr. Sanders is so insistent you work the case."

"Neither do I."

The response took him by surprise, his little eyes changing to the size of a ferret's, or maybe a beaver's.

"Frankly, I wouldn't be averse if you sent me home."

Away from Blain. Away from distraction.

Away from the way he makes you feel.

"I would love to do that, too, Agent Blackwell. However…"

However? she thought, straightening. *However what?*

"We can't ignore the fact that you and Mr. Sanders have come to the killer's attention."

"I know."

"Therefore you'd make good bait."

"Bait?" she asked, actually jerking in her chair. How embarrassingly unprofessional.

"Obviously, one of the best ways to nab the killer would be to draw him out," he explained, as if she were a rookie agent who'd graduated at the bottom of her class. "We can handle the investigative details of the case, but I'm of the opinion you and Sanders would be better served up as bait."

Bait. Oh, great!

"Agent Ashton, with all due respect, I really think I should just go back to San Francisco."

"And why is that?"

Good question. She stared at him. Really good question.

"Mr. Sanders and I—" *nearly boinked this afternoon* "—don't always see eye to eye."

"Are you telling me you wish to quit the case because of professional differences?"

No. Not really. Well, maybe.

"Because if you are, I would remind you, Agent Blackwell, that you are an agent. According to these records, an exemplary agent, although I've noticed the West Coast is a bit more lax in rating their operatives. But be that as it may, your help is needed here. Now, are you going to give it, or go back home?"

Shit and shinola. The man was good. Really good. He had her backed into a corner.

"Sir, surely there's a better solution? And why can't I help investigate?"

"Because we need you with Sanders."

Double shit.

"You can help protect him at his residence."

His residence?

"I…his residence?"

"Yes. We've asked, and he's given his approval. You're to be housed with him," Ashton said, giving her an arch look, as if he knew she and Blain had been bumping and grinding in her hotel room.

Maybe he did.

"It's secluded," he added, "off the shore of a lake. Easy to guard, with nothing but water in the back. And with the two of you staying under one roof, it'll save us manpower."

Two of you under one roof.

Cripes. What a mess. She'd almost had full frontal sex with Blain Sanders, then a wham-bam-thank-you-ma'am farewell, then almost become Cecilius Blackwellius courtesy of a bomb straight out of a Looney Tunes cartoon.

"When do I leave?" she asked in resignation.

"Right now."

Great, Cece thought. Really great. Luxurious accommodations compliments of Blain Sanders. And just what the hell was she going to say to him when she did face him again?

CHAPTER TWELVE

IT WAS A QUESTION that plagued her the whole way to Blain's home, one Agent Thurman driving her there, the lush green North Carolina landscape sliding by the window like movie scenery. Her anxieties only increased when she passed through a wrought-iron gate. In her experience, only truly elaborate homes were to be found on the other side of gates, though why it should make her more anxious to discover that Blain had an elegant mansion was anybody's guess.

And it was elegant. Cece and her new friend goggled at the sight of it. She knew this for a fact because she was staring right at the middle-aged agent when his eyes bulged like a fly's. Then she turned to follow his gaze and her eyes probably bulged, too.

An acre of stucco and glass perched on the edge of a grassy knoll that had obviously been professionally landscaped. Nobody but landscapers could successfully mix daisies and calla lilies. And okay, so it wasn't really an acre, but she wouldn't be surprised if it wasn't half an acre. A blacktop road brought you right up to the front door, with the house on your right. Cece got out of Agent Thurman's standard-issue Ford Taurus, the squeak of the car door breaking the silence of the serene and peaceful Villa Sanders. And that's what it looked like. Red tile roof, beige stucco, lush landscaping that seemed all the more tropical for the North Carolina humidity pressing against her face like a wet rag.

Wow.

"Sanders said to go on in," Agent Thurman said, heading for the front door after chirping his car alarm. Who did the man think would rob him out here? A hard up squirrel? By the looks of things, even the squirrels had it good around here. "I guess we go in the front door."

Cece glanced over at Agent Thurman, tempted to say, "You think?" Only something about the agent's voice, about the way he'd said...

"And I gotta tell you, I can't wait to see the inside of this place."

There it was—confirmation. "You a race fan?" she said.

"I am."

Well, really, was it much of a surprise? This was the heart of stock car country.

But she wouldn't have figured Agent Thurman to be the type. For one thing, he wasn't exactly young, just a few years shy of her boss's fifty years, by the looks of it. But his eyes sure glowed like a teenager's as he opened Blain's front door with a key Blain must have given to him, pulled out a piece of paper and disarmed the alarm that beeped in electronic rage. Cece followed him inside, her steps slowing to a snail's pace as she took it all in.

Holy shlamoly.

The foyer alone was as big as her apartment. Vaulted ceilings with windows above and around the door let in so much light it reminded Cece of a cathedral. Marble floors were done in—what else?—checkered flag. To her left was a living room, the white carpet looking like it'd been poured from a bucket of paint, it dripped down the sunken floor so smoothly. Cream-and-white upholstery with matching drapes, cherry side tables—luxury everywhere she turned, which, at the moment, was to the right. She and Agent Thurman stepped into a less formal family room packed with racing memorabilia plus a flat screen TV nearly as big as her bed back home, wraparound couches in mocha-brown, and a white Berber carpet that must have been hell to keep clean.

"Here it is."

Cece found herself blinking at Agent Thurman's words, having zoned out on her surroundings. He'd moved off to the left, through an arched entry that led to what must be a trophy room.

Agent Thurman looked like he'd found the mother of all drug stashes, the kind agents dream of finding, except this wasn't drugs, this was race stuff.

"I've heard about this room."

All right, she couldn't help herself. She wanted a look-see, too. Cece stepped through the arch and was brought up short by wall-to-wall trophies. But it wasn't just trophies. The room was full of other goodies, too, from a shelfful of different colored helmets to a brightly painted hood to, of all things, a tire propped against a wall, rocks still embedded in the rubber.

"Look at that," Agent Thurman said in awe. "That's the championship trophy right there." He walked over to a case, his awed face reflected back in the glass. Cece resisted the urge to follow. Photos caught her attention. They were on a wall beneath the shelf of helmets. Dozens of Blains looked back at her. Blain wearing a headset as he stared out at a racetrack. Blain in the winner's circle—Blain in a lot of winner's circles—Blain dressed in a tux as he accepted the year-end trophy. Blain with various drivers, celebrities, even TV personalities.

She shook her head, admitting to herself that she was impressed. She'd known he was something of an icon, but nothing brought that home like this room did.

Her hands had started to shake. Whether it was seeing Blain's face again, or because of the sudden realization that he was far, far out of her league, she didn't know.

"I'll be right back."

Agent Thurman nodded, lifting his hand in a halfhearted gesture as he acknowledged her words. Cece crossed the room, heading for the back of the house and, hopefully, the rest room. She needed to splash cold water on her face. *Really* cold.

But the back of the house was a kitchen. Seriously, the whole back of the damn house belonged to a kitchen—well, and a sunroom off one end—but the rest had so much red tile Cece felt like she was standing in Mexico. Brushed aluminum appliances reflected fuzzy half-arcs of light. Windows to her right gave her a view of Lake Norman, which sparkled like a fizzy soda beneath the setting sun. Cece's heels clicked on the tile floor as she crossed to the sink, turning on the spigot so she could splash her face.

Why did her hands shake?

Sure, she'd known Blain was a celebrity. A familiar face to race fans. Team owner. She'd known he'd come a long way from their little town, known he had more money than she'd earn in a dozen lifetimes.

Yet it hadn't hit home until that moment.

She dabbed at her face with a towel hanging by the sink (no paper towels here). Her hands still shook, damn it. Fingers curled into her palms as she took a deep breath and stared out at the lake through the window above the sink. Green lawn stretched almost to the shore, a pier bobbing and swaying like a cork atop the water. She bet if she went out on the balcony, she'd hear the water's rhythmic swish-swoosh-swish of tiny waves.

"Cece."

She jumped.

Oh, jeez. Blain came toward her, the look on his face one she'd never seen before.

"Lord, Cece, you have no idea how worried I've been."

He tried to pull her into his arms, and she wanted to go...she really did. But she shook her head instead, saying, "We're not alone," in a low voice.

He seemed to understand, though the regret in his eyes did something surprising—it tore at her heart.

And then she said more loudly, "I'm fine, Blain, really."

"You're fine?" he asked quietly. "You didn't look fine when you were running around that hotel lobby."

"I was dealing with a bomb threat," she said.

"I know." All he did was stare at her and she could see the myriad thoughts zooming through his mind. They flickered one by one through his eyes like slots on a game wheel. Worry, anger, relief.

"It was nothing, Blain. They took the thing away before it could explode. And now we have some solid evidence to examine."

He continued to stare. Cece grew increasingly uncomfortable.

"How do you do it?" he finally asked.

"Do what?"

"Shut 'em off."

"Shut *what* off?"

"Your emotions."

"I don't shut them off."

"Well, you sure are acting like this is nothing out of the ordinary," he said, "because I've got to tell you, Cece, hearing there was a threat, knowing the target was probably you—"

"It was nothing—"

"And the way you brushed me off in the lobby."

"I didn't expect to see you."

"I came back to see you."

"Bad timing."

"Bad timing or not, it scared me to death," he finished with a shake of his head. "And I haven't been that scared since I saw Randy's car fragment into a million pieces."

Her heart began to pound, the intensity in his eyes as he stared down at her making her want to touch him, to tell him it was okay, that she would be fine.

Except she shouldn't touch.

"Someone tried to kill you," he said grimly. "Maybe me, too, according to one of your colleagues. That same person killed Randy." He turned, moving away from her to stand before a huge bay window to the left of the kitchen counter. She wanted to follow him over there, wanted to lay a hand on his shoulder in comfort.

"Why?" she heard him whisper.

She hated to tell him this, hated the way staring at his face made her feel. Anxious, conflicted, afraid for him. She shouldn't be afraid for a victim.

But she had to be honest. "I don't know."

He didn't like her answer. He rubbed his eyes with the heels of his hands for a long moment before dropping his arms back to his sides.

He stiffened before saying his next words. "I'm going to lose the team."

She felt her head tip to the side. "No, you're not."

He met her gaze. "Yes, I am. I'm going to lose the team, probably my sponsor, maybe my driver, pain in the ass that he is. It's all starting to fall apart."

"Surely you won't lose the team because of this?"

"Maybe, maybe not, but I know for certain I'm going to lose my sponsor."

"What? Why?"

"Because they don't like bad press, Cece, and this is bad. This is very bad."

"Not if you don't tell them."

He shook his head. "They'll find out. Sooner or later they'll find out, and when they do, they'll bail."

"But they've been with you for years."

"So?" he said with a shrug. "It might look all peaches and cream, but behind the scenes racing is just as cutthroat an industry as the movie business. One of my fellow owners won't hesitate to snap up my sponsor should they leave me high and dry. When that money stops coming in, I'll go through my reserves in a month, maybe two. Even if this thing does go away by then, it would take me at least a month beyond that to find another sponsor."

He was right. She knew enough about racing to

know that it took a while, sometimes forever, to get a major corporation to foot the bill.

He rubbed his eyes again. Cece stared up at the man she'd always secretly idolized. All right, she could admit that. She'd had a huge case of hero worship as a teenager. And then later, when he'd gone on to a successful career in racing, she'd been a little bit starstruck, not that she'd have admitted it a couple of days ago. Hell no, if not for that damn bomb, she probably wouldn't be admitting it now.

"We'll catch them, Blain. Whoever's doing this, we'll catch them." And when she looked at him, the way her tummy tightened had nothing to do with pure lust and everything to do with her growing feelings for the man.

He stared back at her, and maybe it was from rubbing his face, maybe it was from exhaustion, but his eyes were red. "I've worked years, Cece, years to get where I am."

"I know."

"I came back east with nothing but twenty bucks in my pocket. Swept the shop floors of any race team that would hire me, worked seven days a week in the hopes of winning a spot on a crew, and when I did finally get that shot, I spent another few years working my way up the food chain. All the hours, all the hard work, all of it about to unravel because somebody thinks I've wronged them."

"But maybe not," she said as optimistically as she dared. "Today's little incident might change that.

We have clues now. Real clues. There are surveillance cameras that caught it all on tape, witnesses, crime scene investigators that might be able to track the blast cap—things that the Bureau can pursue, when all we had before was pretty much bubkus."

She saw the hope flare in his eyes, saw the way it hung against the fear like an anchor too heavy for its boat. He *had* worked hard, and she admired him for that.

"In the meantime we're going to live life under a microscope," he said.

"Well, I, for one, have always wanted to see the inside of a race shop."

"Me, too," came a voice from the family room.

Which made them both smile, and both remember that they had company.

"You know what's really ironic?" Blain asked in a low voice, too low for Thurman to hear.

"What?" Cece asked. "You always wanted to meet a girl who carried a gun?"

Blain found himself almost smiling again. Damn, but he liked her sassy humor.

"I really thought you were something in high school."

She couldn't have looked more surprised if he'd tossed a stick of dynamite at her—although maybe that was a poor analogy given what had happened that day. Damn. He still couldn't believe it.

"It's true. You irritated the heck out of me, but the way you always beat me impressed the hell out of me."

"You're kidding, right?"

He shook his head.

She shook her head, too. "I always thought you hated me."

He resisted the urge to touch her. "I know. I let you think that. Couldn't let on that I got a kick out of racing you. What kind of guy likes to get beat by a woman? Over and over again?"

She smiled before saying, "I'll be damned."

His eyes caught on her lips. Soft. They'd been soft beneath his own. It was such a contrast to the tough-as-nails woman she pretended to be.

Yeah, he had a feeling it was all an act. Or maybe she'd had to be tough for so long she no longer realized it wasn't who she really was. But he remembered how she'd been as a teenager. She'd been like a little puppy, following him around. Remembered the hero-worship in her eyes.

"I used to envy the way you and your dad worked on your car."

The mention of her dad wiped all traces of a smile from her face. He missed it, almost reached out and touched her lips, to maybe tip the edges back up again.

"I always envied your rich-boy life."

"It wasn't what it seemed."

"Really?"

He shook his head. "My dad was always off making money. My mom consoled herself nightly with a gin and tonic, and when my dad did come home, it was yelling and screaming almost twenty-four-seven. I built my cars as a way to escape, no dear old dad to help me out, although that was probably a good thing."

"Your mom ended up leaving him."

"Yup. A year after I graduated high school. They both thought I'd get racing out of my system, then come back home and go to college. When she realized racing was my life, I think she woke up and took a look around."

"Do you ever see your dad?"

"Oh, sure. He's in sales and it's good business to bring a potential client to the racetrack, especially when your son owns the team."

She didn't say anything for a while, while Blain wondered what she was thinking. Not many people knew the story behind the man.

"I would never have blackmailed you."

"Shh," she said, quickly covering his mouth with her hands. She scooted next to him, her hip nearly hitting the kitchen counter. He was silenced by surprise.

"Don't say anything," she hissed.

"Why not?" he whispered back, kind of enjoying their closeness.

"Because." She motioned toward the family room, giving him an exasperated look.

"Afraid he'll hear your little secret about your run-in with the law?"

She glared, her expression clearing saying *don't you dare.*

"Hmm... I wonder how you're going to keep me quiet?"

"I'll find a—"

He covered her mouth with his hand, and as amazing as it seemed, suddenly he felt like laughing.

"You know, it occurs to me that now would be a good time to teach you a lesson."

"A lesson?" she mumbled before batting his hand away, "About what?"

He smiled. "About using me."

"Using you? You're the one who never called me after Las Vegas."

"I didn't know your home number."

Her eyes widened.

"So I figured I'd call you at your office on Monday. Instead you flew here."

"Oh," she said.

"My point being that I never intended not to phone you. Yet I have the feeling that you had every intention of calling it quits between us."

She seemed a bit embarrassed, so he knew he was right.

"I don't like being used," he stated.

"I didn't use you."

"Jumped me like a bitch in heat."

"I did not!"

"Shh," he admonished. "He'll hear you."

She pressed her lips together. Blain had a hard time keeping back a laugh. Funny, a couple hours ago someone had tried to kill her, and it'd scared the shit out of him. Now he found himself smiling.

"You're used to having the upper hand," he surmised. "Calling the shots. Using and abusing the male sex."

"Why, you—"

"Shh," he said, touching her lips again. She tried to draw away, but her butt came up against the counter. He wanted to lift her onto it, to spread her legs….

But he wouldn't. Not yet.

Still, when she tried to sidle away, he found himself asking in a loud voice, "So, what was the arresting officer's name?"

She froze. Well, her body froze. Her face took on a look of fury. She glanced toward the family room as if trying to remind him of the other agent's presence. Actually, Blain had asked the guy for some privacy earlier, but she didn't need to know that.

"You really are an ass sometimes."

"I know."

Her eyes narrowed.

He kissed her. She tried to turn her head away, but he refused to let her. He wanted to kiss her. He didn't care that someone might be listening in, or even watching. He wanted to kiss her, and so he did.

But it wasn't a kiss like those in the hotel. Whether they liked it or not, things had changed between them. He knew her taste now, and she knew his. But it was more than just the physical—so much more. He felt her stiffen, only to abruptly relax, her head tilting as she opened her mouth. This time his tongue probed gently. This time he knew the contours of her mouth, took note of what she liked. She made little sounds in the back of her throat, almost as if she didn't know whether to scream or sigh.

He loved those sounds.

"Blain," she said, wrenching her lips away. "We can't."

"Why not?" he asked, the lingering heat of her mouth making him want to kiss her more.

"Because," she murmured.

He took a step toward her. "We did before," he said in an equally low whisper.

"That was different."

"What was so different?"

"Kissing you didn't mean a potential Internal Affairs investigation."

"Internal Affairs?"

"Yeah. Internal Affairs," she said, eyes gone wide with seriousness. "Getting involved with you is a complete conflict of interest, and if I don't call a stop to this right now, I'll be facing an investigation."

He didn't say anything for a while, and Cece told herself to relax. Obviously, he understood what she was trying to tell him. Getting involved with him would lead to all sorts of complications—complications she didn't want to deal with right now. She didn't want to get involved with anybody. Not like she suddenly wanted to get involved with Blain.

"What are you *doing to me?*" she said in a low voice.

He leaned his head down. "Trying to make you realize that what we have is more than just casual."

"Casual or not, we can't."

"We can if we're careful," he said, his lips just about…oh man, almost touching her own. She refused to move away. Damn it. She would not let him do this to her—whatever *this* was.

"No," she declared. "No more kissing." And this time she meant it—she stepped away.

She expected some flip comment from him about how she hadn't said no earlier, but to her surprise he didn't look perturbed. Instead he looked amused.

"How about petting?"

"No," she said.

"A little ear nuzzling?"

She got shivers just thinking about it. "No," she said firmly.

He held her gaze for a second, thoughts flitting through his eyes that made her skin tingle and alarm bells ring.

"Hmm. A challenge." Said with a smile. "I love a good challenge."

She knew he did. But she was one challenge that was destined to disappoint. "Save your challenges for the racetrack," she said with a brave tip of her head.

Too bad that bravery wasn't echoed in her heart.

CHAPTER THIRTEEN

THE PHONE WOKE BLAIN the next morning in the middle of a very pleasant dream about Cece, making him curse as he reached for the handset.

"Blain," Linda, his secretary, said, "you better get down here. All hell is breaking loose."

He sat up in bed, white sheets falling around his waist. "What's happened?"

"Someone tipped the press about what's going on. The bomb threat's all over the news. Rick Vanhausen called. He and Steve Oxford."

Steve Oxford, VP of Operations for Star Oil. This couldn't be good.

"Did he say what he wanted?"

"He's on his way down," Linda said.

Crap. Definitely not good news. The only time Steve ever made an appearance was if money was involved—as in, he was taking all his money away.

"What time does he want to meet?"

"Two hours."

Blain glanced at the clock. Nine o'clock. The sky had really fallen if Steve Oxford wanted a meeting before noon.

"I'll be right in." He should have been there hours ago, Blain thought with a glance at the clock. His tossing and turning had taken its toll. He wondered how Cece had slept in the room down the hall, then warned himself not to go off thinking about that. He'd only want to head to her room and ask her himself.

He hurried through his shower, his hair still damp as he made his way down to the kitchen to grab a bite to eat. Cece had beaten him, her standard-issue black slacks and white cotton shirt crisply in place.

"Where are you going?" she asked, and he could tell by her heightened color that she was remembering what had gone on the night before, and his parting shot to her. And even though he was dreading the next few hours, he couldn't believe how strong the urge was to tease her, maybe even see if he could make her smile.

He stopped himself. There was a time and place to see where this thing between them would go.

"The office."

"Not without protection."

"I left my condom upstairs."

Damn, he hadn't been able to resist. But the results were worth it because he almost smiled at the way her eyes widened, at the way her lips tightened.

"Relax, Cece," he said, cutting off whatever words she'd been about to say. "I'm not going to jump you."

"Good, because relationships between witnesses and agents are strictly forbidden."

"Yet," he added in a low voice, turning to grab a cup of coffee.

When he glanced back to her it was just in time to catch a *drop dead* glare.

"Seriously, Blain. You better tell Agent Ashton what you're up to."

"And how do I do that?" he asked. "Speak into a lampshade?"

Was that a smile he saw her bite back? Nah. Couldn't be.

"Just go outside and wave your arms."

"Really?"

"No," she said, and it was her turn to look smug. "I'll call him."

"Is it really necessary to check in with him?"

"It is if you want to stay alive."

Someone had tried to kill her yesterday, maybe him. Amazing how he could put that to the back of his mind.

"What about you?"

"I can take care of myself," she said quickly, reaching for her cellphone.

"That's not what I meant," he interrupted.

She paused in dialing the phone, looking up at him.

"I meant what are you going to do today?"

"Go with you."

AND SHE DID, and to be perfectly honest, Blain was glad. Not that he'd put up an argument. He'd figured the two of them would be sticking together, which meant he and Cece would be seeing a lot of each other in the coming days. Too bad it wasn't under different circumstances.

The FBI had provided them what Blain now knew was "loose cover." meaning they hung back far enough to allow the bad guys some breathing room, but not so far that the feds couldn't move in if there was trouble. The fact that they were even there at all was supposed to reassure Blain, but it didn't. Feeling as if he had giant red circles painted on his back wasn't a comforting thing. He didn't know how Cece coped with it as they drove to his office. Granted, she was armed, and maybe that made her feel better. But as for Blain, there was something distinctly disconcerting about being the object of someone's hatred...and having Cece protect him.

How did she do it?

It took effort to separate the two sides of her, especially during times like these when she looked far removed from the tousled sexpot she'd been in the hotel room. She sat in the driver's seat, green eyes alert as she stared around them, a radio and a cell phone strapped to her waist, her FBI badge around her neck.

"You look so serious," he said. And gorgeous. Damn, but he wished he could kiss her. Just one kiss.

She didn't look like she wanted to be kissed. She glanced over at him, the silver hoops in her ears catching the early-morning light. "Protection is serious business."

"I know, and I've got to tell you, I don't like the thought of you in the line of fire."

"That's my job."

"And I don't like it."

He didn't, damn it. He wanted her back at his house, safe, with a full regiment of agents protecting *her.*

"What if there's more than one bad guy?" he added, glancing over at her.

He caught a look of what-of-it unconcern. "We don't have any reason to assume there's more than one. In fact, there's a lot more evidence to support the theory that it's not a group."

"Such as?"

"There still haven't been any claims by terrorist organizations that this is their work, though that might change now that it's gone public. Those groups are always quick to jump on the bandwagon. Plus, if it had been a terrorist cell, they'd have been a lot more professional in the way they put the load together yesterday. Al Qaeda operatives don't use alarm clocks for timers."

"If you're trying to reassure me, it's not working."

"Actually, it should. I'd rather deal with one person than a group of religious fanatics."

One or twenty, the point was someone might have killed her yesterday.

And him.

But he didn't have time to point that out because right then they arrived at his shop, and both Cece and Blain stiffened when they saw the media circus camped out in his parking lot. On a normal day there were tourists around, race fans dropping by the industrial complex in hopes of catching a glimpse of people they deemed "celebrities." Today, however, the parking area was filled with news vans and satellite trucks, people milling about as Cece pulled into Blain's reserved parking spot.

"Great," he said.

"Let me get out first."

He shot her a glare. "Why? So you can get shot at first?"

She rolled her eyes. "Blain, we're surrounded by people. Nobody's going to get a clear shot at me."

She smiled the cocky, nothing-to-worry-about smile he'd come to expect from her. Still, he noticed that she put her hand beneath her jacket as she stepped out of the car. A gun? Blain was pretty certain it was.

Damn.

How could he so hate what she did for a living and yet still admire her brash attitude?

"Step back from the car," she said as people rushed forward. "Mr. Sanders won't be giving a statement today."

Her door slammed with a pop of air pressure, and Blain watched as Cece came around the front of the car. When she opened his door for him, she was in full FBI protection mode, her face expressionless, her eyes scanning, scanning, scanning.

It amazed him.

Especially when she glanced down at him, saying, "It's safe to get out of the car now, Mr. Sanders," in as impersonal a voice as he'd ever heard from her.

His lips formed a bemused smile almost against his will. He couldn't help feeling like a sitting duck as he straightened. But Cece treated it all like another day at the office, and for her, it probably was.

As for him, he rushed into the building. It was weird the way she seemed to relax the moment the door closed, leaving the press milling around outside. But he noticed she still peeked out the glass double doors once or twice.

"Thanks," he said, feeling somehow out of kilter, like his timing chain was off a notch or something. And then it dawned on him that this was the first time he'd ever seen her in protective mode, and he had to admit it was a whole new side of her.

"Doesn't look like any race car shop I've ever seen," she said, turning toward the lobby.

He forced his mind to address her question. No, it didn't, at least from the front. The sprawling five-acre facility wasn't as plush as some of the multi-race teams', but the chrome-and-glass building looked more like an office than a fabrication shop. He'd had the architects hide the shop at the back of the building, more so prying eyes couldn't see into it than for aesthetic reasons.

"Gotta look successful to be successful," he said.

She pulled her gaze away from the trophy case that lauded some of his team's more recent wins. "Well, by the looks of things, you're pretty successful."

He had been, though it'd been a long haul to get where he was. And now it might all go away.

"Thank God you're here," Linda said, her brown hair held back by its customary sixties-style headband. "The phones have been ringing off the hook."

To his surprise, Cece didn't eye Linda up and down. In fact, she seemed coolly unaffected by his receptionist's model-type looks.

"Linda, this is Cece. She's an FBI agent."

Despite how frazzled she appeared, Linda eyed Cece closely. She nodded a curt greeting.

"Nice to meet you, Linda," Cece said.

The secretary turned back to Blain. "Steve Oxford is here," she said.

Blain couldn't conceal his surprise. "Already?" he asked, silently cursing. He'd expected to have at least an hour.

"He was in a hurry."

Bad news. A CEO flying out to see you when you hadn't won a race was always bad news.

"In the conference room?"

Linda nodded, her eyes on Cece.

"Might as well get this over," Blain said.

"You want me to sit in?" Cece asked.

"Sure. You know as much about what's going on as anybody."

But judging by the expression on Steve's face, Blain should have taken the meeting alone. He had always thought the man looked like retired military. Though Steve had to be nearing sixty, he still had the square face, square jaw and buzz cut. But the hard glint in his eyes was more pronounced today, giving Blain a pretty good idea this wasn't going to be pleasant. He shut the glass door to the conference room, glad the vertical blinds had been closed already.

"Blain, maybe we should keep this private," Steve said after he'd been introduced to Cece.

But Blain shook his head, settling himself in a dark green chair that he rolled out from under the glass-covered conference table. "Cece's a big part of the investigation, and since you're no doubt here because of what's going on, I think you'll want her input."

"Is she in charge?" Steve asked, the fluorescent lights revealing his skepticism.

Blain felt his eyes narrow. Something about the way Steve had said that...

"I'm not in charge, Mr. Oxford, but I've been in on things since the very start."

"I'm sure you have," Steve said, in such a placating tone of voice he sounded like a used-car salesman. "But maybe it'd be better if you called your boss and asked *him* to join us."

If Cece had been a dog, Blain was certain that her hackles would have lifted.

"The agent presently in charge of the investigation is busy," Cece said. "I can stand in for him."

"Well, maybe we should reschedule the meeting until he's not busy."

"That would be a waste of time for all of us, Mr. Oxford," Cece said tersely. "Speaking of which, I really need to get to a briefing that's scheduled for an hour from now, so if we could hurry this up…?"

Blain wanted to smile. Steve had always been a pretentious S.O.B., but Blain had never pegged him as sexist. Apparently the gloves were off for this meeting, however, because Blain saw unmasked irritation cross the man's face.

"Very well, then," he said as if he'd given his approval, when, in fact, he'd had no choice. "But I'll expect a written transcript of what we discuss here today."

It was a blatant attempt on Steve's part to put Cece in her place—as if she were nothing more than a glorified secretary for the FBI.

But Blain should have known she'd be able to handle herself. "I'm sure Blain's personal assistant would be happy to come in here and take care of that for you," she replied curtly.

Good for you, Blain privately conveyed to Cece with the hint of a grin. Oh, yeah, she knew how to put men in their place.

"No need for that. What I've got to say will only take a minute."

Then why the hell had he wanted Cece to take notes, Blain almost asked him, but he tried to keep it professional, even though he was fighting the urge to clock Steve Oxford in the face.

"As you know, Blain, Star Oil has been with you for four years now—"

"Cut the crap, Steve. You're ditching me because of all this nonsense, aren't you?"

If Steve seemed surprised by his aggressiveness, it didn't show. He just leaned back in his chair, unbuttoning his suit coat. "We are."

Mother f—

Blain bit back the oath. Sure, he'd suspected the news, but he'd been hoping Steve would deny it.

And as his hopes went sailing out the conference room door, so did the leash on Blain's temper.

"This is bull, Steve. Complete and utter bull."

Blain caught a glimpse of Cece's eyes widening before she glanced at Steve to see his reaction.

"Actually, Blain, it's not," Steve snapped back just as aggressively. "You know as well as I do that things haven't been the same since Randy's death."

"It's only been a month. Give us some time to pull it together."

"But to be honest, this started before Randy died."

"What started?" Blain huffed.

"The losses. Poor qualifying. Poor finishes. Our tracking service claims we've only gotten two hours of network exposure."

He'd known the number was low—his own tracking service had come up with much the same. "Every team goes through ups and downs."

"Yeah, but the words *murder* and *terrorists* haven't been associated with their names."

And there it was out in the open. Blain's fears coming true. "So you're pulling your support because you think consumers will view Star Oil negatively."

"It's subliminal, Blain. Any advertising firm will tell you that. Plus, word is you're going to be grounded, in which case our logo won't see any airtime at all."

"Who told you that?"

Steve smiled tightly. "Barry Bidwell."

Which made Blain sit up in surprise. Rumors were one thing, but if Steve was telling him the truth…

"He told me he's coming over to speak to you about it today."

So then the message he'd left wasn't his way of reminding Blain that he'd promised to keep quiet.

"Mr. Oxford," Cece said, "don't you think your withdrawal is a bit precipitous?"

"I take it you didn't know about that?" Steve asked Blain, blatantly ignoring Cece.

"I only just got in."

"We might catch the perpetrator today," Cece interjected.

Steve turned to her, his expression clearly one of impatience. "Miss Blackwell, with all due respect, this has less to do with Randy's death and more to do with performance."

"Bullshit," she said, which caused Steve's eyes to widen—Blain was looking right at him when it happened. "This is a blatant crap-out by a major sponsor who's too much of a coward to stand by a race team that's proved itself over and over again, and that needs your support now more than ever."

"Cece," Blain warned, even as part of him wanted to lean across the table and kiss her soundly. "I think what Mr. Oxford is saying is that his mind is already made up and nothing we can say or do will help our cause."

Steve's steely eyes had narrowed so much Blain wondered how he could see out of them.

"You're right," the man said tersely, his square face red after Cece's attack. "We have made up our mind. However, I'd appreciate being brought up to date on the investigation so we can address this issue with the press. Miss Blackwell, if I could have the name of your superior for that update."

"Miss Blackwell could update you herself," Cece said, and Blain could tell she was livid...absolutely, positively livid. On his behalf. "But since Star Oil no longer has a vested interest in the case, I won't be able to share that information." She leaned forward, tugging her lips up in a sarcastic smile. "In other words, I could tell you, but then I'd have to kill you."

Color spread into Steve Oxford's wide neck. "Fine. I'll call your superior myself."

"You do that," she said, tipping her chin. "But he's only going to tell you what I just told you."

"And while I'm at it," Steve added, "maybe

we'll have a little conversation about you and your unprofessionalism."

"Go ahead. Maybe they'll fire me. I'd kinda like to go home instead of handling bomb threats."

Steve pushed himself to his feet, the buttons on his jacket catching on the table. "Blain, our attorneys will be in touch."

"I'm sure they will," Blain said.

And that was it.

All the years of sponsorship. All the friendships he'd made within the company—all gone—like that.

"That arrogant, sexist son of a—" Cece got up from her chair, splayed her hands. "How can he pull his support like that?"

"Racing," Blain said with a shrug.

"Well, racing sucks," Cece said, pressing her palms flat on the glass. "And I don't know how you put up with it."

"Actually," Blain said, "I've been pretty lucky. Star Oil has been with me for almost five years. That's longer than a lot of teams get to spend with one sponsor."

"And that's supposed to make me feel better?" Cece asked, swiping an irritating strand of hair out of her face. "I'm supposed to just pat you on the back and say 'tough luck, Blain'?"

She crossed her arms as he came over to her side of the table. On the walls around them were pictures of his race cars, most of them with the Star Oil logo painted on the hood. Cece looked like she wanted to toss them out after Steve Oxford.

"Cece, you amaze me."

She raised her brows. Blain lifted his hand to stroke the freckles he remembered from their childhood, but she darted away before he could do it.

"No touching," she reminded him.

"At least not here," he said in a low voice.

"Not anywhere," Cece corrected even as her stupid body warmed at his words. He'd just been fired by his sponsor. She'd just lost complete control of herself in front of said sponsor and acted in a way she probably shouldn't have, and yet all she could think about was that she wished Blain would try to touch her again. Jeesh.

"And what do you mean, I amaze you?" she asked, pressing her lips together as she peered up at him suspiciously.

His smile widened a few notches. "When we were first reunited you practically spat on my shoes, and now here you are defending my team and my abilities to a man most people are afraid of."

"Afraid of that overfed pile of pig meat?" She raised her chin. "I've eaten men like him for breakfast. Sexist—"

Blain bent down and stopped her words with his mouth.

"Hey," she said, jerking back. "No fair." But her lips tingled.

"Thank you," he said, his silver eyes suddenly serious. And this time when he lifted his hand, she didn't move. "Thank you," he said again in his soft drawl, his thumb brushing her cheek. "I appreciate your righteous indignation."

That almost made her smile, except she wasn't *really* liking the way his finger made her feel. She didn't *really* want him to go on touching her. She didn't *really* feel the urge to tug his head down so he could kiss her again—

"Mr. Sanders, you have Mr.—oops," Linda said, Cece glancing over at the conference room door just in time to see the flashy brunette stiffen, the woman's eyes narrowing as she took in the scene.

Blain's hand dropped, but he didn't blink as he said, "Mr. Oops?"

Linda's lips tightened. Cece watched them go as flat as a heart monitor. Ah...so that was it. Not that she blamed Linda for having a crush on her boss. "Mr. Bidwell is on line three," she said.

Blain finally looked her way. "Great," he muttered sarcastically. "I'll take it in here."

"That's the president of the racing association, isn't it?" Cece asked after Linda-of-the-big-boobs left.

"It is," Blain said.

"You think he's calling to tell you you can't race?"

"I think there's a good chance that he is."

"But...they can't do that!"

"Yes, Cece, they can."

"It's not fair."

"That's—"

"Racing," she finished for him. "I know. But it sucks." And at the look of resignation on his face, Cece found herself touching his jaw, despite telling herself no, no, no. "We'll break this case, Blain. Soon. You'll be out there racing again before you know it."

"Yeah, with no sponsor."

"Are you kidding? Once this is all done, you'll have sponsors lining up at the door."

He smiled, but it wasn't a very convincing one. "From your mouth to God's ears, Cece."

"I mean it, Blain. We'll catch this guy. I promise."

CHAPTER FOURTEEN

BUT SAYING THE WORDS was a lot easier than doing it, especially when it was obvious Agent Ashton really didn't want her investigating, something that became more and more apparent after her cellphone beeped later that day, the preprogrammed display revealing the big cheese of the Charlotte office himself. Damn.

"I just got off the phone with Steve Oxford," Agent Ashton said without preamble.

Cece sank down in the conference room she'd appropriated as her own little office. Jeesh. What'd Oxford do? Race out and go tell Mommy?

"Agent Blackwell, would you say that you acted professionally this morning?"

It was a leading question. Cece hated leading questions. "I would say that I acted honestly, Agent Ashton."

"And so professionalism does not go hand in hand with honesty—is that what you're telling me?"

"No—"

"Because I have to say I don't find it very professional to tell a civilian that his company was 'crapping out.'"

Cece winced. Yeah, yeah, yeah. He had a point. "The man treated me like a junior secretary," she said, but she knew it was a weak excuse at best.

Agent Ashton picked right up on it. "The man is a civilian whose impression of the FBI is now less than favorable, especially when it appears to him that I was taking your side by refusing him information."

"But surely he understood that as a civilian, he doesn't have a right to know."

"What he *knows* is that an agent under my direction started mouthing off to him."

Cece tipped her head down, rubbing her temples as she spat out the inevitable. "I know. And I'm sorry." And even though she technically worked for Bob and the San Francisco office, she said the words with as much sincerity as she could muster. "It won't happen again, sir. The stress of yesterday must have affected me more than I thought."

She had to stay on good terms with the Charlotte office. They were her only "in" to the investigation, and if she stared alienating people, they'd keep her "out."

"See that it doesn't happen again," Agent Ashton said.

"Any word on who tipped off the press?" Cece asked.

There was a pause, and for a moment Cece thought he wouldn't answer. To her shock, he said, "It appears one of the perps did."

"*One* of the perps?" she asked.

"We're going under the assumption that this is a terrorist faction we haven't heard of before."

Terrorists? But that didn't make a lick of sense... unless they knew something she didn't know.

"Did we get another communication from them?"

"We did."

Well, what did it say? "Is it possible to have a copy faxed to me here?" she asked.

"Negative," Agent Ashton said quickly and firmly. "You're to continue in your capacity as protection for Sanders."

"But I can still help with the investigation while I'm doing that."

"Frankly, Agent Blackwell, my office is more than capable of handling the investigation on its own. This has now moved to our jurisdiction, thanks to the attempt on your life yesterday. We're not a bunch of backwater rednecks here, contrary to what you might think."

Whoa! Where the heck had that come from? "Of course not," Cece said. "I don't know what gave you the impression that I thought that."

"I've had dealings with the San Francisco office before."

Oh, jeesh, so that was it. This wasn't personal, this was politics. Someone from her office had stepped on Ashton's toes before. Was it Bob? Was that the reason for this thinly veiled hostility? She sighed.

He must have heard it, because he said with more

venom than before, "So while I appreciate your offer of help, your orders are to stay glued to Sanders's side."

Glued to Blain's side. Terrific. Just what she didn't want to become—a human Post-it note. She'd hardly be able to help with the investigation that way.

"Surely there's something—"

Click.

Cece folded her own phone closed. *Jerk.* She wrapped her hands around the cellphone as if it was Agent Ashton's neck, shaking it for good measure. She'd like to toss the thing on the floor and stomp on it, but that was just a nice fantasy. Besides, there was more than one way to skin a cat.

She turned on her sensibly short heel, heading for the fabrication shop. She didn't know where Blain was, but she didn't need his help for this. In fact, she'd rather he be out of the loop.

She found Mike Johnson, Blain's crew chief, right where she thought he'd be, standing in front of a giant red toolbox organizing the contents of its drawers. Cece doubted that he was their suspect, but she hated the fact that she couldn't be sure. She'd run into him earlier when she'd poked around the place, and wasn't surprised he hadn't moved from his spot. The drawers were a mess, as was the whole shop. It looked as if a tornado had come through—or the FBI.

He glanced up when she walked in, seeming less than pleased to see her.

"I had nothing to do with this," she said, lifting her hands, having to squint against the light reflecting off the cement floor, thanks to an open roll-up door. When she'd reconnoitered earlier, she'd gauged the back of the shop to be secure enough that she didn't have to worry about explosives being tossed inside.

Mike flung a shiny socket that probably cost a couple hundred bucks into the drawer, where it bounced and tinged off other sockets.

"Can't they search a place without destroying it?" he asked, his Southern drawl much more pronounced than Blain's. "I swear they dusted everything in this place for prints."

They probably had. "They were looking for evidence," Cece said. The room was huge, bigger than the average home, with light blue walls and spotless red toolboxes around the perimeter. Numerous race cars were lined up near the toolboxes. On the shorter walls were doors that led to different departments: engine, fabrication, dyno room. She could hear a motor being tested now, despite the fact that the walls were supposed to be soundproof.

"Well, what the hell am I supposed to use to clean this stuff off?" he asked. He held up a hand black with powder.

"Hand lotion will get rid of it." He didn't look pleased to have to use *anything* to take the stuff off. "I'm sorry, Mike, but it had to be done. We're running pretty low on clues."

The crew chief looked away, but not before she saw his resigned expression. "You guys have any idea who's doing this?"

"Can't say," she replied.

He nodded and picked up another socket, wiping it down before snapping it into place next to a slightly smaller version, and for a second Cece thought about how many people this thing had affected. These men might be forced to find new jobs if the Charlotte office couldn't break the case in a reasonable amount of time. Hell, the whole sport might suffer with tighter security, no more pit passes, no more autograph sessions, no more shaking drivers' hands. She could only guess at the kind of security measures that would be put into place this weekend. If they even held the race, which was all the more reason why she should work the case on her own, something she intended to do, starting now.

"Hey, I need to speak with whomever the Charlotte office planted undercover."

He looked up at that. "You don't know?"

She frowned in frustration. "I haven't been told bubkus."

Mike's eyes widened.

"That's the reason I can't tell you anything, not because I don't want to." Not precisely true, but she needed to treat him like a suspect. "I think it's because I'm an outsider. Stupid. So I'm going to take matters into my own hands, starting with a little chat with whoever's working the case here. Hopefully, they can tell me something."

Mike nodded, and for the first time he smiled. "Nothing wrong with that." He pointed with a ratchet toward a doorway. "They've planted a couple of people. One of them's in the dyno room."

"Thanks," Cece said, heading off in that direction.

"He should be out here helping us clean up," he called after her.

She couldn't help but smile. "I'll tell him that."

If Mike said anything else, Cece didn't hear him, because the moment she opened the dyno room door she wished she had a set of earplugs. Good Lord, she couldn't believe how loud it was. Even with the engine being tested behind a thick wall of what she assumed was soundproof glass, it sounded like the inside of a tornado, not that she'd ever been inside one of those.

Two heads turned to her when she entered, one of them Agent Thurman.

"Hey," she said in surprise. "I thought you were doing surveillance."

"Are you kidding?" he said. "When I could be undercover at the corporate headquarters of Sanders Racing?"

Cece shook her head. The other guy looked back at the controls of the dynometer, the sound of the engine abruptly lowering after he dialed one of the knobs.

"I see your point," she said, noting that the guy

at the controls looked more like a computer geek than a motorhead, with his skinny face and wire-rimmed glasses.

"Can I talk to you?" Cece asked Agent Thurman.

When they were outside the room, she couldn't resist saying, "I see you've made yourself at home."

"Can you believe it?" Thurman said. "That engine might be used at Daytona."

Yeah, yeah, yeah, neat. Cece wasn't exactly in a rah-rah racing mood today. "Listen," she said. "I need to know what's going on with the investigation."

Apparently, Agent Thurman hadn't been told not to talk to her because he said, "We found a few things yesterday that look promising."

"Like what?"

"A few fingerprints that don't match our list of latents. A broom handle that looks like it was used to push the load into place."

In other words, not much.

"But our biggest break was a former employee with a criminal record who was fired two months back."

Cece perked up.

"Apparently, he went ballistic when he was let go."

Definitely good news.

"They took him into custody early this morning."

Cece turned on her heel.

"Where you going?" Agent Thurman asked.

"Out," she answered.

IT DIDN'T TAKE but a few minutes to find out who the suspect was—thanks to the steely-eyed Linda, who looked only too happy to give her the address if it meant Cece would leave. A stop at a vacant computer terminal and she had driving directions. When she told Blain she was leaving, he didn't even ask what she needed his car for, probably because he was too busy meeting with his general manager, and it didn't look pretty. In fact, the place was as grim as a dentist's office, not surprising given what was going on.

And so Cece found herself on her way to the Charlotte Bureau's number one suspect's home—or apartment, as the case may be. She called her real boss on the way, but Bob wasn't in and so she left a message telling him what she was up to. To hell with Agent Ashton. She reported to Bob, and she'd do exactly that.

Beep. "Five Bravo Five, where are you going?" The voice rang in her ear as she started the car.

"Just a little errand, boys," she said cheerfully.

"You're not authorized to leave—"

She shut off her radio. They were just going to tell her she couldn't go. To hell with them. Maybe they'd follow her, maybe they wouldn't. Chances were they'd stay with Blain, since they'd figure she didn't need protecting, and by gum, she didn't.

It didn't take her long to get to one Brian Johnson's two-story apartment complex. It was the kind of complex frequently featured in *Cops,* one with a flimsy wrought-iron rail across the top landing and parking spots in front. She pulled in, and when she got out, a glance to the left and right revealed no feds parked nearby. Gone. Humph.

The door to the suspect's apartment was closed, but it took her less than a second to jimmy the lock.

"Jeez-oh-peets," she said, staring around at the dim interior. The place was messier than her own apartment, which was saying a lot. Mr. Johnson appeared to be something of a slob, because it hadn't been her fellow agents who left the place like this. Tossing a suspect's home only happened on TV.

She closed the door behind her. To be honest, Cece didn't know what she expected to find. Any evidence would have already been taken away. But there was always the slim chance the Charlotte Bureau might have missed something. Hell, in the movies they always missed something. But, Cece reminded herself, real FBI life rarely worked that way. Like she really had a chance of finding a race car schematic with a giant X circled where a bomb should go.

So she didn't hold out much hope of spotting anything. But she *did* hope to get a feel for the person they had in custody, maybe get a sense of whether he was good or bad. There were ways to do that. A look at the kind of stuff the person read—*Guns & Ammo* or *People? Guns & Ammo,* she noticed, along with race magazines, a couple of them dog-eared. She turned the pages to see a picture of

Blain and his team in the winner's circle, with Randy Newell grinning from ear to ear.

To her surprise, she felt a brief stab of sadness. Such a talented driver to have been snuffed out.

Was she standing in the killer's home?

She put the magazine down, absorbing the place. There were no photographs. Another telling clue. Loner. Fit the profile.

All firearms would have been taken away, but she looked for a gun safe. There wasn't one, but that didn't mean a pistol couldn't have been hidden beneath his mattress.

Not only had the place been dusted for prints, swabs had been done, too—likely looking for signs of nitrates. Nothing appeared to have come back positive. Interesting.

Further poking around revealed little else. Frankly, she didn't know much more than before, except the suspect appeared to fit the profile of a killer, but that didn't mean much. A few combat magazines and a pink slip did not a killer make.

Sighing, she let herself out. *Damn.* At this rate she'd be better off buying a game of Clue.

"Colonel Mustard in the library," she muttered to herself.

The apartment was on the second floor, and so she had a good view of the space where Blain's fancy import was parked. No sign of her fellow agents. Not surprising. Their primary focus was Blain, not her. And so she was careful as she headed toward her car, her hand poised over the pistol she carried beneath her jacket, her heels clicking down concrete steps to the street.

The pistol turned out to be useless, because things happened so fast Cece didn't have time to react. A car made a sudden, screeching halt at the back of Blain's vehicle just as she took the last step. She pulled her weapon, but it wasn't exactly FBI policy to shoot at reckless drivers, and—damn it—she couldn't see through the car's tinted windows.

One window rolled partway down.

Cece removed the safety.

Something flew out of the car.

Bad guy.

"Damn it!" she yelled in outrage, squeezing the trigger at the same time she dove to the ground.

If felt like a giant stomped on the earth. Cece landed hard. A thousand earthquakes, a hundred rock concerts, a million degrees of heat.

And then silence.

But only for a second. Then the din of car alarms, someone screaming—

The screamer was her. She howled in outrage as she came to her knees, looking for her weapon, diving for it, but when she came up, it was too late.

Gone.

The perp was gone.

She pushed to her feet, ran a few steps. No use.

And then she saw Blain's car, or what was left of it. The shiny new import was nothing more than a burning hulk, the cars on either side of it partially decimated, too.

"Oh, shit," she said. "Shit, shit, shit."

Frustration made her want to toss her weapon to the ground. Instead she took a deep breath, her knees aching where they'd hit the pavement, and reached for her phone.

CHAPTER FIFTEEN

IT REALLY RANKLED to be brought home by Agent Ashton. Cece felt like a teenager who'd been caught drinking on prom night. It didn't help that the man was thoroughly, completely pissed. They'd had words. There'd been the mention of writing her up. She had a feeling the only thing that stopped him was his need for bait, otherwise she'd have been sent packing.

"Disobey me again, Agent Blackwell, and I'll have you suspended."

The words had been dropped into the dense silence that had filled the car. Cece wanted to tell him to go ahead and suspend her. But she was in the wrong. She'd almost gotten killed today. If she'd been in that car...

But she hadn't been, even though the killer had obviously thought Blain was. And if either of them had, all that'd be left of them now would be atoms floating in the atmosphere. The realization that someone might have killed Blain today twisted her insides into knots.

"I understand," she said, doing her best to stay calm.

Agent Ashton's watery blue eyes held her own for a second, his age-spotted hands clenching the steering wheel in such a way as to let Cece know that he was envisioning her neck.

"Go," he said.

She went, opening the car door so quickly, her hand slid off the handle so that it snapped back and pinched her skin. Damn. That hurt. No, damn the whole day. Damn the whole week. It wasn't supposed to happen this way. The bad guys weren't supposed to get one off on her. She should have been more alert. And dammit, she shouldn't have left Blain's side.

Cece walked up the brick path to Blain's front door, wondering how many agents were watching her, and what they were thinking. Probably that she'd blown it. And that she couldn't apprehend a suspect to save her life.

Damn it.

She opened the door.

Blain stood in the hallway.

A very unhappy Blain.

A very *angry* Blain.

Oh, crap, just what she needed.

"Tough day at the office?" he asked in a calm and level voice.

It was so completely the opposite of the tirade she'd been expecting that she found herself nodding.

He opened his arms.

Cece went still. No, that wasn't true. Her mind spun in a million different directions, only to settle on one thought; she, Agent Cecilia Blackwell, was feeling really, really sorry for herself.

"Come here," he said gently.

And from nowhere came the urge to cry. It was totally ridiculous, that urge. Why the heck did she want to start bawling? She was a tough-as-nails FBI agent, one who'd worked her way up to the top of her class, who—until this case—had proven herself over and over again to her fellow agents.

She went into his arms, her eyes stinging by the time she got there. And the man she wanted to forget, the dratted man she'd spent a decade despising, just folded her up in his embrace. It felt good to have that sheltering security. Felt good to have someone to lean on.

He shook.

Cece could feel the tremors rack his body. She pulled back.

The worry she saw in his eyes took her breath away. Yes, he was livid. She could see that. But he was also very, very scared.

"Blain," she said, part question, part concern.

He didn't say anything for a moment. She knew it was because he didn't trust himself to speak.

And the comforting lilt of his Southern drawl washed over her as he said, "Shit, Cece, next time you ask me for the keys to my car, I'm goin' to have to tell you no."

Something tumbled end over end inside of her for a moment. "Oh, Blain."

He bent down, and this time when he tried to kiss her, she didn't move. She couldn't have moved if she tried. This man, this crazy, silly man—who up until a few weeks ago had had the world at his feet—was shaking, his emotions for her were so strong.

But she had to pull back. Couldn't kiss him. She was in enough trouble as it was. The last thing she needed was Internal Affairs on her ass, so she drew back gently—almost as gently as the words she murmured. "Don't worry, Sanders. I could still blow your doors off driving a race car."

He seemed to know what she was doing, even though she could see the disappointment in his eyes. He didn't want to let her go. She didn't *want* him to let her go. But he had to.

"Oh, yeah?" he asked softly, slowly releasing her.

"Yeah," she replied, reluctantly stepping away.

For long seconds he just stared. Cece wondered if he might pull her into his arms again, or maybe place her carefully in a chair…do something that made her feel girly—because, damn it, she needed that right now.

But he didn't. Instead he whispered, "Prove it."

She lifted her brows, gratitude surging through her because, bless him, he obviously understood that a show of sympathy would shatter her control.

"How? You got a couple of '69 Camaros in your

garage that I don't know about?" she asked with a cocky tilt of her chin.

"No, but I've got something else," he said, his finger drifting down her cheek in a way that conveyed a world of tenderness.

"What's that?" she asked, her voice suddenly hoarse.

"Come here." He tugged on her hand.

Cece wanted to cry. She wanted to turn him back to her and sink into his arms. But instead, she followed him up the steps.

"Here."

He led her into a game room that overlooked the lake, the pewter waters gleaming like molten lava beneath the setting sun. The room's walls glowed orange with reflected light, which was probably why she didn't initially see the thing as she walked into the room; that, and because a cherrywood pool table with a stained-glass lamp hanging above it blocked her view.

"Put your money where your mouth is, Ace," he said with a grin.

She followed his gaze, an unexpected huff of laughter escaping her when she saw the arcade-size video game in one corner.

"You have your own personal SEGA?"

"I do. And this ain't just any video game," he said, his Southern accent poured on. "This here is the actual, real-deal, SEGA Daytona USA video game, complete with interconnected game modules and built-in hydraulics so I can bump, nudge and draft you right off the racetrack." He leaned toward her, lifting one side of his mouth up along with a brow. "If you're up to it."

She almost laughed. She almost cried. She wanted to kiss him on the spot.

"You're on," she said.

He smiled. "I was hoping you'd say that."

And as Cece adjusted her seat, familiarizing herself with the controls, she found her hands shook just a little less. Her heart began to thud more regularly, and her breathing returned almost to normal.

"Ready?" Blain asked as he started the game.

"Ready," she affirmed.

"Just remember you're on my turf now, baby. No more zipper racing. No more straight tracks. Left turns from here on out."

"Won't make any difference," she said, glancing up at the game's giant screen, a part of her still stunned to be sitting here next to Blain, playing a video game when not two hours ago she'd been knocked flat by a car bomb.

"Keep telling yourself that."

"Prepare to qualify," the game's electronic voice said a moment later, and Cece all but laughed at the burst of adrenaline she got.

She kicked his butt.

He took it like a man, though, promising to get even with her when they actually raced. And he almost did pull his car even with hers—once—Cece giggling like they were in high school again as his car "bumped" hers from behind, causing her seat to jump beneath her in an almost realistic way.

"No way," she told him as she swerved her wheel, all thoughts of bad guys, bombs, and Internal Affairs gone from her mind. "You're staying behind me, buddy. Right where you belong." Her face actually hurt, she was grinning so hard.

"You're hogging the track," he complained.

"Wuss," she said, feeling him nudge her again. "You're going down."

And he did.

"Ha," she said as she crossed the finish line in front of him. "Beaten again," she said, bounding up from her seat and doing a wiggle dance of victory.

"You do that when you bring down bad guys, too?" he asked from inside his "car," but there was a twinkle in his eyes as he said the words.

"Only if they're lucky."

"You're the lucky one for beating me," he said.

"No. I'm just better," she answered back.

"Luck," he said again.

"All right, wise guy," she said. "If you think I'm so lucky then let's race again."

"Only if we make it a little more interesting."

"Interesting how?"

"How about a little wager?"

"Ah. I see." God help her, her body quickened as

if Blain had promised his touch—and by the look in his eyes, that's exactly what he'd done.

"That desperate, soldier?" She felt bold enough to tease.

"I'm just saying we should make our last race a little more interesting."

"What do you want?" she asked, crossing her arms and trying to assume a stern expression of don't-you-dare-suggest-what-I-think-you're-going-to-suggest.

"If you win the game I'll give you something you want."

"You don't *have* anything I want."

"Not even hot passes to the Daytona 500 next year?"

Ooo, that was low. "Well, maybe that," she admitted.

"And if I win, I get something I want."

"And that would be?" she asked in her best raised eyebrow, schoolmarm look of pubescent admonishment.

"Dinner with you downstairs in my sunroom."

That was all? Cece felt an unexpected stab of... disappointment.

"Fine," she said, heading back to her car.

And that was when Cece realized she'd been had. Royally, thoroughly had, because the Blain Sanders she'd raced up to now was not the same Blain Sanders she raced now. This Blain beat her qualifying by six spots. And when the race started, he overtook her in a matter of seconds.

"Hey," she said, concentrating on the big screen as she tried to find him in the field. "Where'd you learn that move?"

"I've had this game for nearly two years."

She darted a glance over at him, the screen in front of him tinting his face an alien blue-green. "Why, you—"

"Careful," he said with a glance at her screen.

She crashed, her seat doing the video game equivalent of a demolition derby wreck, it vibrated and pitched so much.

"Why, you sneaky, slime-mongrel of a male!"

He laughed, and Cece wanted to laugh, too, never having heard his uncensored version. Eyes as blue as a Montana sky glittered and sparkled, his tan face wreathed in a smile.

Thank you, she wanted to tell him.

"C'mon," he said, the moment passing. "I'll make you some dinner."

And she found herself smiling back, and even laughing a little bit. You gotta love a man with a sense of humor.

Love?

Well, not that kind of love.

So when he took her downstairs, she didn't mind. And when he led her to the kitchen, she didn't mind that, either. But when he took her to the sunroom, she had a moment's thought that this didn't seem right. There was a perfectly good kitchen table…

He turned back to her in the glass room, the last of the sun's rays ebbing though the blinds, which had been closed earlier against the North Carolina sun.

And then he kissed her.

"Blain," she protested in shock, trying to draw away.

"Oh, no," he said, and even though she could see the remnants of laughter in his eyes, her heart still thudded as if she'd just come face-to-face with an AK-47. "Time to pay up."

"You said dinner."

"I said dinner in case one of your buddies had a listening device trained on us."

"You—"

He kissed her again.

"They'll still hear us," she whispered against his lips.

"The walls are glass," he said in a low voice. "And so there's no place for listening devices."

"You think."

"I know. I checked earlier."

"Oh, and so now you think you're James Bond? You think you know what a listening device looks like? We have things that let you hear into a house from a quarter mile—"

He kissed her again.

"Blain," she protested, drawing back. Again.

Only this time he didn't say a word. This time he lifted a hand to her face, touched it gently, the look in his eyes changing so quickly it was as if he'd become a different man.

"Let me kiss you, Cece," he said. "Let me *hold* you. Let me try and forget for a moment that someone tried to kill you today, and that if that had happened, the world would have lost one of the bravest women I've ever known."

Oh. Oh, oh, oh.

"Will you?" he asked. "Will you let me hold you? Will you let me make love to you?"

She stared up at him, and Blain could see the indecision in her eyes.

"But if someone finds out—"

"They won't."

Her eyes searched his, and he knew how hard this must be for her. He knew Cece well enough to know that her job was everything to her. Asking her to risk it was tantamount to asking him to risk his race team.

"I don't think I can," she said softly.

Yup. By the book—that was his Cece.

His Cece. He liked the way that sounded. And he liked the way staring at her made him feel. At home. One. With his soul mate.

"Please," he said, brushing his hand against her face. "Let's worry about the future tomorrow."

He expected her to balk again, expected her to turn away. To his surprise, what she did was close the door to the sunroom, her shoulders squaring as she faced him. There was hardly any light in the room, just a muted gray glow that perfectly captured the green in her eyes. It amazed him that a woman so small could face down bad guys. But that was the first of many things that amazed him about Cece—her loyalty, her determination, but most of all, her courage.

That courage had almost gotten her killed today.

His hands started to shake once more. He covered it by gently pulling her toward him. He saw the brief flare of concern that must have followed a thought that they shouldn't be doing this. He didn't give her time to reconsider, just bent down and captured the world's softest lips.

"Cece," he whispered against them, his breath wafting back on him, mixing with her own. "Little spitfire."

And then he pressed his mouth against hers again, urging her to open, wanting to feel that warm heat of hers again, to taste her and know that she was there in his arms—and safe.

When she started to kiss him back—really kiss him—he stopped thinking. No. That wasn't true. He had one thought on his mind. To make love to her. And so he pulled the cushions from his rattan furniture, creating a makeshift bed on the sunroom floor, then laying her down on top.

She smiled up at him, and Blain's heart tipped sideways. For just a second, he had a memory of when they were teenagers. The same soft expression. The same piercing green eyes, the same challenge shining from their depths.

You think you can beat my car? she'd asked.

Piece of cake.

Only *she'd* beaten *him*. And if he was honest, he'd found that fascinating.

He reached up and touched her chin, something that was quickly becoming a habit, and he marveled at how soft her skin was, how utterly feminine. And those adorable freckles…

"If you'd been killed today, I would have made it my mission in life to catch who's doing this—to make them pay."

"But I wasn't," she said softly.

"Thank God," he murmured.

Her look changed to one of tenderness and gratitude, and, he thought, perhaps even surprise. And then he did what he'd been longing to do: he covered her, his body protecting her, their faces inches apart. He sheltered her. Tried to keep her safe from harm.

If only he could.

When she reached up and stroked his cheek, he tipped his jaw into her hand, then lowered his head, bringing them closer together as he slowly, softly kissed her. And there was something different about kissing Cece. Something special. Something unique. It felt…right. As if he'd been kissing her since forever.

She sighed, lifting her other hand to frame each side of his face. He pulled back and kissed her palm, making her eyes widen. He smiled, then bent and kissed her cheek, her temple, her ear…such a sweet ear, Blain thought, licking her lobe, then tasting the inside. She wiggled and he stopped.

"No. Don't stop," she said.

He bit back a smile, then nuzzled her ear some more, nipping, teasing, suckling. And she reciprocated, her hands skimming down his sides, one of them sneaking between their bodies. And when she touched him—Lord help him—when she touched him, he almost came unglued. He pulled back to catch his breath, the same breath he'd hissed out between clenched teeth as she worked him, stroked him, teased him.

"Lord, Cece," he said, closing his eyes.

Her other hand lifted the edge of his shirt. He needed no prompting to tip back and take the thing off. But she wasn't content with just the shirt. Her eyes never wavered from his face as she encouraged him to kneel alongside her, those nimble fingers of hers releasing the catch on his pants. He couldn't move. Gasped as he felt her fingers touch him again when she lowered the zipper. Held his breath as she slowly worked his pants down, then his briefs.

She stroked him with her tongue.

Blain threw his head back.

She glided her lips up his shaft.

He looked down at her, cupped her head with his hands, showed her how to work him, how to use those lips of hers to make him come.

But, no, this wasn't right. *He* wanted to make love to *her.*

"Get undressed," he ordered.

She lifted a brow. "No."

"No?"

"In due time," she said with a secret smile, her head lowering toward him again.

"Cece, no," he said.

She looked back up at him, surprised by the expression on his face. There was firmness there, and determination.

"I don't want it to be like this."

And oddly enough, her heart seemed to stop beating at his words. "Like what?"

"Sex," he said, cupping her face again. "I don't want this to be sex. I want this to be making love."

Her body went still.

He reached down and pulled her up so they were kneeling face-to-face. His expression was utterly serious as he said, "Let me make love to you, Cece. Let me touch you and caress you and show you what I'm feeling inside. Let me show you how much losing you today would have hurt me."

She didn't understand. Or maybe she did. Maybe she knew exactly what he meant, because she was feeling things that she'd never felt before, too. Things, she admitted with a touch of panic, she didn't want to feel for him.

For anybody.

Heaven help her, she was falling in love with the guy.

CHAPTER SIXTEEN

SHE LEFT HIM KNEELING there.

And even as she did it, she felt horrible. And guilty. And damn it—something she hated to feel—panicked.

"Cece," he called out.

But she needed air. Fresh air. Great big gulps of air.

She opened one of the kitchen's French doors, the humid North Carolina night feeling like a force of its own. It wasn't quite dark yet; the crickets and frogs starting their evening serenade. Cece headed toward the lake's rippling edge, the liquid-silver waves gently lapping at the pebbled shore.

"Cece, wait."

He'd followed her. Damn it. If they were under surveillance, they'd be found out for sure, what with him half-dressed, shirt thrown on and untucked, no shoes on his feet.

He caught her right at the shoreline. "What the hell is going on?"

She looked up at him. The side of his face was

bathed in color—gray and orange and muted blue. His eyes looked silver, or maybe that was light refracting off the lake. She didn't know. All she knew was that she didn't need this. She didn't want to—feel. And that concerned her all the more. She wasn't a coward. She wasn't afraid of anything. And yet she sure feared the way she felt about Blain.

She straightened her shoulders, determined to confront this problem like she did all others in her life. Directly and with no apologies. Still, it took her a moment to quell the urge to squeeze his hand, because the worry and disappointment she saw in his eyes made her heart do things it had no business doing.

"I can't."

"Can't what, Cece?" he said with a tiny shake of his head.

"I can't do this."

Her words shocked him, she could tell. He rocked back a bit, his mouth compressing into a line. For the longest moment he didn't say anything.

"Because of your job?" he said. "Because if you're worried about getting into trouble, don't. We can wait until this is all over. I don't mind."

And that made her heart melt even more. *Man*, he was the complete opposite of who she'd thought him to be. Why did he have to be so nice?

"You don't understand," she said.

His eyes asked her to *help* him understand.

"It's more than my job, Blain. It's…everything."

But it was obvious he still didn't understand.

She tried to pull her thoughts from the dank air, tried to gather them around so they made some sort of sense. "It's…you. You're too…" Damn it, why was this so hard to articulate? "Nice," she said at last, because really, that's what it boiled down to.

Unfortunately, her words had the opposite effect than what she'd wanted. His wrinkled brow smoothed, his eyes softened. "That's it? That's what has you so worried? I'm too nice?"

"Yes." A mosquito buzzed around her ear with a high-pitched whine. She swatted it away. "I mean, no. Actually, that's most of it. I'm starting to care for you, and that's not good."

He closed the distance between them. "Yes it is good," he said, touching the line of her jaw. "I care for you, too, Cece."

Lordy, she wished he'd stop touching her. It did things to her insides. No, it did things to her heart. Everything about him did things to her heart, from the look in his eyes to the tender way his fingers stroked her face.

"But that's just it, Blain," she said softly. "I don't want you to care for me."

"Why not?"

"Because our lifestyles are too different."

"So? We can work that out."

"No, Blain, we can't. Your job doesn't involve going undercover, pretending to be someone else, becoming someone you really aren't for weeks at a time, just so you can flush out a bad guy."

He shook his head, and it was apparent he didn't understand.

She tried to help him. "Sometimes, because it's a part of my job, I have to pretend to be someone I'm not, and it's hell, Blain. You have to do and say things that are so completely *not* who you are. And if you're in for a long time, if you're forced undercover for months, you almost become that person, and then, when you come back home, you have to shut it all off, and it's hell on the people you love. But that's my job, and it's a job I'm committed to, a job I've worked years to get. It's who I am. I won't give it up for anybody."

"I'm not asking you to."

"Oh, yeah? You really don't mind what I do for a living?"

He didn't answer for a moment, and she knew he *did* mind. To be honest, she kind of expected that. Though he wasn't Southern-born, he'd adopted Southern ways. And in the South, women didn't become FBI agents. They joined country clubs and had babies.

"You don't like me being in danger, do you?"

"You know I don't," he admitted. "But I'd never ask you to quit."

"No?"

He shook his head. Her respect for him went up a notch. But that wasn't really the point, was it? "What I'm trying to say, Blain, is that I don't want to hurt you, and eventually, what I do for a living *would* hurt you."

She gave in to the urge to grab his hand, to squeeze it so that she had his attention. "My partner, the one that died—remember me telling you about him on the plane?"

He nodded.

"Well, what I didn't tell you was the way his widow reacted to his death. I had to tell her, Blain. I had to break the news. I wouldn't let anyone else do it. I'd been over to their house for dinner. I'd gone to their children's christenings. Watched their kids on weekends. I wasn't going to let some perfect stranger break the news that Bill was gone."

She clenched his hand, part of her realizing she would probably end up hurting him, another part of her suddenly desperate for the lifeline anyway.

"It was the worst thing I've ever had to do, Blain. She couldn't comprehend what I was telling her, and then suddenly her eyes changed and I knew she *did* understand. Bill was dead." Cece released his hand, looked out over the lake, crossing her arms in front of her. "Her heart broke that day, Blain. I saw it shatter. And I was partly responsible. We were partners. I should have been watching out for him."

"It wasn't your fault, Cece."

"That's what the shrinks said, too. And I know that. But I've seen that look before." Cece turned back to face him. "I'd seen what my dad's death did to my mom, too. I'm not going to do that to someone *I* love."

"Ridiculous."

"Maybe so, but it's the way I feel."

Blain couldn't believe his ears. That she would live her life like that? Didn't she realize you didn't get anything out of life without risk? Granted, he didn't know where their relationship would lead. Friendship? Marriage? He surely didn't know. He doubted Cece knew. But how would they *ever* know if she didn't open up?

"So you're closing the door? Refusing to feel anything more for me because you're too afraid?"

"I'm not afraid for myself," she said. "I'm afraid for *you*."

"Don't you think *I* should make the call as to whether or not I want to take the risk of getting hurt?"

"You can't make that choice."

"The hell I can't."

"No, you can't. You don't know a thing about what it's like to live with an FBI agent."

"I'd like to try."

She shook her head, and Blain felt almost as frustrated as he had when his sponsor dropped him earlier that day. Damn it. What the hell had happened to his life?

"I'm sorry, Blain," she said, stepping back from him.

"Cece, wait."

She turned.

"C'mon, Cece, don't."

But she walked away, which pissed him off even

more. If anyone could understand the dangers inherent in a job, he could.

He crossed his arms, turned back to the lake, debating. But what could he say? There would be no reasoning with her right now. He'd have to work on her tomorrow. And the next day. And the day after that.

Because there was one thing he knew for certain—he wasn't about to give up. When he saw something he wanted, he went after it.

And he wanted Cece Blackwell.

CHAPTER SEVENTEEN

THE NEXT FEW DAYS went by in a blur for Cece, mostly because she kept herself busy any way she could, and that involved learning the inner workings of a race shop—while somehow avoiding Blain.

And she did manage to avoid him, though she had a feeling he let her. The man didn't act like someone who'd been dumped. No. He was entirely too nice. Granted, they were forced to work together out of necessity, which meant she drove with him everywhere, slept in a room down the hall, ate breakfast, lunch and dinner with the man. And through it all, he smiled, conversed with her and otherwise behaved like a big brother. That should have reassured her. Instead it made her feel edgy, off balance—maybe even a little mad. Darn it, she wanted to touch him, to hold him, to forget for a moment what she did for a living. She couldn't.

So when it came time to head out for the next weekend's race—Blain having delayed their departure as long as possible—she wasn't exactly in a great mood. All right, she could admit it—she was in a terrible mood.

Granted, part of her irritation stemmed from someone having tried to kill her. Twice. Sleep didn't exactly come easy when you were worried about explosives being lobbed through the window. But so far, their suspect was lying low. She expected that to change at Atlanta Motor Speedway, where they held the Cutmax 400, and where Blain was racing on his own dime. Unfortunately, that meant a long time with Blain in a car—make that a Hummer, Blain having selected his new vehicle with bricks of C4 in mind.

"Jeesh," Cece said when she caught sight of the bright yellow vehicle outside his house. "You thinking of going to work for Chiquita Banana?"

"What do you mean?" he asked, following behind her, an overnight bag flung over his shoulder.

Overnight. With Blain.

Ay yi yi.

"It's yellow."

"So it is," he said.

"Bright yellow…as in the Space Shuttle can see us from orbit yellow."

"I wanted a color that your friends tailing us would be able to spot in traffic."

"Mission accomplished," she grumbled.

She thought she heard him chuckle, but she didn't look back to check. Even when she opened the car door, the smell of freshly unwrapped Hummer greeting her, she didn't look at him.

"An armored tank probably would have been cheaper."

"They don't come with cruise control."

She glanced over at him. He gave her a crooked smile. She hated that crooked smile. It reminded her of what a great guy he was—and how hard a time she'd been having remembering that she didn't get involved with great guys.

"What? No leather?" she said, hopping into the thing, doing her best to appear dignified as she contorted herself into the vehicle's small interior.

"No, but it has a diamond-plated underside."

"No kidding," she said, thinking Blain must not be doing too bad financially if he could afford a Hummer, and one with the bomb-proofing option at that.

But, see, that was just it. He appeared to be taking everything well. Have someone blow up your fancy import, buy a Hummer. Have someone kill your driver, hire another one. Lose your multimillion-dollar sponsor, race your car without a fancy logo on the hood. Actually, what he'd put in place of that logo had made her laugh: Your Name Here.

But she didn't *want* Blain to make her laugh. She wanted him to do things that made her think she'd been right to call it quits between them.

"I still think the color's all wrong." But she was grumbling more about her internal monologue than the color of the car.

"You'll get used to it," he said with a smile, and Cece's heart did that little flippity-flop.

Oh, brother.

IT WAS A LONG, long, *loooooong* drive to Atlanta. Cece wished for about the hundredth time that they'd flown, but FBI higher-ups had advised them to keep their feet firmly on the ground—they didn't want any airplanes falling out of the sky. She glanced over at him, and instantly wished she hadn't. He'd forgotten to shave this morning, the result being that he had a light dusting of black hair on his handsome, square and thoroughly masculine chin. She'd always been a sucker for men who looked good in business clothes. And while Blain didn't wear a suit and tie, he *did* wear a white button-down shirt that highlighted the tan he'd gotten while working outdoors. Masculine legs were defined by dark blue slacks that would look preppy on a lesser man. Not on Blain. By the time they reached the track, the Hummer felt about the size of a wheelbarrow.

"The entrance to the infield is over there," he said, pointing toward the gate.

And a good thing, too. But when she took the time to actually look around, she was surprised by how much foliage surrounded the track. Somehow, she'd always pictured racetracks in industrialized areas, but Atlanta's rose up from a sea of trees. VIP suites, press boxes and the track's private offices ran along the front stretch, hundreds of seats visible beneath them.

"Did Linda give you a copy of our schedule?"

Linda of the low cleavage would sooner hand her a vial of bubonic plague than give her something as useful as a schedule, or so Cece surmised.

"Actually, no," Cece said.

"I asked her to."

"She must have missed me on the way out." Hah. She'd probably withheld the information.

"Okay, well, the first thing we need to do is have a meeting with Barry Bidwell."

"The president of NASCAR?" she asked.

Blain nodded. "That's the man."

"I thought you'd worked everything out with him last week in Vegas."

"He called this morning and requested a meeting."

And something about the look on his face alerted Cece that this would be no ordinary meeting, and she couldn't believe he'd waited until now to tell her about it. Didn't he believe in the intimacy of sharing?

You're the one who'd called it quits.

Oh, yeah, she'd forgotten. "What do you think he wants?"

"I don't think he wants anything. I think he's going to pull my license."

AND HE WAS RIGHT.

"You can't do that," Blain said calmly, though Cece could tell the words rankled.

"Actually, we can," said a man who'd introduced himself as the head of PR, Rick Something-or-other.

"We have the right to pull anyone's license. It's in the rule book."

"Yeah, but that only applies when rules have been broken."

"Not necessarily, Blain," the PR guy said. "We reserve the right to pull a license for *any* reason."

Blain just shook his head. "Why the about-face?" he asked.

"We didn't take the threat seriously before. Now we do," Barry Bidwell said. "And with someone out there targeting your team, and those affiliated with you—" he glanced in Cece's direction "—we really feel it's better for the fans if you're not around this weekend. We'd hate for the killer to miss you and hit someone else instead."

And even though Cece hated to admit it, she could see their point.

"When can I have it back?" Blain asked.

"As soon as this crazy son of a gun is caught," Bidwell said.

"That might be awhile," Cece muttered under her breath.

Barry glanced at her for a second, then back at Blain. "It might," he said, his vowels sounding longer, like Blain's. Southern. "But we can't do anything about that."

"Son of a bitch," Blain said. "By the time I get back to racing, I'll be millions in the hole. Crap, I may as well shut the whole operation down."

"That's certainly an option."

"No, it's not. I can't tell my guys that they're out of a job—what about their families?"

Silence followed. Outside, the drone of race cars rose in volume, higher and higher, a million angry bees roaring down the homestretch. Practice time.

Cece spoke up. "Mr. Bidwell, with all due respect, perhaps this decision is a bit precipitous. It might be weeks before we solve the case—months, even. Asking Mr. Sanders to ground his team is tantamount to asking him to give up racing."

"We can't help that," the PR guy said. "We're just trying to do what's best for the sport, and the fans' safety."

"Bullshit," Blain shot back, slamming his palm down on the table. Cece jumped. Everyone in the room did, except Mr. Bidwell, whose eyes had never left Blain's.

"What would be best for racing is if you canceled the upcoming races until this guy is caught."

"We can't do that," Barry said instantly, "any more than the NFL canceled the Super Bowl when there was a terrorist threat."

"The Super Bowl was *one* event. You have a whole list of events where a killer might strike."

"And we're increasing security to counteract that threat."

"You think that will help?" Blain asked, his face turning as red as the flag they used to stop the cars. "You think you can protect one hundred thousand race fans?"

"The airports do it every day."

Blain just gave him a look of disbelief. But unlike Blain, Cece could understand the association's position. If they let terrorists rule their lives, they'd never race again. In fact, she wouldn't be surprised if her friend Agent Ashton hadn't advised Mr. Bidwell to do exactly as he was doing: increase security and ditch the biggest threat—Sanders Racing.

Shit.

"This isn't an airport," Blain said.

"No, but we're using the same measures to protect our fans. Given the circumstances, it's the best we can do."

Blain fell silent, but Cece could see how upset he was by the white brackets around his mouth.

"Son of a—" He got to his feet, crossed to the bank of windows that overlooked the track, and stared outside at the vehicles roaring by. "I have a car out there practicing right now, and a driver who expects to race day after tomorrow. What am I going to tell him?"

"As to that, we have a solution," Rick said.

Blain turned and faced the men at the table.

"We're not without sympathy, Blain," Barry said. "You've been in this industry a long time, and we realize you need to keep up a presence, maybe even collect some purse money so that sponsors might get interested. We asked Pat Pearson if he'd like to manage your team in your absence."

"Are you out of your mind?" Blain said, and Cece

could tell if he'd been furious before, that was nothing compared to his anger now. "He's my biggest competitor, and a man who'd love to get a glimpse of how I do things just for the advantage it'd bring him once this is over."

"It's your choice."

"Well, it's a shitty choice—"

"Then don't race."

"That's not an option."

"Not from where we sit—"

"Gentlemen," Cece interrupted, straightening up a bit as she put on her most professional smile. "I mean, really, what difference does it make who's managing Mr. Sanders's team? The driver and crew might still be targeted—"

"Since none of the other teams, nor their friends, have come under fire, we're not of that opinion," Bidwell said, "and so the only solution we're prepared to offer is the one we just suggested." He looked at Blain. "Either you do this or leave the track. Today."

Cece had a fantasy of jumping up on the table, pulling out her pistol and saying, "Make us, you varmints," just like they did in the cartoons.

But when she caught a glimpse of Blain's profile over by the window, her heart broke instead.

Oh, jeesh…

"I can't believe you're doing this to me," he said, arms crossed.

"We have no choice," Bidwell said.

Yes, they did, but Cece knew trying to convince them otherwise would be an impossible task. She was a racing outsider. She had about as much clout in their eyes as the conference room windows.

"Then I guess we're leaving."

"If that's your choice."

He nodded, and they all stared at each other for long seconds before Blain turned toward the door. Cece got up, too, shooting Bidwell and the PR guy her nastiest look. By the time she and Blain emerged into the Atlanta sunshine, he was ten feet ahead of her.

"Blain."

He kept going.

"Blain, wait," she insisted, catching up to him, touching his arm. He jerked away, and she tried not to get angry at that. She'd walked away from him enough times, that's for sure. And he was furious. She could understand that. But she also expected him to know she knew how he felt.

"Blain, stop," she said, taking a firmer grip on his arm, stepping in front of him.

There were tears in his eyes.

Cece felt as if the ground dropped from beneath her feet.

"Oh, Blain," she said, her hand tightening on his arm.

He tried to step around her again. She wouldn't let him, placing a hand against his chest in spite of the agents who might be watching. And beneath her palm, she could feel the furious thump of his heart, her own heart tearing in two at the look on his face.

"They're going to ruin me, Cece."

"No, they're not."

"It'll take me years to recover from this."

And before she could think about the consequences, before she could remind herself that someone might be watching, she found herself wrapping him in her arms. He let her.

"We'll find out who's doing this, Blain. I promise. You'll be out there racing before you know it."

"What am I going to tell the guys?"

She drew back. Tears still hovered on the rim of his lower lids. If he'd been any other man, she would bet he'd be hiding his tears. But Blain wasn't that type of man, and the way he fearlessly allowed her to see how he felt touched her in a way she'd never been touched before.

"Tell them the truth, Blain—that you've been grounded. Tell them you're sorry, and if they want to find positions with other teams, that you'll understand. Tell them the FBI is going to solve this case and then everything will be back to normal."

"What if you don't solve it?"

"We will, Blain." And, Lord, how she wanted to reach up and kiss him. How she wanted to wrap her arms around his neck, pull her to him and comfort him. But she couldn't, partly because she didn't want to risk an Internal Affairs investigation, and partly because she didn't trust herself to touch him that way. God help her, she was feeling things right now that should have sent her scurrying away.

"Let's go tell your crew," she said, grabbing his hand.

"YOU'VE GOT TO BE KIDDING," Lance Cooper said, the look on his face as incredulous as the rest of the crew's.

They were standing near their garage stall, their plate car still hot from practice—a practice that'd been preempted.

"I wish I was," Blain said to his team and driver. "We're packing up."

Twenty faces stared back at him, most of them with various looks of disbelief, a few in obvious disappointment. Blain glanced over at Cece. She'd made no attempt to disguise the fact that she was an FBI agent, from her standard-issue black jacket and black pants that must be smoking hot in the Atlanta heat, to the tightly drawn back hair.

We'll catch these guys. Her voice rang in his ears. He sure hoped so.

"Look," he said, turning back to his crew. "I know you expected to race this weekend, and that you'd hoped to win the bonuses that go along with a top finish. That isn't going to happen. So if you want to work for another team, you have my permission. I won't hold you to your contracts. Not anymore." He met the gaze of one of his longtime employees. "I know the number sixteen car is looking for a tire changer, Brad. You might be able to go over there," he said to the man, who nodded. Blain then addressed the crew in general. "I'm sure there'll be a lot of other teams that'd be glad to have you, and I'm not going to stop you from finding those jobs."

Seeing nods all around, Blain looked at Lance. "I'm sorry, Lance," he said to the wiry driver. "I'll understand if you want to go drive for someone else, but I'll continue to pay you if you decide to wait it out."

Blain knew what his answer would be, for there was one universal truth about all drivers—they wanted to drive.

"I'll let you know," the kid said.

Blain felt even more disappointment. He sensed something about the guy, something that he suspected might lead to greatness one day. If they could only get it together, figure each other out...

There'd be no chance to do that now. At least not for a while, and by then Lance would be driving for someone else.

"That's it then, guys. I just ask that you stick around long enough to pack up the hauler. After that, you're on your own. But I'll still pay your salary no matter what."

There were looks of relief at that, mostly because the odds of all of them finding work elsewhere were slim to nil this late in the day. But the good ones would be snapped up soon, and it pissed Blain off to the point that he felt like punching something.

"See you back at the shop."

When he turned away, Cece stepped into position next to him. It chafed to have her protecting him. It chafed to have her witness what had gone on upstairs. It chafed that she'd seen him lose control.

But as he glanced down at her, he realized he was glad. He needed her in a way he'd never needed a woman, wanted to lose himself in the comfort of her arms.

"Where are you going now?" she said, her green eyes peering up at him. She had a wisp of light blond hair that kept drifting down from her forehead. He reached up and swept it behind her ear. Those eyes of hers widened.

"Relax, none of your buddies saw."

"I'm sure they did," she corrected, frowning. "This place is crawling with agents." She glanced around the garage.

And it was. For the first time in Blain's racing career, he'd had to show a photo ID to get inside. Usually, security just waved him through. Hell, half the time he was recognized. Today had been different, and it reminded Blain that someone, somewhere, was watching them. And not just good guys. The bad guy was out there, too—or *guys*. Was it one of the fans who'd come to the track early to watch them set up? Someone from another team who had it in for him? Someone who didn't even like racing? One of his crew?

"You'd think they'd try to blend in a little bit better," he heard Cece mutter under her breath.

He had to force himself to remember what they'd been talking about. Oh, yeah, the number of agents.

"You think with everything they have on their plate that they're keeping an eye on you?"

"After that hug an hour ago, I'm sure there are more than a few raised eyebrows."

"Screw 'em," Blain said.

She frowned, and Blain knew that'd been the wrong thing to say. Cece's job meant everything to her. He knew that. His job was to convince her that *he* could mean just as much to *her*, and it looked as if he'd have plenty of time to do that in the coming weeks.

Once again he felt the acidic heat of dread hit his stomach.

He might lose it all.

He might, but he wouldn't. By God, he'd sell everything before he let that happen. Maybe rebuild from scratch…if it came to that.

"I'm going to get a hotel room for the night," he said.

She looked up sharply.

"Don't worry, we don't have to share it."

She lifted a brow, and was that a tiny smile he saw hovering on her lips? "I *wasn't* worried."

Dread slipped away as he stared into Cece's eyes, as did the persistent sensation of being watched.

"Oh, that's right. You've decided to shut off your emotions where I'm concerned."

The smile faded. "That's right."

"Well, then, I guess there's nothing to worry about. You can share a hotel room with me, after all."

She stopped, hands on her hips. "I will not."

He almost laughed.

She realized he was teasing her and smiled back, and beneath the hot Atlanta sun, Blain felt his anxiety slip away. Damn, the way she made him feel when she smiled up at him...

"Seriously," he said, advising himself to be patient. "I don't feel like driving back tonight."

"Yeah, neither do I."

"Then let's get a hotel. We can kick back, use the spa. Order some champagne."

She rolled her eyes.

"And I promise not to touch," he added.

"I told you, I'm not worried about that."

You should be.

"But if you're set on this idea, then I suppose Bravo Team can set up security."

Oh, yeah—protection. Funny how easy it was to forget about that for a few minutes.

"Well, tell Bravo Team that I want to stay at the Renaissance downtown."

Her brows lifted at the mention of the Renaissance; even she'd heard of the luxurious hotel. "Hey, if I'm going to have to give all this up, I might as well go out with a bang," he added.

She frowned. "You don't think it'll really come to that, do you?

"It might."

She looked away for a second, only to pull her shoulders back, tip her chin up and smile at him tightly. "Then I guess we're off to the Renaissance."

"Atta girl."

CHAPTER EIGHTEEN

BUT BY THE TIME Cece arrived at the Renaissance's Presidential Suite, she was a nervous wreck. Words kept repeating themselves over and over again in her head.

Blain. Hotel room. Alone.

It wasn't that she thought he'd pull something. He'd been a perfect gentleman all week, after all. Still, she was as jumpy as a rookie on her first day on the gun range.

"Here we are," Blain said as he stopped before a double door with the name Presidential Suite etched into a brass plaque next to them.

Blain. Hotel room— Stop it, Cece!

But her first words weren't, "Unhand me, you fiend," which she'd half-hoped would be required. They were, "Jeez-oh-peets," as she set her stuff down by the door. "Does the Shah of Iran live here?"

Blain walked in behind her, tossing his room card on the marble-topped entry table guarded by a giant mirror mounted above it.

"Nah," he said, "suites are all the same. They

only make them look like a million bucks. The frames are all plastic, the carpets made in China and the furniture pressed wood."

Cece crossed to the window, stepping back quickly when she realized how high up they were. Okay, so the altitude didn't make her feel any calmer.

"But the view can't be faked," he said.

"If you like views," she grumbled.

"Don't like heights?"

"Don't like being close to windows that are high up," Cece clarified, and it was true, though her edginess had more to do with being in a hotel room, alone, with Blain.

"You *are* afraid of heights," he accused.

Cece sighed. "Just a little," she confessed.

"I'll be damned," she heard him murmur.

"Probably you will," she quipped wryly.

He shook his head. She looked back at the window, telling herself to calm down. "I noticed in my travels that the price of a room is usually commensurate with how far off the ground it is."

"Good point."

"Bet you've been high off the ground a few times."

"A few."

And that was part of the problem. High off the ground in hotel rooms with how many other women?

And why had he given up on her so easily?

"I'm going to search the place," she said, suddenly fed up with herself. She was sounding as fickle as a woman, which she was, but, well—forget it.

"Don't you think that might be overkill?" Blain asked as she turned away. "I sincerely doubt that a bad guy had time to booby-trap the room in between our checking in and coming up here."

"It's my job," Cece said. It really was, she reminded herself. "But I'm also making note of entrance and exit points." And in a two-thousand-square-foot suite, there were a lot of those.

"Places where you can hide, if need be, and places where you shouldn't stand in the event someone slides something under the door." She glanced back at Blain. "By the way, you might want to move. Never a good idea to stand near a main entrance."

She would have smiled at the way his eyes widened except she was too edgy to summon even the tiniest of tilts to her lips. The fact of the matter was they had agents watching the floor through surveillance. If someone was making his way toward the private suite, Cece's radio would beep, warning her. Frankly, they were safer up here than they were at Blain's home. More secluded, too. There really was only one way in, maybe two if someone decided to rappel down to the balcony, although she doubted that would happen. This wasn't a James Bond flick.

She took a deep breath.

Blain was safe. For now. Maybe that's why she was so tense. She'd been worried about him.

"I think you're going to be fine," she said, heading for the front door.

"Where are you going?" Blain asked.

"I'm going to check into my own room."

"Seriously, Cece, you can stay here. There's plenty of space."

"No," she said quickly.

"I promised not to touch."

"No," she said again, but only because she had to quell the instant "yes" that wanted to rise to her lips.

"Can't concentrate with me nearby?"

Something like that. "No. I just prefer my privacy."

He started to move toward her. Cece felt her spine prickle. Usually the feeling preceded a bullet whizzing by her ear.

"What are you doing?" she asked warily.

"I want to give you a hug."

"A *what?*"

"A hug," he said with a small smile.

She turned, saying, "Goodbye," over her shoulder.

"Oh, no, you don't." He assumed a look of innocence as he stepped in front of her. "What? Am I not allowed to thank you for all you've done?"

"Send me a letter," she said, trying to sidle past him.

"Cece, wait." He caught her before she'd taken two steps, his big hand encompassing her own. "Don't go," he said, tightening his grip.

"I have to," she said.

"No, you don't."

"Yes, Blain, I do. I told you I wasn't going to go

there with you. I can't believe you refuse to respect that wish."

Yes, you can, a voice argued. *You're thrilled he refuses to give up. Go on. Admit it.*

"I'm not going to let you get away so easily."

And if she needed confirmation that she truly wanted his pursuit, all she had to do was feel the way her body tingled at his words.

"I want to make love to you."

"Forget it," she said.

"Cece, please…I don't want to be alone tonight."

"That's a really good line, buddy."

"It's not a line," he said. "It's the truth. I'm about to lose everything. I don't want to lose you, too."

Cece froze. She knew she should step in the other direction, or at least pull back, but instead her breath caught as she looked into his eyes.

"I need you, Cece. Now more than ever. No more games. No more keeping my distance. I want to hold you, to feel your warmth, to know you're in my arms—where I've been longing for you to be."

No, the voice screamed. *Don't let his words sway you.*

"Damn you," she said, tears of frustration filling her eyes. She didn't want this. She couldn't handle a relationship. Not now. Not ever. There were things he didn't even know about her, important things.

He bent down and gently, tenderly, kissed her, and all her objections melted away.

To be honest, she'd come up to his room half

wishing for his kiss, and to hell with Internal Affairs. So when he slid her jacket off her shoulders, she let him. And when he slowly began to undo the buttons of her white blouse, she let him do that, too. And the further he undressed her, the further away her protests drifted, until she felt only his hands, their gentle, tender touch making her realize how much she loved the reverent way he caressed her. And her breathing—she was aware of that, too, of the way she sucked in a breath when he slipped off her bra. The way she gasped when his lips moved away from her own to lightly suckle the side of her neck, and then her collarbone, and then—oh, lord—her breast.

She watched as his tongue darted out and flicked the tip of her left nipple, flicking and flicking…

How, she wondered, how did he know how to touch her so perfectly…so right? Her knees grew weak, but she'd never felt stronger or more alive in her life. His tongue dove in and out of her mouth, over and over and over again, in a rhythm that she wanted matched between her thighs.

He must have felt her sag against him because he picked her up. Cece came back to earth then, but only for a brief second, during which sanity returned and she wondered what she was doing letting Blain Sanders carry her to a room with a massive bed.

"Blain…" His name escaped her lips part sigh, part panicked moan.

But when he laid her down, when he sat on the edge of the plush bed and looked down at her, his hand lifting to caress her nose, she felt herself melt all over again. His intensely tender yet possessive gaze made her feel more feminine than she could remember feeling in a long, long time.

"I want you naked," he said.

She didn't move.

"And I want you to watch me undress, too, Cece. I want you to see what you do to me."

He stood. And Cece watched as he removed his shirt. Watched as he pulled down his slacks, the bulge beneath his briefs springing free when he removed those, too. Her body spasmed at the sight of him, a spasm that turned to liquid desire. When he undid her slacks, then urged her out of them, she didn't protest. The only time she moved was when his mouth found the top of her thighs, and then only to convulse in pleasure, especially when that wonderful mouth of his moved closer to her core. And then, oh Lord, he was there, his tongue drifting up the center of her, lapping at her and suckling her moisture.

She almost came right then. She rose up on her elbows. "Blain, no...not yet."

His tongue sank deep inside of her, and she couldn't stop it. She came at the intimacy of his touch.

Tremors rolled through her body, her moans matching the rhythm of her pleasure. She fell back on the pillow, wishing the feeling would never end, knowing that it would.

She felt him stir. Opened first one eye and then

the other. He smiled. She couldn't help it—she smiled back.

"Good?" he asked.

"Yeah," she sighed. "Oh, yeah."

She moved her legs to the side, wanting him to come up next to her. He stopped her.

"What are you doing?"

"We're not done yet."

"I know, I just thought—"

He spread her legs again. "I want to be inside of you, Cece. Deep inside of you. I want to pleasure you. To make you feel things you've never felt before. To show you just what you do to me."

He sucked her again, lapping away the juices of her release, and she'd never had a man do that before, never, ever known how erotic it could be to have him lick her like that.

Oh, jeesh—

He moved up her body while Cece was still reeling from the eroticism of his kiss. The tip of him found her, and it felt erotic in a whole new way. Every muscle in her body strained as he entered her.

He kissed her, and the essence of herself was in his mouth, salty and tangy and heightening her sexual pleasure. She knew then that he'd understood her craving to be *taken*. She was tired of always being in control, always having to take charge. His erection slid deep inside. She moaned.

He withdrew.

No.

He pushed back inside.

Yessss…

And then he shifted a bit, finding a spot that brought her to a level of pleasure she'd never experienced before, just as he'd promised.

"Blain," she panted.

He thrust against that spot, his butt flexing as he worked her.

She came again, in a second orgasm that was even more amazing than the first. And he kept pumping into her, prolonging the sensation, making her think that maybe, just maybe, she might come again. No. Impossible.

She convulsed once more.

"Jeesh—" she lost the ability to talk, to think, to move.

"Cece," he moaned. Then he stilled, his whole body trembling as he reached his own release, his erection throbbing and throbbing and throbbing inside of her.

She held him, felt his heart beat against her own, realized distantly that they were both sweaty. But she didn't care. She just didn't care. That had been—

Incredible, she thought with a mental sigh. Simply incredible. And from the way his erection stayed firm, she had a feeling there was more on the way.

CHAPTER NINETEEN

CECE WOKE UP near dawn, the pleasure she'd received from Blain's lovemaking suffusing her in a warm glow. If she were a cat, she'd have done one of those paw stretches, claws extended, back arched. Content. That's the way she felt. And she hadn't felt that way in a long, long time.

It was an effort not to stare at Blain, to look at the contours of his face and simply marvel that he lay next to her. Never in a million years would she have thought she'd end up in bed with Blain Sanders.

She slipped from beneath the covers and into a hotel bathrobe, wandering into the living area of the suite. She'd kill for a cup of coffee right now. She thought about calling room service, but she didn't want to wake Blain. What she wanted to do was think.

You think too much.

Yeah, most of the time that was true, Cece admitted, settling on a couch that sat before a huge window. The sun was just breaking the plane of the horizon, turning the sky a deep purple that would eventually fade to gray and then blue.

She had fallen for Blain.

There was no sense in denying it. Not after last night. He'd swept under her defenses, charmed her with his Southern accent and his tender concern.

She sighed, tucking her feet beneath her, because as much as she wanted a life with Blain, she knew Cece Blackwell, Federal Agent, couldn't have it. And that tore her apart.

"What are you doing up so early?"

She started, shocked to see Blain come around the edge of the couch, a similar bathrobe thrown over his large frame.

"Did I wake you?" she asked.

"Nah," he said. "What are you doing?"

"Thinking," she admitted, the instant surge of happiness she felt upon seeing him dimming, the peacefulness she'd felt upon first waking evaporating like water on sand.

"C'mon back to bed." She could tell by his expression what he had in mind. It amazed her how just that look could get her heart pumping, make goose pimples rise on her arms. The back of her neck tingled as she imagined him kissing it.

"I have too much work to do," she lied.

"Don't work," he said, leaning forward to cup her face.

But that was the problem. She *was* her work…always would be.

"You're thinking about work again," he said, his voice faintly teasing. "I can tell."

She looked him in the eye, feeling her stomach knot. The sun had started to rise, the night was over; time for the realities of the day.

"Blain, we can't do this."

"Can't do what?"

"This," she said, motioning to herself.

"Use the hotel's bathrobes?"

He was teasing her, she could tell, but she didn't smile. "Get involved," she said.

"You're going to give me that speech again, aren't you? The one about how dangerous a job you have and how you can't ask me to live that kind of life?"

She shot up from the couch. "Damn it, this is nothing to joke about."

"Cece, c'mon," he said, following her up. "It's a little late to be telling me we can't get involved."

She swallowed, looking into his masculine blue eyes.

"We already *are* involved. I'm involved. And nothing you say is going to change that."

She looked away, but he tipped her chin up again, forcing her to meet his gaze. "I know you're worried about the effects your job might have on us, but it's a risk I'm willing to take. I hope you're willing, too."

Was she? Was she willing to give up her hard-won independence? And was that really the issue at hand? Was it her independence she suddenly feared losing, or her fear of losing Blain should their relationship fail?

"I told you that I lost my partner," she found herself saying, looking away from him because suddenly it was hard to meet his eyes. "And I told you how horrible it was to tell his widow that Bill had died. But what I didn't tell you was just how close I was to Bill and his wife."

"Cece, whatever happened in the past, it doesn't matter—"

She held up her hand. "Yes, Blain, it does matter. It matters when you have a front row seat to the effects of your job. I've never been deeply involved with someone like Bill was. But he would tell me about what it was like, about how hard it was to turn back into himself after going undercover, especially with his family looking on. They can send you to all the psychiatrists in the world, but it's not easy. I saw what it did to Bill and his marriage. I saw what it did to his kids."

"Then we won't have kids."

"We…what?" she asked in shock, the gears of her mind grinding to a halt. "What did you say?"

"We don't have to have kids," he answered tenderly, lifting his hands to her shoulders, squeezing them. "Hell, Cece, we don't have to have a dog if you don't want to."

Oh, Blain.

But she didn't say the words aloud. That he would agree to that, that he would make that sacrifice… And yet still. Obviously he didn't understand.

"I help her out, you know."

His brow wrinkled, the expression of tenderness fading into confusion. "Help *who* out?"

"My partner's widow."

"How?"

"With money."

She could tell that surprised him. Well, and why wouldn't it? There were days when she didn't understand why she did it. Then again, she did. It had to do with losing her own father, and then her mother. It had to do with struggling for years to put herself through college. It had to do with five little kids who needed their mother hale and hearty, not working her fingers to the bone—as her own mother had.

"She doesn't know it," Cece explained. "She thinks the money she gets comes from a pension. I had a bank set it up that way. She's not the type who would accept charity."

"So you send her financial aid?"

"I do," Cece admitted. "They had five kids, Blain. Five wonderful little kids who were like nieces and nephews to me before Bill died. Afterward—" she shook her head "—afterward it was too hard on his widow and me. We drifted apart, but not before I saw how hard she struggled to keep her family afloat. Five kids are a lot of mouths to feed, and Bill's death benefit only went so far. It was like my childhood happening all over again. So I set up an account, diverted money from my checks. She thinks it's a special fund."

She didn't think it was possible, but the look in his eyes softened all the more. "Unbelievable."

"Actually, it was pretty easy. Especially when I

was determined that the same thing that happened to my mother wouldn't happen to her. Every little bit helps. I called her the day after my bank sent her the first check. She called it pennies from heaven."

"You amaze me, you know that?" he said at last.

She didn't move, couldn't move because of the look in his eyes. They held so much awe, so much amazement, so much admiration.

"The more I learn of you, the more I see how remarkable you are."

He pulled back, looked down at her. He was going to kiss her. She stepped out of his arms.

"No, Blain. Don't," she said, "Just don't. I can't do this with you. That's what I'm trying to tell you. I made a promise to myself that I wouldn't get involved with anybody, *anybody*, unless I had a desk job."

"Then get a desk job."

"I don't *want* a desk job. I want to keep doing what I've been doing—getting bad guys off the streets. My life was almost ruined by a kid working for some two-bit car-theft ring. I almost went to juvenile detention for something I didn't do. That pissed me off. So I got even, not with the crooks that almost sent me away, but with others like them. And I'm good at it. Only, I realized early on that the job entails some sacrifices."

"Like falling in love?" he asked softly.

Oh, man, was she so easy to read? "Like falling in love," she answered back.

He didn't say anything for a long moment, his blue eyes nearly black in the half-light of the hotel room. "How can someone be so brave and yet so scared?"

"I'm not scared," she lied.

"Then I guess this is it."

"I guess so," she said.

"Shame," he said.

"What is?"

"It's a shame that you're afraid to love."

HE LEFT HER ALONE, and damn it, Blain was kind of tired of backing off. He liked tackling problems head-on, and the way he felt about Cece... Well, he wasn't prepared to treat it like a casual affair. But she needed time to think, and so he gave it to her, ordering room service since they weren't in any hurry to leave. She was thumbing through some papers by the time their breakfast arrived. Work, by the looks of things—he was familiar with the method of losing yourself in your job. Hell, racing being as stressful as it was, he was practically a workaholic.

Work he might not have for much longer.

With that thought foremost in his mind, he kept his distance for the rest of the morning. So it was something of a surprise to have Cece call out to him an hour or so later, "Blain, come here," in a voice unmistakably tinged with excitement.

The sight of her still in her bathrobe, hair tumbled down her back, made him want to go to her, to maybe kiss the back of her neck or tousle her hair.

She gave part of her not-that-sizable income to her partner's widow. He couldn't quite believe it. And yet, to be honest, it didn't really surprise him.

"Check this out," she said, turning to her laptop, which she'd plugged into the suite's Internet connection. She was completely unaware of the effect she had on him.

And then he saw what she was looking at. And he froze at the image on the screen.

It was Randy's car after it had exploded, fire and debris frozen in time before the screen faded to black.

"I went over the notes from our first meeting," Cece said, clicking on something that started the image rolling again. "You told me just before Randy wrecked he'd been complaining of a vibration."

Blain didn't say anything. He couldn't speak, not when he was face-to-face with the worst day of his life.

"My notes said he reported a problem with a tire."

She glanced back at him and saw the look on his face. He hadn't moved, hadn't taken his eyes off her brightly colored monitor.

"Oh, jeesh, Blain," she said softly. "I'm sorry. I should have warned you."

He blinked, looked away, shook his head. Out of the corner of his eye he could see what happened next. If he *closed* his eyes, he could see what happened next. Randy's car bobbled. It started to pitch, heading toward the wall at the worst possible moment.

Boom!

A fireball. On the other side of the catch fence, fans looking on with horror. Flames. Black smoke. Debris.

"If you don't want to watch it, Blain, I'll understand. Jeesh, I'm sorry. I was just so focused on what I was doing…"

He looked into the eyes of the woman he'd made love to over and over again last night, the woman he was starting to fall in love with.

Only he'd forgotten about her job. What was it she'd said?

Eventually, what I do for a living will hurt you.

He hadn't believed her at the time, but glancing back at her computer monitor he realized she was right—because if she could so easily push aside what they'd done last night, she must be harder on the inside than he'd thought.

"What did you discover?" he asked.

She looked as if she wouldn't answer. Looked as if she might tell him to forget it.

He made his face go blank, made himself say the words, "Go on. Show me."

Reluctantly, she faced her monitor again, though she peeked at him one last time.

"It's not what I discovered," she said, "so much as what it is I'm thinking." She moved her hand to press the replay button. For a second, a brief moment that he might have missed if he hadn't been looking for it, she hesitated. But he saw her stiffen almost imperceptibly before she went ahead and clicked.

Dark screen. Bright light. Randy's car in the center of the screen.

"As I was saying, just before the wreck, Randy was complaining about a tire."

Think we've got a tire goin' bad, Randy had said.

Don't say that, Mike, his crew chief, had groaned.

Gonna have to come in…shit!

Who'd said the word? Blain still didn't know. Randy orMike—someone had cursed just as Randy had started to slide…and slide…and slide.

Boom!

Dear Lord, would he ever get that image out of his mind? But this was different. This was watching it again, something he hadn't done since before going to the FBI.

"We now know the car exploded just before impact."

With Randy inside. Randy, who'd climbed up the ranks of stock car racing alongside Blain. They'd been a team, amassing six championships, the two of them hoping to find the magic again so they could win a seventh.

Boom!

"What I've always wondered was if the killer had a scanner. If maybe he'd heard Randy say you had a bad tire. At which point our killer was faced with a decision. He must have seen Randy sliding, must have realized he was going into the wall. The speed he was traveling, the angle he was going in at would have taken Randy out of the race. All that hard work getting the explosives into the car, all that planning, wasted. Unless—" she glanced back at Blain, her eyes seeming to shine "—unless the killer detonated the bomb right then, right at that very moment."

Randy. This was Randy she was talking about.

Eventually, what I do for a living will hurt you.

Yeah, Blain hadn't thought she meant personally. But reliving all this, going through the motions again—it hurt.

"So he detonated the thing just before Randy hit, thinking that a car erupting into flames before it hit a wall would surely garner attention."

She clicked Replay again.

Not again.

"Only it didn't," she said. "And that must have pissed our killer off. It didn't happen the way he'd planned. Nobody cried foul. Nobody said a word." She reached into her pile of papers. "And so he sent this."

It was the note.

"The first line says: 'I killed Randy Newell, and I will strike again.'"

Blain glanced at the piece of paper, which looked like the ransom notes you saw in movies. Letters cut from the newspaper had been glued to form the words, a picture of Texas Motor Speedway on the bottom.

"But what strikes me about this note is something no one's noticed before," Cece continued. "It's been assumed that the letters used were all random—whatever the killer happened to find in the newspaper. But look at the *I*. It's different from the rest. Bold. '*I* killed Randy Newell'. It's personal. *I* killed him, no one else.

"This whole time we've been working under the assumption that the threat was to the team, when, in fact, I believe all along the target was Randy. This was between the killer and him. But everyone dismissed Randy's death as an accident. The killer couldn't let that happen, so he sent the note, after the event—something that always puzzled me about the case. Why do that? Why not tip your hand first? But if his target was Randy, he wouldn't want to risk the murder being foiled, so he sent the note afterward."

She looked back at Blain, an expression of pleasure on her face.

Pleasure at Randy's death.

God, how did she do it? How did she separate herself from such tragedy? And from *him*.

"But that's not all," she said, turning back to her monitor. "I mean, really, my hypothesis doesn't mean a hill of beans. I can't prove the killer meant 'I' as in 'me'. No. What I find interesting is this."

She picked up the note again, swiveling on her seat so Blain could see better.

"This is just a copy. The photo on the bottom isn't as clear as the original, but you can still see it. A standard PR shot of a racetrack's name taken from the infield, complete with flag stand and the bottom portion of the grandstands."

She looked up at him, her eyes all but sparkling. "Only this isn't the track whose name is on that wall," she said, pointing to the black letters. "This is a different track. I found a picture of Texas Motor Speedway on the Internet. And look." She turned back to her computer, clicking on a new window. "It's not the same."

Blain felt himself stiffen, and against his will, he leaned toward the computer screen, looking from the note to the monitor and back again.

"That's Atlanta Motor Speedway," he said.

"Atlanta?" she said in surprise. "But that's—"

They met each other's gaze, saying at the same time, "Now."

THE THRILL OF FINDING important evidence was a buzz Cece always reveled in, but IDing Atlanta Motor Speedway was bittersweet. Blain's friend had died, and now the killer might be at work again.

It didn't help that Agent Ashton ignored her. Cece didn't know what pissed her off more—that he'd judged her so unimportant that he wouldn't answer his cell phone when she called, or that nobody would tell her what frequency to use to contact him on the radio.

The only good thing about the situation was that her discovery eliminated all that "morning after" awkwardness. Blain seemed distant and withdrawn, which, considering she'd told him she didn't want to get involved, not to mention watching the replay of his best friend's death, was to be expected. Cece told herself not to feel guilty about that—this was an investigation—but as they headed back to AMS, she couldn't help but wonder if she shouldn't have waited to break it off with him.

But it was too late. They had to find Agent Ashton. Granted, she'd already passed what she knew to a Bravo Team member, but she wanted to speak to Ashton personally. She wanted to be allowed to investigate, damn it.

They found the man of the hour in the spotting stand all the way at the top of the Atlanta Motor Speedway grandstands—all the way, as in on the roof of the announcer's stand, because why be at ground level when you can be on a roof?

Cece had no choice but to climb the narrow stairs to the precariously perched platform, constructed to give crew members an unobstructed view of the track.

"Agent Ashton," she said, trying not to look down. And trying not to clutch at Blain's hands.

Why the hell did he have to be up here?

Even though there was a cool breeze blowing today, Cece broke into a sweat.

"Agent Ashton," she repeated when he continued to look down. Granted, cars were out there practicing, so the whine of motors might have drowned out her words, but somehow she doubted it.

"Agent Ashton," Blain said.

The man turned. And the look he shot Cece perfectly conveyed his irritation at being interrupted, his eyes narrowing like a Jack Russell on the scent of vermin. Terrific.

"Mr. Sanders. What are you doing here?"

Cece stepped in front of Blain, which, unfortunately, brought her closer to the edge of the roof.

She gulped, forcing herself to say, "Did you get the message?" she asked.

"Message about what?"

"About this track being a target?"

She saw the derision in his eyes, the way he seemed to shake his head a bit before he said, "Yes, Agent Blackwell, I got it. But I also seem to recall that you're not supposed to be looking over evidence. You're supposed to be protecting Mr. Sanders."

Son of a— Cece bit back a comment, but just barely. "I understand that, but I saw no reason—"

"No buts. In the future, keep your fingers out of my case."

"But…what are you going to do?"

"Nothing," he said in as condescending a voice as she'd ever heard. "We've always been operating under the assumption that *every* racetrack is a target. What you've learned is nothing we haven't already surmised for ourselves."

"Yes, but now we know for certain Atlanta is a target. We need to close the track, increase security, get some bomb-sniffing dogs out here."

"With the exception of closing the track, that's already been done, Agent Blackwell."

She was going to push the man off the roof. She really was. That chip on his shoulder was so big he'd land like a boulder.

"And we're not about to close the track," he said, "any more than we advise that airports be closed when they receive threats."

"This isn't a terrorist cell. This is a person," Cece said calmly, yet firmly. "Look at the bomb threat letter. The 'I' is bold. We overlooked that before, too, thinking it was arbitrary, but I think it's telling us that this is one person, someone who's trying to trip us up."

"Duly noted," Agent Ashton said, glancing back at Blain. "Now, if you wouldn't mind taking Mr. Sanders off the roof…? He's too easy a target up here."

Target?

"And the next time you feel the need to confront me, I would suggest you leave him in his hotel room."

Okay, that did it. She *was* pushing him off the roof.

Blain's hand stopped her. (Not that she was really going to do it, but still…)

"C'mon, Cece," he urged.

Just one push…one tiny, little nudge…

"Forget it," Blain said.

Cece's teeth clamped together. She had to physically relax her muscles in order to move. Well, okay, part of her inability to move had to do with her fear of heights, but the minute they'd climbed down the narrow steps, she felt the rage.

"That no-good, sexist son of a—" An Atlanta breeze tugged at her hair. She swiped at it angrily. "I want to hit him...I really do."

They reached the announcer's stand and found a TV crew pointing a camera in their direction. Cece looked right at them and said, "If you want some *explosive* footage, keep your cameras trained on the grandstands."

"Cece..." Blain warned.

Yeah, yeah, yeah...she should probably keep her mouth shut. She turned away, so furious she wanted...she wanted...ooo, she didn't know what she wanted.

"What are you going to do now?" Blain asked a moment later.

She thought about it for a second. "I'm going to ignore the slimy bastard and do some snooping around on my own."

CHAPTER TWENTY

BUT SHE WAS BOOTED OUT of Atlanta. A couple of agents gently but firmly told her to leave, a hint being dropped that if she continued to ignore her duty to Blain, there'd be a disciplinary hearing in her future.

Cece had never been more humiliated or frustrated in her life.

So they headed back to Charlotte, and it was a testament to how distracted they both were that not one word was mentioned about the night before. Well, okay, Blain had glanced over at her shortly after they'd left, and asked if she was tired. And when she'd said no, he'd given her a wicked grin and asked, "Sore?" which had made her blush and wonder what the hell she'd been thinking to jump into bed with him. Twice. Well, more like five times— or six. And just what the heck was he doing teasing her when she'd all but broken up with him earlier?

It didn't help matters that the whole drive back he was sweet. So sweet and concerned and, darn it all, understanding, that she found herself wanting to kiss him just because. He let her vent her frustration without complaint. Tenderly took her hand when someone had cut them off and she'd thought it might be the bad guy and she'd gone into defensive driving mode.

She darted a glance at Blain. He must have felt it because he looked over and gave her a small smile. "Okay?" he asked.

And, damn it, she wished he'd stop being so darn solicitous. "Fine," she said, looking out the window under the guise of keeping an eye out for bad guys. And so that was what she did the whole way back: think about Blain and keep a lookout for thugs— only *they* were all back in Atlanta.

They arrived back in North Carolina without incident, and by the time they got there, Cece could tell Blain was as tense as she was. They'd spent the time brainstorming, and Cece had to admit Blain's quick mind impressed her. He had a knack for seeing things from a different perspective, of taking something she said and twisting it in a way she would have never thought of.

They decided to head straight to Rebecca Newell's home.

Randy Newell's widow lived a few miles from Blain. Actually, by the time they arrived, Cece had learned from Blain that most of the drivers, crew members and their families lived in the same area. If a disaster ever befell the Mooresville district, the racing industry would be decimated.

"Nice home," Cece said.

"Randy was smart with his money," Blain said, obviously comfortable enough with the widow Newell to pull into the driveway of the two-story brick mansion that, like Blain's home, backed up to Lake Norman. "He invested in things, including a truck team that his wife now manages."

"Really?" Cece said. Of course, she'd heard of Rebecca Newell. When Randy had died, her face had been plastered on magazines and newspapers across the nation. It seemed surreal to be meeting her.

With a glance behind to make sure their surveillance team was trailing them, Cece followed Blain up the granite walkway. Lush shrubs and white-framed windows sparkled in the aftermath of the thunderstorm they'd driven through on their way north. Once again the weighty North Carolina humidity pressed in on her. But come to think of it, she was starting to like the way it made her skin feel—soft—which was as womanly a thought as she ever allowed herself.

"What if she's not home?"

"She's home," Blain said, ringing the doorbell, an elegant bell chime that reminded Cece of church.

"How do you know?"

Right then the door opened.

Cece's first thought was that she didn't look like a widow. She looked like a model on her way to a photo shoot, the jeans she wore decorated with black lace that swirled and spiraled up her legs. A white tank with tiny rhinestones around the neckline matched the diamond studs in her ears, her famous red hair piled atop her head.

"Blain," she said, and there was no mistaking the warmth in her smile.

And for a second, just a second, Cece felt jealousy rear its ugly head. Lord, but she would never look that good while lounging around the house. Maybe the woman had been on her way somewhere.

"I hope we're not interrupting something?"

"Oh, no," Rebecca said breezily, glancing at Cece with unmistakable curiosity. "Today is my at-home day."

Today was her "at home" day. Jeesh, so she really *did* look that good on a daily basis? Cece told herself not to hate her.

"This is Cecilia Blackwell," Blain said, giving Cece a smile that made some of her jealousy wane.

"This is Cece?" Rebecca said.

What ho? Huh? Had Blain told the woman about her?

"In the flesh," Cece said, trying to sort out the way that made her feel.

"Wow. It's *so* nice to meet you, Cece," she said, her Southern accent more noticeable when she said her name. Ceeeceee, not the short and sharp syllables people used to pronounce her name in the West. And it was obvious she *was* glad to meet her. Rebecca smiled widely, reaching out to take her hand.

Cece shook it, wondering how the heck the woman kept her palms from sweating.

"Come on in," she said, stepping aside.

Add gracious and personable to the list of traits Cece should be jealous of. Yet, strangely enough, she wasn't. There was something so instantly nice about Rebecca, a generosity of spirit that Cece instantly warmed to.

The house was every bit as lovely as the outside promised. Like Blain's home, it was richly furnished, but whereas Blain's home looked, well, guyish, this home spoke of a woman's caring touch. Floral patterns graced the couches and wallpaper, and fresh flower arrangements brought a fragrant whiff of summer to Cece's nose. Shelves and tabletops held cute little mementos that Mrs. Newell must have collected during her husband's racing career.

That reminded Cece of why they were here, and she suddenly felt sorry for the woman.

"Look, Becca," Blain said, taking a seat on a tapestry couch in a giant family room. "I'm not going to sugarcoat it. Cece needs to ask you some questions about Randy."

The shadows that drifted into Rebecca Newell's green eyes were unmistakable. Damn, Cece hated this part of her job. Widows and widowers—they were never easy to talk to.

"What do you need to know?" the woman asked.

Cece tried to think of the best way to phrase her

questions so that she didn't bring Rebecca's pain to the surface. But it was hard. Damn hard.

"I need to know if your husband had any enemies."

To her shock, Rebecca smiled, a sultry, very Southern laugh falling from her collagen-injected lips. (Okay, maybe *that* was a bit catty.)

"Randy had lots of enemies, Ms. Blackwell."

"Cece, please," she said.

"Then you must call me Rebecca." And then her face turned serious. "Randy made a living pissing people off."

The word *pissing* had no business being uttered by Rebecca Newell's (maybe) naturally plump lips. No business at all.

"He received hate mail all the time."

"Anybody cross the line?"

Rebecca shook her head. "I gave your co-workers the letters, though, just in case I might have missed something."

Co-workers. Yeah, right. "Did you keep copies?"

Rebecca shook her head. "I was glad to get rid of the things."

Shit.

"What about non-fans? Anybody in his personal life that might stick out?"

"You know," she said with a pleasant smile that included Blain, "I already answered these questions for your friends."

"They won't share anything with Cece," Blain explained.

Cece resisted the urge to jam her foot into his instep. She didn't need Rebecca Newell to know about her problems.

But apparently, it was the right thing to say. "Are those sexist S.O.B.s giving you a hard time?" she asked with a raised brow of commiseration.

Cece couldn't help but smile. "They are."

"I'm not surprised. You should see how Barry Bidwell treats me. I think the man only tolerates me as an owner because he knows I'm the type to raise a fuss if he pulls that crap on me."

"At least he hasn't grounded you," Blain said.

Rebecca turned to him, concerned. "What do you mean?"

"They pulled my license yesterday."

"They *what?*"

"We were in Atlanta and they told me I couldn't race."

"Why?"

"They're worried we'll attract trouble."

"Will you?"

"He might," Cece admitted. "And that's part of the reason why we're here. We think there's going to be another attack. This weekend."

"This weekend?" Rebecca asked in shock. "Why don't they cancel the race then?"

"Becca, really. Do you think they'd honestly do that?" Blain asked.

The two shared a private look that had Cece's jealousy gremlin rearing its ugly head.

"You're right," Rebecca said. "One thing you've got to understand," she added, turning to Cece, "this industry is all about money. Canceling a race would cost them plenty."

Cece had gathered as much from Blain.

"Well, I wish I could help you, I really do, but I don't have anything more to go on than I did last week, when I was told that Randy's death was actually a murder."

She spoke the words with so little emotion Cece knew she'd had plenty of practice. And she probably had. Cece would bet her phone hadn't stopped ringing since the news broke.

"Is your phone off the hook?" Cece asked, with a sudden flash of insight as to why they couldn't reach her on the phone earlier.

"It is," Rebecca said. "I've had a heck of a time keeping news crews away, too. They refuse to leave me alone."

She would just bet. Damn media. "They're camped out at Blain's shop as we speak."

"I'm not surprised."

And even though she hated to do it, Cece redirected the conversation back to Randy. "So your husband never received any death threats."

"Practically every week."

Cece stiffened.

Rebecca smiled. "The other drivers hated my husband, Cece. He was fond of what we in racing call "bumping" and "nudging." Sometimes he'd nudge people into a wall." Her smile turned almost cynical. "Usually on the final lap. I don't think a weekend went by when I didn't hear one his fellow drivers threaten to kill him, but it was always uttered in the heat of the moment."

"It usually is until the threat turns real."

She looked surprised. "You think a driver murdered my husband?"

Cece didn't know what to think. She looked at Blain. He was shaking his head. "Doubtful, Cece," he said. "Drivers are hot-tempered, but I don't know a single one I'd say would be capable of killing— and who's an explosives expert, for that matter. Most of them have families, go to church, attend barbecues at other drivers' homes. I just don't see it happening."

"He's right," Rebecca said. "Randy had enemies, but only on race day, never afterward."

Then who? Cece wanted to ask. Who would do this? And who would try to kill her, too? And Blain? Honestly, it was the attempt on their lives that convinced Cece the perp wasn't a driver. She doubted a driver would hold a grudge against an FBI agent. That didn't make sense. None of it made sense. And obviously this was a dead end.

"Well, we've taken up enough of your time," Cece said, standing.

"Oh, no. You two aren't going anywhere. You're having dinner with me."

Dinner? With Randy Newell's widow? Funny

how these people she'd seen on TV went from being celebrities to ordinary people in seconds.

"I don't think that's a good idea. Blain and I are considered targets."

"Don't you have people keeping an eye on you?"

"Yes, but—"

"Well, invite them, too."

"I don't think—"

The squawk of the radio filled the room, the noise making everyone who heard it wince. And then her cellphone rang. Cece stiffened. Anytime her radio and cellphone went off at the same time, it wasn't good.

"Bravo twenty-four." She cut the radio off midstream and answered her cellphone. "Agent Blackwell," she said, shooting Bryce and Rebecca a strained smile as she got up from the couch.

"Agent Blackwell, Agent Ashton here."

As if she didn't know that from her caller ID.

"We have a situation."

Cece tensed, and thankfully, Agent Ashton didn't make her ask what had happened. "Two hours ago, Atlanta Motor Speedway suffered an attack."

Cece wished she hadn't left the couch. Her knees felt suddenly weak.

"What kind of attack?"

"One of the grandstands is gone."

"Gone?"

"Demolished. By a bomb."

CHAPTER TWENTY-ONE

AGENT ASHTON ORDERED a meeting later that day, something that didn't surprise Cece at all. What surprised her was that Blain insisted on going with her, and that he looked disappointed when she told him no. He compromised by insisting she drive the Chiquita Bananamobile, so she agreed, only to have him suddenly clutch her to him and kiss her so thoroughly that she was certain the surveillance team outside had to have seen. Jeesh, she'd be lucky to have a job by the end of the week. And damn it, he wasn't supposed to be kissing her. She'd told him that, too, for all the good it had done. He simply insisted that he wasn't about to give up.

And so as she drove to her appointment with Agent Ashton, Cece let her thoughts roam—in between checking her mirror to make sure no one was following her, and wondering where the investigation was leading…and what exactly to do about Blain. What if someone did lob something at her? What if she didn't survive? What if Blain got hurt? What if *she* got hurt while on the job…or worse, died? Granted, if she died, she got the better part of the bargain. It was Blain who would suffer...Blain who would get the knock on the door.

Stop!

She wasn't going there, she firmly told herself. They weren't a couple. Not now. Not ever.

So Cece forced herself to focus. She had a meeting to get to and a killer on the loose.

Not a killer, exactly, she thought, checking her mirrors once more while she changed lanes. Granted, Randy Newell had been murdered, but nobody since. And that struck Cece as odd. Usually, a killer got more bold as the death toll mounted. And that was something niggling at the back of her mind—for a killer, he was pretty inept. Why deliver flowers to a room when you could use a gun? And for that matter, why not make sure someone was inside Blain's car before blowing it up? And the grandstand that had been blown up today—it'd been empty, too, and small. Why blow it up during practice? Why not wait until the thing was full?

Something felt off. Something felt *really* off.

It bothered her the whole way downtown. Cece's mind kept spinning and spinning, shooting out one thing after another, only to discard the reasoning a second later. She was missing something—something vital, something right at the edge of her awareness, but which she couldn't reel in to save her life. Damn it.

When she arrived at the Charlotte field office,

Agent Ashton didn't make her wait to see him, thankfully. She showed her badge to the gal at the front desk and was practically run to the private conference room. Agent Ashton arrived moments later, looking worse for wear after his harried day dashing between Charlotte and Atlanta. And within seconds it became apparent to Cece why she'd been shown to the conference room, and not his private office. The conference room had a TV and VCR.

Uh-oh.

He popped in a tape, stepped back from the tiny screen, crossed his arms and watched.

Cece's face materialized on the screen, an angry face, one that turned toward the camera and said—

No...

"If you want some *explosive* footage, just keep your cameras trained on the grandstands."

Damn. Damn, damn, damn. She hadn't been summoned to Charlotte to be welcomed into the investigative fold. She'd been brought in for a buttwhuppin'.

"And so the real story," the newscaster said, a man whose face looked as grim as Agent Ashton's as it stared into the camera, "is whether or not the FBI had knowledge that a bomb had been planted."

She was toast.

The look in Agent Ashton's eyes confirmed it. Frankly, he looked like he wanted to bump her off himself, especially judging by the way he stabbed the off button on the TV, the VCR still whirring in its wake.

"Agent Blackwell," he said in a calm, even voice, one that managed to convey all his disgust, all his anger, all his revulsion. "I have spent the last four hours fielding calls from the media." He let his words sink in, as he stared at her, unblinking.

Bet he played a hell of an I-can-keep-my-eyes-open-longer-than-you game.

"I've also spent time on the phone with Director Roberts."

Director? Uh-oh.

"He's not pleased."

Shit. Shit, shit, shit.

And when all he did was continue to stare at her, she swallowed, saying, "Do I still have a job?"

Agent Ashton took a moment to answer, and Cece thought it might be because he didn't trust himself to speak.

"As of right now, you're on paid administrative leave."

Suspended. Crap. Shit. Damn.

"Pending a full investigation of your inability to keep your mouth shut."

She deserved that. She knew she did.

"What about Sanders?" she asked.

"We'll take over his protection. You've been released from the case. You're free to go back to San Francisco."

Released from the case.

"And frankly, I'd leave on the earliest flight."

She tensed, licked her lips, wondered if she

should slip off without a whimper or try and plead her case. She decided on a combination of the two.

"Agent Ashton, I accept full blame for what I did. I was…angry—" at *you* "—but that's no excuse. I should have controlled my temper."

He didn't say anything, just crossed his arms. "I need your badge," he said.

"But I've had some thoughts about the case—"

"Keep them to yourself."

"But I—"

"Your badge, Agent Blackwell."

"This is ridiculous. Granted," Cece plunged onward, "I accept full responsibility for speaking to the press, but I can still help with the case. As a matter of fact, I don't think the perp wants to kill anybody—"

"Not another *word*," Agent Ashton said, his lips framed by brackets of displeasure. He turned for the door, but not before shooting her one last look of extreme and total scorn? fury? before leaving the room.

Cece just sat there. Okay, she'd blown it. Really, truly, honestly blown it. But that didn't mean he shouldn't at least hear her out. Yeah, he was angry at her, but what if she really did know something that might help the case? Not that she did, but she might, and if she'd been allowed to sound it out, maybe Agent Ashton could have helped her piece it together.

She inhaled deeply, suddenly more depressed than she'd ever been in her life. To think, all that worry about getting canned because of her relationship with Blain, and in the end it was her own big mouth that had done it.

She reluctantly removed her badge from around her neck. For a second the polished metal blurred before her eyes, but she blinked the tears away. This wasn't permanent. Once the review board heard her side of the story, they'd reinstate her.

She hoped.

And so she left, slinking out of the Charlotte office like a beaten dog heading toward the doghouse. By the time she reached Blain's Hummer, she felt even more depressed. For the first time in her career, she'd be meeting with a review board.

And it was while contemplating her future that it hit her.

Actually, it was the brief thought that her mom would have been *so* disappointed.

Mom.

HE'D WAITED UP FOR HER, something that made Cece's heart do a little flip. She'd never had a man wait up for her before.

But she stifled the emotions he aroused, just as she stopped him from pulling her into his arms, though she longed, absolutely longed to sink into him, to take a deep breath, to tell him everything that had happened.

Instead she said, "Blain, I need to talk to you."

He stopped a couple of inches away from her, and

the look in his eyes as he anxiously scanned her face made her heart tumble some more.

"What happened?"

She shook her head slightly, indicating with her chin the surveillance team outside. "Not here," she mouthed, giving him what must have been a weak smile before turning away and heading toward the back of the house.

The sun had gone to bed for the evening, Carolina humidity cooling the air in a way that clung to her skin as she stepped outside. A bug light *zzzz-zapped* to her left, and Cece found herself thinking she felt an awful lot like that bug. One wrong turn and *zzzzap*, on administrative leave.

"Cece, what happened?" he asked again, and this time he didn't give her a chance to protest as he pulled her into his arms. And that was one of the things she loved about Blain. He took charge. Cece had had a lifetime of being in charge—sometimes she got tired of it. Like now.

His big hands came around her, his palm cradling the back of her head, and she loved it. She loved how warm and secure she felt when he did that. She wished for just a moment that this was any other night and that she could enjoy the way the moonlight poured over the landscape, the crickets chirping their evening song.

But they had a killer to catch. And she had no business letting Blain touch her.

She drew back. "Blain, I need to ask you a question."

In the darkness, she saw his concern fade to consternation. "What kind of question?"

"Two years ago Randy was involved in a wreck, one that took a driver's life."

Nothing like talking about murder to kill a romantic moment. Cece watched as Blain stiffened, then crossed his arms as if trying to ward off the coming discussion.

"Yeah, Curt Tanner."

The Wonder Kid. That's what people used to call him. A kid with more talent than anyone had seen in a long, long time. He'd been Rookie of the Year his first year of Cup racing. The next year he'd won the championship. From there it'd been one winning season after another, until Randy Newell had pitched him into a wall.

"It was ruled an accident, though, wasn't it?"

Blain nodded, his eyes dark. Or maybe it was the reflection off the surface of the lake—Cece didn't know. All she knew was that suddenly it felt cold outside. She shivered.

"But Curt's family didn't believe that, did they?"

Blain shrugged. "There was some talk of the nudge that sent Curt into the wall being intentional—but it was just racing. The talk died down as fast as it'd started."

Cece absently shook her head as she stared out at the dark waters of the lake.

"What's this all about?" Blain asked.

She met his gaze again, wondering how much to

tell him. She decided to tell him everything. "Something hit me while driving to my meeting with Agent Ashton. Actually, it's bothered me for a while now. The explosion today just brought it all home.

"See, that alarm clock timer was so obvious. It never made sense, not when digital clocks are available. It was almost as if the killer wanted me to find the bomb. Plus, there are better, easier and far more simpler ways to kill someone. A gun, for instance."

He nodded, and she could tell by his expression that he'd thought the same thing.

"And then today—why the heck did our perpetrator blow up empty grandstands? If your intention is to kill people, wouldn't you wait until tonight's race?"

"The newscasters think the detonation was an accident. I've been watching the reports all evening."

She shook her head. "But see, that makes no sense. You blow up someone's car while they're driving in a race—in fact, you're so organized, you're able to remotely detonate the explosives when you realize the car is about to wreck, and yet you're saying that same person 'accidentally' blew up the grandstands on the wrong day?"

"I'm not saying that. The newscasters are."

"I know, I know. And I'm saying it makes no sense. Neither does using an alarm clock for a timer. I detected the thing with hours to spare."

"Thank God."

"My point is that the killer *gave* me that time,

Blain. Just as he waited until I came out of that apartment complex before blowing up your car."

"So you're saying what? That he's trying to scare us?"

"That's exactly what I'm saying, although I don't think it was to scare us. I think it was meant more as an attention-getter."

"Whose attention?"

"The press. And I know I'm right because we know for a fact that the perp alerted the press at least once before."

"Why the hell would someone want the press's attention?"

"To hurt racing."

His brows darted toward his hairline.

"We always assumed the bad guy was some crazy who wanted to kill you and a few thousand fans. But what if that's really not the killer's goal? What if his aim is to scare people? That's all. Just scare them away, thereby reducing ticket sales and sending the sport into a financial spiral."

"I'll be damned," he said.

She smiled faintly. Now he was beginning to see. "There's no doubt that Randy's death was intentional, but that's been the only death—his and nobody else's, even though there's been three times when the killer could have struck at you, or me, or even race fans."

Blain's mind reeled. Was she right? Could it be as simple as that?

"See, something else hit me, too. Actually, it'd been floating around in the back of my mind along with this other stuff, it just took something to trigger the memory."

"What?" he asked, having to fight the urge to nudge a lock of hair out of her eyes. She was so focused she probably didn't even see it there.

"I remember watching a special on Curt's death. They interviewed his family, and I remember his mother saying how let down she felt by everyone involved with racing. No one seemed to care that her son had been all but murdered, and rather than a full-blown investigation, everything had been swept under the carpet."

Curt's mother had said that? "I know she was bitter," he mused aloud. "Everyone knew it. Curt was her only child. When he died, everyone expected she'd be devastated. And she was. She grieved, looked for someone to blame."

"She blamed Randy. What's more, she was furious at how quickly her son was forgotten. One minute he was racing's cover boy, the next he was yesterday's news. I remember the fury in her eyes when she told the reporter about how nobody down in Daytona would return her calls."

"You think…" He left the thought unfinished.

But Cece was nodding. "I looked something up on the Internet on my way home."

"On your way home?"

"I have Internet access through my mobile

phone," she said with a dismissive wave. "And here's the thing. Curt's family had money."

"Yeah. I knew that."

"But did you know where their wealth came from?"

He shook his head.

"Demolitions."

It felt as if someone sat on Blain's chest.

Cece nodded. "His great-grandfather was a wild-catter. Made a mint capping rogue wells. Curt's grandfather expanded the business. He liked to blow up other things—old bridges, buildings, abandoned mines. And this is what clinched it for me. The grandfather's only child was a daughter, Curt's mother. She learned the business from Daddy."

Blain shook his head. "Holy shit."

CHAPTER TWENTY-TWO

BUT ONCE AGAIN Agent Ashton didn't want to talk to her.

Well, that wasn't precisely true, Cece admitted. Bob wasn't answering his cellphone and Agent Ashton might well be off the clock. It was late on a Saturday night, after all. Getting someone on the phone became an exercise in frustration, and so Cece did the only thing she could do.

"Come out, come out, wherever you are," she called, stepping out of Blain's front door.

"What the heck are you doing?" he asked, following her outside.

"Trying to get someone's attention."

"Can't you just wait for Agent Ashton to return your call?"

"He's not going to," she worried aloud, halting at the edge of Blain's driveway.

"Why the heck wouldn't he?"

Okay, she hadn't wanted to admit this to him, not yet, anyway, but she supposed there was no point in keeping it from him. "Because I got fired today."

"Fired?"

She frowned, wondering if she should walk up the private drive and find the surveillance vehicle that was no doubt somewhere nearby. "Well," she admitted, "not exactly fired. More like laid off."

Blain stepped in front of her, halting her progress up the drive. Light from inside the house illuminated his puzzled face. "Laid off?"

"Yeah. Put on administrative leave."

"Why?" he asked, and damn it, there he went looking all concerned for her again. If he kept this up, he'd make her go all soft on the inside, maybe slip under her guard and get her to rethink a relationship with him.

"Remember that comment I made to the news crew earlier today?"

He lifted his eyebrows, only to lower them a second later.

"Yeah, that one," she said. "They got a little mad at me for that."

"Lord, Cece, you're kidding me."

"I wish I was," she said grimly.

"So they fired you?"

And though his face remained expressionless, his eyes did not. For a moment, just a brief second, she saw it. Relief.

"You're happy I might be losing my job," she accused.

He drew back. "What makes you say that?"

"I can see it in your eyes."

She expected him to deny it, and so it floored her when he said, "Yeah, well, can you blame me for being happy that you'll no longer be in danger? And maybe now you can drop the relationship ban you've placed on us."

"I would expect you to understand that that's part of my job. And there is no 'us.'"

"That's what you think, and I do understand about your job, but I don't have to like it," he retorted, his Southern drawl more pronounced when he was agitated.

"You sexist pig."

"Cece, I'm not sexist. I'm in love with you."

Thump.

That's what her heart did. Once, twice—harder and harder each time.

I'm in love with you.

"Oh, jeesh."

"Yeah, 'Oh, jeesh'," he repeated, his voice suddenly tinged with amusement. "For the first time in my life I tell a woman I'm in love with her and she says 'oh, jeesh.' Tell me that's a good thing."

"I don't know what to say."

"You could say you love me back."

And here it was, the moment she'd half expected, but never dreamed of, certainly not with Blain Sanders.

Blain Sanders was in love with her.

"Oh, Blain," she said.

"Do I take that as a 'yes, I love you, too, Blain'?"

he asked, stepping up to her, his hands doing what they'd done so many times before—tipping her chin up. Gently, sweetly stroking her.

"I think I do," she admitted, the flipping of her heart suddenly settling into a warm weight that made silly, girlish tears enter her eyes. "But it doesn't make my fear subside."

"I'll just have to work on that, then."

She felt the sting of tears again. "You make it sound so easy."

"Cece," he interrupted, his hands framing her face again. "It *can* be easy."

But could she do it? Could she really let go of her conviction that loving Blain would lead to disaster?

Yes.

"We'll take it one day at a time," he said, seeming to read her mind. "One day at a time," he repeated, the soft brush of his lips causing more tears. Why did she even bother fighting it? She'd been half in love with him since forever, even during her anti-Blain years. Why did she—

And then she stopped thinking, just allowed herself to *feel*—to remember that this incredible feeling he aroused in her was part of the reason she loved him.

"Were you looking for me?"

Cece screeched. It was as feminine a sound as she'd ever made, her hand reaching for her gun, only to freeze halfway there.

A man dressed all in black, night vision goggles

on his head and black paint on his face, stood a few paces away.

Agent Thurman.

"I'm going to pretend I didn't see that kiss," he said, his smile a shock of white against his black face. "Especially since I was told to report any romantic activity between you two."

"You were *what?*"

He nodded. "We were all told that."

"How the heck—"

"Did we guess? It's pretty obvious there's something between you two. But don't worry, I'm not going to report it."

"It wouldn't matter if you did," Cece grumbled, stepping away from Blain—and was that a blush she felt on her cheeks? Criminey, what other lost feminine traits had she picked up in recent days?

"What do you mean, it wouldn't matter?"

"She's on paid administrative leave." Blain answered for her.

Thurman looked back at her with wide eyes. "You get busted for flapping your jaw at the TV crew?"

Apparently, Agent Thurman was better informed that she'd thought. "I did."

He shook his head. "Agent Ashton's a complete ass. I'm not surprised you lost your temper. The man's famous for sitting on information too long, usually to the detriment of whatever poor victim is involved. Rumor has it he lost his edge when he acted too hastily on some bad information. Ever since then his dick's shriveled to the size of a peanut."

So it wasn't just her. Cece didn't know if that made it better or worse. "I tried to tell him today that I think I know who's behind this, but he won't return my calls."

"You know who the bad guy is?"

"I think so. But he doesn't want to hear it from me."

"Because of what happened today," Thurman said with a shake of his head.

"I'm sure of it. But I can't sit on this information."

"Tell it to me, then."

Cece filled him in quickly, happy to concentrate on something other than the way her heart went *pitter-patter* every time she looked into Blain's eyes. When she finished, Agent Thurman was nodding, his eyes alight.

"I remember all that," he said. "But I'd completely forgotten about it until now."

"It's worth looking into, isn't it?" Cece said.

"It is," he agreed. "In fact, I think I'm going to do just that."

"You'd do that for me?"

"Hey, we're paid to act on hunches, and this is a damn good hunch."

And from nowhere Cece had the urge to hug him.

"But it might cost you something," he said with a smile.

Cece raised an eyebrow. She glanced back at Blain, who looked equally wary. "Cost me what?"

"You? Nothing," he said, grinning at Blain. "Him, a couple of garage passes."

"Done," Blain said immediately, a smile breaking out on his own face.

"*Hot* passes," Thurman clarified.

The smile spread. "No problem."

"Good. Then I'll be right back."

IT WAS LIKE *Mutiny on the Bounty* without the ship. Or Captain Bligh. Or the water. But who cared? The point was that Agent Terrance Thurman had the ability to act on a hunch when Cece couldn't. What was more, he could bring other agents into the fold, not that they were exactly planning to bust down the door of Lilly Tanner's house. First of all, they couldn't do that without a warrant, and Terry, as he liked to be called, would rather err on the side of prudence. Just a few questions of the mom, maybe a few agents watching the house to see what she did afterward, and then they'd see what happened. Cece liked the plan. It helped that Agent Thurman happened to know a judge, one who didn't mind being called in the middle of the night to see if he'd arrange a wire tap on the phone.

They used Blain's dining room as a command center, pulling up whatever information they could find on Lilly Tanner while they waited for the judge to give them an answer, and the further they dug, the more promising a lead it appeared, so much so that Cece hardly felt the effects of a near-sleepless night.

"Still no word from the judge?" Blain asked in the wee hours of the day.

"He wanted to wait until morning to make a decision."

"So you're at a standstill?"

"Yup."

"Did you get any sleep? Maybe you should use one of the rooms upstairs," he offered, the worried look on his face making her want to slip into his arms. She couldn't, though, partly because the other agents were still up and in the next room, partly because in recent hours she'd been thinking.

Thinking too much.

She didn't want to be with him right now. She needed to sort things out. Needed to understand why she was still so afraid.

"Blain, did you really mean it when you said no kids?"

She hadn't meant to ask the question. Lord, she must be more tired than she thought to be blurting out words, but she couldn't take them back, so she held her breath and waited for him to answer.

He didn't reply right away. Instead, he clutched her hand. She released a breath she hadn't known she'd been holding. She wanted to squeeze his hand in return, to slip off and make love with him like they had the other night. To forget, for a few hours, everything that was far from normal.

"Yeah, I meant it. If that's what you want."

Pregnant. Children. With Blain.

She'd never thought about having children before. Well, she *had,* but not in the way most women thought about it. Cece had merely assumed she'd never have any, and she'd been okay with that. Some women wanted families. Cece had chosen a career. And yet suddenly she wanted Blain's child with a fierceness that made her heart ache even more.

Which meant no career.

No, it didn't have to be that way….

"You look upset," he said tenderly, trying to pull her into his arms.

She resisted, glancing in the direction of the dining room as an excuse. He seemed to swallow it, though he still frowned down at her.

"Cece, what's wrong?"

"Nothing," she lied. "I'm just tired."

But that wasn't it at all. She was terrified, terrified of what being in love might mean. Marriage. Children. Changes.

"Cece," Agent Thurman said, startling them both. "We've gotten approval to go in."

And this was the problem she and Blain would have. A romantic moment. A phone call. *Sorry, Blain, gotta go.*

"When are you doing it?"

"We're assembling a team right now."

"Does your boss know?"

"Had to call him," Terry said.

"Well, at least he's listening to you."

"Yeah, but he wasn't pleased to hear you were still around."

"Tell the bastard that Cece is my guest—he has no say in whether or not she's allowed to stay."

Terry shrugged, the skin under his eyes likely as discolored as her own.

"Keep me informed, will you?" Cece asked.

"Of course," he said. "I'll let you know just as soon as we find out anything."

And that was that. He turned away without telling her what kind of warrant they'd gotten, whether or not they were bringing Lilly Tanner in for questioning, or had just dropped by as they'd discussed. Nothing. Of course, now that Agent Ashton was back in the picture, Terry had probably been told to button things down.

And if ever Cece had a moment when she realized just exactly what it meant to be suspended from her job, watching Bravo Team leave was it. That was when Cece realized she might never go out on an op again. She might never get to suit up. Might never go out and bring back the bad guys. She'd blown it. Big time.

So when Blain said, "Let's go upstairs," her instinctive reaction was to lash out at him and tell him the last thing she wanted was *sex*. But then he said, "I just want to hold you," as if he'd read her mind.

I just want to hold you.

And if she'd been the kind of woman to burst into tears, she might have cracked up right then and there. But Cece wasn't, and so she just shook her head. "I'm afraid I won't wake up if they call."

"You that tired?"

"I am."

"Then maybe some food will wake you up." And then he gently took her hand, led her to one of his couches and said, "Sit. I'll make breakfast."

She sat, resting her head in her hands, realizing at that moment that she was too tense, too upset to fall asleep.

It turned out not to be true.

CHAPTER TWENTY-THREE

To say that Blain was surprised to see Curt Tanner's grandmother on his doorstep would have been an understatement. He'd seen her around the shop a few times, but her visits had always been short and somewhat strained, especially after her grandson's death.

"Grandma Matty," he said, because that's what he always called her, and because he really didn't know what else to say when faced with the mother of their number one suspect at his door.

"Well, are you going to let me in?" she asked in that no-nonsense way of hers. She was pushing seventy, gray-haired but still spry, with silver eyes that were every bit as sharp as they'd been when he'd first met her all those years ago.

"'Course. Come on in," he said, so completely thrown by the events he didn't know what else to do.

"Place hasn't changed a bit," she said as she stepped through. She hadn't been to his house in years, despite her occasional appearances at the shop.

The shop.

Good Lord—could she be the one....

Blain glanced toward the couch where Cece slept. She was gone.

He stiffened, glanced left, thinking maybe she'd moved to his living room, but she hadn't. Gone.

At that moment, Blain regretted letting Matty inside. Did she know about her daughter? Why else would she be here?

To kill him?

"How you doing, Grandma Matty?" he asked.

She didn't look like a killer, and it was her daughter who had the vendetta. Cece and the other agents had found scores of interviews that pointed to Lilly Tanner being the culprit.

"I've heard some disturbing rumors, Blain," Grandma Matty said, stopping just inside the door.

"Oh?"

She had an old lady's purse, big and brown with wide shoulder straps.

Hiding a gun?

Blain shook his head. No, no, no. Grandma Matty wasn't the culprit. She couldn't be. She was an old lady. But Blain had to admit she didn't look her age. Sure, she had gray hair, but it was the white-blond of someone who took care of herself. Her body had never been bowed by the years; she was still tall and lithe and elegantly clothed. Blain had known her his entire racing career—the Tanners were a second-generation racing family.

And then Blain stiffened. Ah, hell. Matty even knew about Cece. He'd told Matty about the spirited girl who'd blown his doors off as a kid, then gone on to become an FBI agent.

Holy shit.

"Is it true that Barry Bidwell pulled your license?" Matty demanded.

Blain told himself to relax. That's all this was about. She wasn't a killer. And she didn't know about her daughter. Yet. For a second he contemplated telling her, but he had a feeling the FBI wouldn't approve of that.

"It's true," he said, realizing he'd forgotten to answer her question, and she'd started to look at him strangely.

"Those sons of bitches," she said, reaching for her purse. And despite his self-reassurance, Blain tensed. She opened the flap, reached inside....

And pulled out a cellphone.

When she caught him looking at her, she said, "I'm waiting for a call from Lilly. We're supposed to go to town together."

Won't be doing that today, he almost said, but he held his tongue.

"That's part of the reason why I'm here," she said. "Lilly hasn't been herself lately and I'm thinking something's wrong."

Lilly hadn't been herself. Well, that made sense, given what the FBI suspected her of.

"Mind if I sit down?" she asked.

"Not at all." He followed her to his wraparound couch, where Cece had been resting up until the knock on the door.

Where was she? And why was he suddenly grateful that she was somewhere nearby? And armed?

You're overreacting, Sanders. There's nothing to fear from Grandma Matty—it's the daughter you need to worry about.

"Would you like some coffee?" he asked, thinking maybe Cece was in the kitchen. He might catch her there.

"Don't drink the stuff."

"Oh," he said, settling down. But she didn't follow suit.

"Hell. Haven't seen that stuff in a while."

Blain jumped back up and followed her to the trophy room, stealing a glance behind him as he did so.

Where the hell was Cece?

"Must be worth a fortune."

Blain shrugged. Tried to concentrate. Tried not to be so jumpy. He wasn't about to be blown away by a gun-toting granny.

Was he?

"I have a bunch of Curt's old stuff," she added.

"Yeah?" Blain asked, standing by the archway.

"Probably not worth much now. Not many people remember my grandson."

"Now, that's not true," he instantly reassured her.

She turned on him, and for a second he saw something that made him stiffen. But just as quickly as it came, it was gone. The smile she gave him next was vintage Grandma Matty. "C'mon, Blain, we both know that's not true. In fact, it's one of the reasons why I'm here—"

Her phone rang.

Blain glanced at her purse. What if that was Lilly? What if she told her mother what was going on?

Matty reached for the phone.

"IT'S MY DAUGHTER."

Cece heard the words from her position behind the kitchen door.

No. Not now.

If Matty Tanner found out her daughter was in custody, it would blow everything, because one thing Cece knew for sure.

Matty Tanner was their suspect.

It wasn't just Cece's gut that tipped the scales, it was something that had nagged at her throughout their research last night. Lilly Tanner had never signed in at Blain's shop.

But someone named "Grandma Matty" had.

For a split second indecision warred within her. Should she take the old lady down? Did she have enough probable cause?

"Hello?" the old woman said.

Shit!

"What?" she said next, her voice tinged with disbelief and shock. "No. That *can't* be."

Cece reached for her— Shit! Where was her

weapon? She'd taken it off when she'd felt herself getting sleepy, which meant—oh, balls, it was in the flippin' family room.

And then the voice said, "No. I'll take care of it," sounding dead calm.

Take care of *what?* Cece stood motionless with indecision.

In the end she couldn't risk letting Matty Tanner go.

She stepped out from behind the door and froze.

Grandma Matty had a gun.

If Cece hadn't seen pretty much everything during her career with the FBI, she would have found the sight of a little old lady holding a gun ludicrous. But she *had* seen everything, and so when Matty Tanner began to turn in her direction, when that gun quickly followed suit, Cece reacted out of instinct. She dove to the ground.

Bam.

Holy shit, the old bat just tried to kill me!

Cece rolled beneath the table. "Run!" she yelled at Blain as, on all fours, she crawled toward the other end of the table. Black pant legs stopped near the table as Cece eyed the kitchen door, gauging the distance, wondering if she could push the chairs out of the way.

Then the feet began to move around the long side.

No time to think, Cece…move!

"Put the gun down, Grandma Matty."

She froze again. *Put the gun down?*

A glance at the legs revealed they weren't moving. Actually, what they did was face the other direction, quickly and suddenly.

"I mean it, Matty. Put it down or I'll shoot."

Her weapon. Blain had found her weapon.

Oh, thank God.

Cece closed her eyes in relief, only to have them pop back open again. The safety was on her gun. Did Blain know that?

"You bastard," Matty said. "You knew, didn't you?"

"I knew they'd taken Lilly into custody for questioning, yes, but I didn't think it was my place to tell you."

"Liar," the woman said, and something about the way the legs were flexing, the way they rocked back a bit…

"Blain, look out!"

"Matty," Blain warned.

Boom!

Cece charged Matty's legs.

Boom, boom, boom.

She shoved at the chairs in her way. Unfortunately, they didn't move. Pain slammed through her right shoulder. A chair tipped.

Matty's legs were gone. What the—

Blain flung away the chair she'd crashed into. "Cece, are you all right?"

"Go after her," she ordered through lips gone taut with pain. What the hell had she done to her shoulder?

The front door slammed.

"Damn it, Blain, go after her." Cece realized she couldn't go after the woman herself; she'd dislocated her shoulder.

Damn, damn, damn.

"You're hurt," he said, gently pushing her back down when she tried to get up.

"It's nothing, and she's *getting away.*"

He set the gun down. Cece tried to get up on her own, which was hard to do with only one arm, especially when the other one was in agony.

"Damn it," she cursed. *"Don't let her get away."*

But then she looked into his eyes—and saw that terror had drained the color from his face.

"You're not going to go after her, are you?" she asked.

"No," he said.

She tried in earnest to move then.

"Are you shot?"

"No, I'm not shot. Let me go. I have to go after her."

"No, you don't."

"Did you hit her?" she asked.

"I wasn't trying to hit her."

"You *what?*"

"Wasn't trying to hit her."

"Why the hell not?"

"I…couldn't do it."

CHAPTER TWENTY-FOUR

SO SHE GOT AWAY.

Cece didn't know what pissed her off more—that Blain had forced her to go to a hospital (because he refused to let the paramedics reset her shoulder), or that Agent Ashton showed up right after they'd fixed her shoulder so that he saw her at her absolute, crack-the-mirror worst: eyes red (okay, so she'd shed a few pain-induced tears), hospital gown gaping open, hair hanging half up, half down (because really, it was hard to fix one's hair when you only had one arm).

"Agent Blackwell," he said, stopping at the foot of her bed.

Jeesh. Just what she needed. "Agent Ashton," she said, trying hard to appear dignified in a light blue, flower-spotted gown that allowed suspiciously cool air access to her backside. "What brings *you* here?"

Okay, so she wasn't exactly being nice, but she was furious that Grandma Goofball had gotten away, and that ten minutes after bringing her to the E.R., Blain had trotted off with the local police to answer questions.

"I see we're still as outspoken as ever."

She gave him a *drop dead* look, and she didn't feel guilty about doing it, either. The man had single-handedly blown this investigation more times than she would wager Agent Ashton could count. Cece was fed up. She'd hit the wall. Jumped off the pier. And she was ready to call it quits.

"You'll have to excuse my bad mood, Agent Ashton. In less than twenty-four hours, I've been put on administrative leave, shot at and hospitalized. I'm not exactly feeling social." *Especially toward you.* But she didn't say that last part.

Agent Ashton moved around the end of the bed. Cece's eyes narrowed. Almost...almost, she put her foot out to stop him, but she didn't want to suffer the further indignity of having him see her bare toes.

"Look, Cece..."

Cece?

"I came here to make sure you're all right."

"Ah, shucks, boss, that's so sweet of you." Too sarcastic? Cece didn't care.

He didn't say anything for a second, and something about the way he looked around the perimeter of the room, at the floor, out the window, at the walls, made Cece squint at him.

"And to tell you we need you back on the case," he added.

She thought she'd misheard him. "I beg your pardon?" she said, tipping her head, which made yesterday's hairstyle shift even more to the left.

"Look," he said, grabbing one of the blue visitor's chairs and sitting down. "I'm taking some heat about the way the investigation has gone."

She had to stop her brows leaping skyward.

"And frankly, Barry Bidwell has asked that you be put back on the investigation."

The president of NASCAR wanted her back on the case?

"After this morning's incident at Sanders's residence, the pressure's on. I don't think I have to explain to you that it looks bad for us that you were on hand and we weren't."

"It was just a coincidence that the real perpetrator stopped by the morning you were apprehending her daughter."

And to her absolute shock, Agent Ashton looked somewhat grateful for her defense. "I know, but it doesn't look that way to the press."

"It's on the news?"

"Sanders is outside talking to broadcasters right now."

So that's where he was.

"Bottom line, we think Matty Tanner is on her way to Atlanta Motor Speedway."

Cece sat up—bad move. Pain radiated down her arm.

"We have a jet standing by to transport us."

"Let me get dressed," she said quickly, not about to let this gift horse kick her in the teeth.

He nodded, and when he got up and left, Cece

saw him pause at the small table opposite the bed. He left her badge behind.

Hot damn. She couldn't stop herself. She smiled.

BLAIN WISHED HE COULD be as enthusiastic. When he came back to Cece's room, and noticed the FBI badge back in place around her neck, his stomach turned as if he was on the last lap of a race.

"What're you doing?"

She looked at him without a hint of sorrow. "I'm going to Atlanta. Agent Ashton seems to think Matty Tanner is on her way there."

Matty Tanner, a killer. He still couldn't believe it. Nor could he believe that Cece was all set to go tearing after her.

"But you're injured."

"It was just a dislocated shoulder. A little bruising, some soreness, but I'll be all better in a few days."

She was going after Matty. Matty, who'd tried to kill her earlier that day.

"Cece, do you think that's wise? What if you can't draw a gun?"

She rolled her shoulder, trying to convince him that she was fine, but she couldn't hide the resulting wince. "Just a little sore, Blain. I'll be fine."

No, he thought. She wasn't fine. And he couldn't believe the FBI would call her back to duty after she'd just been hospitalized. "I thought you'd been fired."

"Not fired, just suspended. They reinstated me today, thanks to Barry Bidwell."

"Barry?"

"He demanded I be put back on the job."

Of course he would. With a big race going on today, Barry wanted to appear as if he was doing everything he could to apprehend the suspect. "What he should do is cancel the race."

Cece shook her head. "Too late for that now. It starts in less than two hours. The stands are already filled."

"And you're heading off into danger."

She couldn't have looked more shocked if she'd tried. "Of course I am, Blain. That's my job."

He knew it was.

And yet seeing her on the floor earlier—wounded, him holding a gun in his hand and pointing it at someone—had suddenly changed things.

"You understand that, don't you?"

"Of course," he said, but he couldn't help thinking that it was a lie.

She smiled, stepping toward him. "Then I'll see you when I get home." She pressed a kiss against his check. "Hopefully with Matty Tanner in custody."

If Matty didn't kill her.

Because Cece hadn't seen the look in the old lady's eyes. She hadn't seen the fury that had tightened her lips right before she'd turned and pointed the weapon in Cece's direction.

He didn't move when Cece stepped away, and she looked momentarily puzzled.

"Be careful," was all he felt capable of saying.

I love you.
Don't die.

"I will," she said, smiling. And with one last kiss on his cheek, she turned and walked out the door.

Blain felt as if she took his heart with her.

IF CECE WORRIED something might be wrong with Blain, she didn't have time to think about it. The minute she hopped into Agent Ashton's car, she was briefed on what they knew so far—and it surprised the hell out of her.

Matty Tanner had hitched a ride to Atlanta on a private jet. Apparently, she'd called up a driver she was close to and asked for a ride. She'd shown up at the Concord Airport toting two pieces of luggage. There'd been reports that she'd gone to the race-track after landing in Atlanta, but there was no way to confirm that just yet. The green flag had dropped on the Atlanta 500 a half hour ago and the teams were a little too busy to be questioned.

"So what's the plan?" Cece asked after being ushered into a waiting helicopter.

"We try to determine if she's at the track to kill someone, or as a way to cover her trail while flee-ing the country," Agent Ashton said, his glasses reflecting the flash of the sun as he put on a pair of headphones. Cece did the same.

"But if she's fleeing the country, why not leave as soon as she landed at Atlanta International?" Cece asked.

"That's what worries us," Agent Ashton said.

And it worried Cece, too, but for one more reason than Agent Ashton knew. When her cellphone rang five minutes after they'd landed at the track, her worry tripled. It was the call she'd been waiting for.

"Blackwell here," she answered, Agent Ashton shooting her a look as they headed for the black sedan that would take them to the infield.

"Cece, it's Bob."

Bob, her boss from San Francisco. She wasn't surprised to hear from him after all the calls she'd placed to his office this weekend.

"Talk to me," she said.

"You were right," he said, verifying that he'd been brought up to speed. "Three weeks ago Matty Tanner bought herself a light anti-armor system," Bob said. "And the juice to go with it."

"A LAW rocket? Crap."

"You going to break the news to Ashton, or should I?"

"I'll do it."

"Roger," he said, hanging up.

Cece decided not to mince words. "Four weeks ago, our San Francisco office got a report that someone who stood out a bit was trying to buy themselves a rocket launcher."

"Let me guess," Ashton said, leaning against the cloth seat. "She was an old lady."

"Our undercover op confirmed the ID two minutes ago."

Silence. He looked out the window at the racetrack, which rose up like a giant bull ring.

"We need to stop the race," Cece said, following his gaze. "Matty Tanner may be an old lady, but it doesn't take much more than a shoulder to balance a LAW rocket."

"We can't stop the race," Ashton said. "It's too late. The fans would panic. Plus it'd take hours to evacuate a hundred thousand people, not to mention we don't even know if she's here or if she's fled the country."

"Then what do we do?"

"We find her," Agent Ashton said. "Fast."

THEY BROKE UP INTO TEAMS, wearing ball caps and T-shirts with various team logos so that they blended in better. But these shirts had Velcro strips on the back that when reversed, read FBI. Badges and weapons were concealed, to be pulled out when needed. North Carolina agents mixed with their Georgia counterparts as they were rapidly briefed.

As quickly as he could, Agent Ashton updated them on all aspects of the plan. But really, Cece found herself thinking, if Matty was at AMS, there were only a few places she could hide out with a rocket launcher. If she were to use the top of a hauler to site her target, someone would see her. Ditto somewhere in the garage. So they would search rest rooms, infield buildings, crew member parking— everywhere someone might be able to hide out and point a weapon at the same time.

They came up with nothing.

Around them the race went on, but none of the agents paid any heed. They were too busy trying to figure out where the hell Matty Tanner had gotten to.

"If she's here, she has to be in with the fans," Cece reasoned aloud.

"Yeah, but she'd be just as noticeable there as here," Terry Thurman said.

"Not if she were in a private suite," Cece said, her eyes catching on the row of windows at the very top of the homestretch grandstands. They were mirrored, revealing vague outlines of what must be people in the seats near the front.

Terry lifted a brow and within seconds radioed Agent Ashton. They had approval to check it out, one of their helicopters overhead moving in for a closer look, too.

There was a good chance Matty Tanner was up there, maybe even looking down at them as they frantically searched the infield.

The crowd roared. Both she and Agent Thurman turned. Smoke came from turn three. Cece's heart stopped. And then, at the far end of the track, looking like it skated along the roof of the garage, a car slid toward the infield.

Just a wreck.

She and Agent Thurman looked at each other. No need to say what the other was thinking. When they turned, their steps took on new urgency as they met up with the rest of their team, and Cece took comfort in the familiar faces. A night spent working by their sides had proved that she could trust them if things got sticky. The problem was how to keep the situation from getting sticky. They had forty-four boxes to search, Cece knew. Forty-four rooms where a killer might hide. Forty-four rooms where fans might be mingling with said killer, or held hostage by her.

But was Matty Tanner a killer?

So many things didn't make sense, Cece thought. Why take the trouble to plant explosives and then detonate when no one was around? Why use a LAW rocket on race day when you'd had a perfectly good grandstand to blow up the day before? What the hell was going on?

That was the expression on some of the fans' faces as Bravo Team emerged from the tunnel and burst into the concession area, badges pulled from beneath their shirts now, the chrome catching the light as it was meant to do.

"We'll check the suites one at a time," Agent Thurman told them. "Standard search and seizure, but I want caution, people. Nobody's going to be expecting us, and if our suspect isn't there, I don't want people staring at a gun pointed in their faces."

The ride to the VIP suites was a long one, though it gave them time to attach bold letters proclaiming them to be FBI on their shirts, and to pull out their weapons. The elevator doors opened. Before them stretched a long corridor, metal louvers on the right flinging a zebra pattern of shadows on the floor. And as they looked down the bank of doors, the pitfalls of their task became apparent. There were forty-four suites on two levels. Doors were opened by private keys, which meant they would have to knock or force each one open. Thurman radioed down for a pass key, which made it only slightly easier. After searching two suites, they realized it'd take them close to an hour to do it right.

The clock ticked.

"Son of a bitch," Agent Thurman said after searching the fourth. "This is going to take forever."

Cece couldn't agree more. So many suites, all of them occupied, the roar of the crowd reminding them that lives could be in danger.

"Maybe we should break up into two teams," Cece suggested. "A few of us can do the suites above while you guys continue searching down here."

"Good idea," Terry said. "You—" he pointed to a younger agent Cece had never met before "—and you," he said, motioning with his thumb to another man she recognized from Blain's house. "Go on up with Cece. If you find Tanner, pin her down and wait for reinforcements to arrive."

"Roger," Cece said, turning to follow. On her back she could feel her FBI ID flap around a bit. She ignored it, the adrenaline surge that had been pumping since the moment they'd landed causing her nerve endings to almost burn. Matty was here. Cece knew it. No place else made any sense, because with all the fans running around, she would have been seen. But here, in the halls leading to the suites, hardly anyone stirred, race fans barricaded in their private boxes equipped with bathrooms, kitchens and a whole host of other amenities that made leaving the suite unnecessary.

They caught the elevator up. Cece pushed the button to the floor they needed over and over again, as if that might speed things up. It didn't, and as the doors whooshed closed, her grip tightened on her weapon. Her palms were sweaty, and she was breathing a bit rapidly.

Calm down, she cautioned herself. Just routine search and seizure.

She eyed the glowing button she'd just pressed... and her spine stiffened.

"What was Curt Tanner's car number?" she blurted.

"Does anybody remember?" She stared at the man she'd met at Blain's house. Mike was his name. "I remember seeing it in our research last night."

"Forty-one," Mike said. "It's my age. You think—"
Cece nodded. "I do."

Her two partners nodded in turn.

When the elevator doors opened, they headed for suite 41, calling down to Thurman for reinforcements.

Cece's pulse pounded as Mike inserted the key. Right away she knew something was different. The previous suites they'd checked all had voices coming from the other side. Not so this one.

Mike glanced over at them, nodding just before he swung the door wide.

The first person Cece saw was Blain.

CHAPTER TWENTY-FIVE

"TAKE ANOTHER STEP and I'll let this thing fly."

Cece froze, her gaze moving left. Matty Tanner sat in the second row, her shape hidden from probing eyes below by the empty seats in front of her, a rocket launcher balanced on her shoulder.

Granny had a rocket launcher.

For a second the whole situation seemed ludicrous. The woman was almost seventy years old, and yet there she sat, holding the heavy tube on her shoulder like a parasol.

"Put it down," Cece ordered, darting a glance at Blain.

"Shoot me and the last thing you'll see is me pulling the trigger."

"That would be a big mistake," Cece said. Mike pressed up against the wall, one hand holding his weapon, the other a radio into which he softly spoke.

"Matty, in less than five minutes our helicopter will be here and a sniper will have you in his sights. He'll take you out the moment he sees your finger tighten on the trigger."

"Then I guess I'll have to blow this joint before then."

"Matty, don't say that," Blain said. "I'm telling you, this isn't the way to get even with Barry Bidwell."

"Bullshit," Matty said. "This is the best damn way to make those bastards pay, and you know it. The fat man up in smoke. My heart rejoices at the thought."

"Look, Matty," Blain said. "Like I told you earlier, if Curt were alive, he'd disapprove."

"If Curt were alive, we wouldn't be here," Matty said, her aim never wavering. "So you can thank that no-good bastard driver of yours for the little fireworks display I'm about to set off."

"Randy is dead," Blain said. "There's no reason for anyone else to die."

"Yes, there is," Matty said. "There's plenty of reason. Those bastards let my son's killer go unpunished. Told everyone it was an accident. It wasn't an accident. We both know that, and today that bastard Barry Bidwell will go up in flames like Randy did."

And that was when it hit Cece. She met Blain's eyes, knowing he'd reasoned it out, too. Probably before her. Matty *hadn't been* trying to kill race fans, or Blain, or her. She'd been targeting Barry all along. Barry and the sport he was such a huge part of. Barry, the man who'd let her grandson's killer go unpunished. Barry, who'd left Daytona to come to Atlanta, thanks to her machinations. Barry, who'd fallen right into her trap—he was scheduled to award the trophy personally in a public display of bravado.

Son of a bitch.

"Red flag the race," Cece ordered Mike.

That got Matty's attention. For the first time the old woman moved—well, flinched was more like it. She kept the rocket trained on the infield, but she cocked her head a bit to look at Cece. "Do that and I swear to God I'll target the fans."

"And the minute you move, I'll put a bullet through your head." But Cece motioned to Mike to wait a second nonetheless.

"Not before I squeeze the trigger."

"There won't be time to squeeze." Cece tried to bluff. Actually, there would be. Shit, a sniper shot might cause the woman to flinch, to pull on the lever that would launch a rocket.

"Matty, please." Blain tried again. "I came here to reason with you."

"You came here to save your girlfriend's life."

"Cece can take care of herself," Blain said.

"Then why didn't you call her and tell her you knew where I was?"

"Because I was trying to save *your* life."

Matty Tanner glanced at Blain. "My life's over, Blain."

"No it's not, Matty."

"You think I stand a chance of surviving prison?" the old woman said with a derisive snort. "C'mon, Blain, I always figured you for an intelligent man.

You had shitty taste in drivers, but I never held that against you."

Out of the corner of her eyes, Cece saw Mike motioning. "Sniper," he mouthed. They had a man in position. Before the end of the race, Matty Tanner would be taken out…unless they could get her to surrender.

Footsteps sounded in the hall, but Cece didn't look over her shoulder to see who'd arrived. If she moved, she might set Matty Turner off, and she didn't want to risk that. Not yet.

"Look, Matty," she said. "We understand why you did what you did. Hell, race fans all over celebrated the day you took Randy out."

"Damn straight," Matty agreed.

"The man was a putz. Huge ego, bad attitude, dirty driver."

"You got that right."

"But you've done what you set out to do. You took him out. It's over. There's no need to take this to another level."

"That's where you're wrong," Matty said. "Because just look at what's happened so far. I took out a whole grandstand yesterday. An entire structure. And did it scare anybody off? No. Because the fans believed Bidwell's lies—they believed the threat was over, believed the fat man would protect them. Well, I'm here today to prove that nobody's safe, not even the president of the stock car racing association."

"And when *you're* taken out," Cece said. "When

fans hear you were killed seconds after you launched your rocket, do you think they'll believe the threat is over then? Because it will be, Matty. You'll be gone. The fans will realize that. They'll come back."

"Yeah, but the industry will suffer. Attendance will drop off. Revenue will go down. They'll be made to pay, just as my daughter and I paid when Curt died—paid with our hearts."

And what about your daughter? You going to leave her behind to absorb the fallout of your actions?" Cece asked.

"My daughter would be the first to tell me to pull the trigger."

And that was when Cece realized they were fighting a lost cause. The woman didn't care. She'd checked out. Cece had seen it before—serial killers who made last stands. Cult leaders who took their members out with them. Drug dealers who just didn't care.

Blain must have realized it, too, because he started walking toward Matty.

"Don't you come near me, Blain Sanders," Matty said just as Cece was about to call out a warning.

"I'm coming near you because I can see from here that your arms are about to give out from the weight of that thing."

"No, they're not."

"And because I want you to look me in the eyes and tell me you don't mind blowing up a couple hundred innocent bystanders in your quest for revenge."

"I don't care," Matty said. "At this point, I don't care about anything."

Cece glanced at Mike. Agent Ashton stood in his place.

"We're taking her out," he mouthed.

They had no choice. "Blain, do as she says," Cece warned.

He didn't listen.

"Listen to your girlfriend," Matty said.

Agent Ashton began to count down with his fingers. Five…

"Put it down, Matty," Blain warned.

Four.

"No."

Three.

"I can see the thing shaking from here. You're not going to make it until the end of the race."

Two.

"Watch me."

Blain lunged. Cece cried, "Abort, abort, abort," into her radio at the same time she dove for Blain. But it happened. Glass shattered. Matty Tanner cried out. So did Cece when she hit Blain dead center. Pain burst through her injured shoulder.

The launcher!

Cece looked up from her sprawled position on the floor. Matty Tanner's head lay against the back of the chair, motionless. But it was the launcher that caught her attention. It was sliding off her shoulder, tipping backward, Matty's hand still on the lever. And as the thing tipped back, Cece knew instantly what would happen.

No!

She covered Blain, covered herself.

Pop!

A flash of heat. They should be burned. But they weren't. She would remember later finding that odd. And then she heard noise. An odd sort of groaning that she thought might be Blain. She rolled off him, got to her hands and knees.

"Cece—"

Pain. Her back.

"Cece."

It was the last word Cece heard.

"IT'S NOT GOOD," Dr. Martin Washburn told Blain. "But it could be worse."

"How bad is it?" Blain asked, trying to disguise the shaking of his hands by clenching them into fists.

"She broke the bottom two vertebrae. From what we can tell right now, it's an incomplete paralysis probably caused by a contusion to the cord. She responds to stimuli, but she can't move. The movement might come back, but I think you should prepare yourself for the worst."

Dr. Washburn's face blurred.

"You going to be okay?" the doctor asked.

No. Blain wasn't okay. He gasped in a breath, tipped his head against the wall and struggled to retain control. It'd be okay. She hadn't severed her spinal cord.

And all the while the doctor gazed at him, the look of compassion and sympathy on his face making the tears spill from Blain's eyes.

She'd walk again. "She *has* to walk again," he said aloud, trying to make them understand that they had to fix her. "Being an FBI agent is her life. If she can't walk again…"

He let the words trail off.

"We'll do the best we can," Dr. Washburn said. "I wish I had better news. I really do."

Blain put his head on his knees, just concentrating on breathing in, over and over again. The doctor slipped away as, a few doors down, Cece slept behind a door—an artificial sleep, brought on by the drugs and painkillers they'd given her.

"Blain," a male voice said. He looked up and saw Agent Thurman. "What'd he say?"

"She broke her back," he told the man.

"Will she walk again?"

"It's too soon to tell," Blain told him.

But Blain could see the fear in Thurman's eyes. They'd both watched the launcher fire, had seen it hit the wall, severing a beam on its way out. The missile hadn't exploded, but it might as well have as far as Cece was concerned. The damn beam had fallen right on top of her.

"She *has* to walk again," he heard himself repeat.

"I don't know," Thurman said. "I really don't know."

CHAPTER TWENTY-SIX

CECE WOKE WITH THE WORST taste in her mouth. *Must have been sleeping with my mouth open,* she thought.

And then she remembered.

She tried to sit up.

And she couldn't.

For a moment, she thought it was one of those really horrible dreams you had every once in a while when you couldn't move. Your eyes opened, your mind raced, but nothing worked.

Only she could move her arms.

And when she did, she saw the IV strapped to one, saw the hospital ID bracelet. Then she registered other things—white curtains and blue vinyl chairs—furnishings that seemed obligatory for hospitals. In the left corner of the room was a door, closed, its aluminum handle catching a beam of light so that she had to squint for a second.

And then she saw Blain.

"Wha—?" But she never finished the question. In a flash she remembered. The racetrack. The launcher.

The pain.

She looked down. A cast encased her torso. She couldn't move.

Horror made her heart pound. The frantic beep-beep-beep echoed on the heart monitor.

"Blain?" she moaned, the word part question, part panic as she tried to move her toes.

"Hey, Cece," he said, grabbing her hand. She could feel that. Could feel his warm palm engulf her cold one. But she couldn't feel anything below the cast.

"I can't—" But she couldn't finish.

"I know," he said.

Maybe drugs? Had they sedated her somehow so she couldn't feel…?

And then she saw the look in his eyes. No, what she saw was redness, and the shimmer of tears.

Oh, no…oh, God, no…

She tried to move her legs again. Tried so hard it sent spasms of pain up her back and into her shoulders.

"Don't move," he warned, his hand tightening, his other hand covering the first. "Cece, please. Don't move. You're injured."

The beam. It had fallen.

On her back.

"How bad?" she asked, the sound coming from a long, long way away.

"Not bad," he answered, his hand lifted to the side of her face. "You'll be walking in no time."

But she could tell he didn't actually believe the words. She could tell by the way he all but prodded a smile onto his face, a smile that started to wobble. "Cece?" he asked.

But she turned her head away. That caused the world to spin, and Cece welcomed the darkness, welcomed it with a fervor that made her wish for oblivion to follow. It did.

SHE WOKE AGAIN a few hours later, and this time Blain pressed the call button immediately. By the time Cece's eyes got more lucid, a nurse was already there, injecting a sedative into the IV. Within seconds Cece's eyes went glassy, but she didn't go completely under. Instead she stared at him, and Blain's heart broke into a million little pieces.

"Permanent?" she asked in a groggy voice.

"They don't know," he said.

But she must have seen the fear in his eyes because she blinked.

"Cece, don't think that way," he said, squeezing the hand he'd never let go. "It's too early to tell anything yet." And his heart nearly broke all over again at the way she swallowed, at the way she gave him a brave half smile.

Oh, Lord, why'd this have to happen to you?

He almost started crying. Instead he gave her a brave smile, too.

"Hey, if you'd wanted some time off, you could have just asked instead of letting a beam fall on you."

But the smile had started to wobble and Blain knew her brave heart was about to take a beating, knew the eyes filling with tears weren't going to stop crying. Not now. Maybe not for a while.

And so he did what he'd done a hundred times in the past few days. He leaned forward and softly, gently kissed her. And as he did, Cece's breathing changed. She started to cry. To be honest, they both did.

BLAIN INSISTED ON TAKING her home when it came time to leave. The dining room she'd once shared with four FBI agents became her bedroom. Ramps were put on the front door and back. Cece gained strength by wheeling herself around the lake, all the while reminding herself it could be worse. The accident could have happened in San Francisco, where she had no family and very few friends. What would she have done without Blain? Blain, who'd been such a rock. Blain, who couldn't stare at her without pity, because the truth of the matter was—she wasn't getting better.

They'd talked about what had happened, talked about why he hadn't called her to let her know where Matty Tanner was. He'd been trying to protect her, he'd said. Unspoken was the admission that he hadn't done a very good job.

The only perk of her invalid condition was her new role as darling of the racing world. The first time a famous driver came by to visit her, Cece had been

filled with awe. Too bad that awe had faded to embarrassment when she'd seen the pity in his eyes. She
didn't want to be pitied. She wanted to walk again,
dammit. And so, while she appreciated the racing
crowd's support, she didn't necessarily want it. All
she wanted was to get on with her life.

So that's what she tried to do in the weeks that followed, all the while ignoring the fear that Blain's
constant reassurances that he loved her stemmed
from guilt. But that fear was nothing compared to the
one that she might lose him.

They hired someone to help her—though she'd
gotten good in recent weeks at taking care of herself—
and had found a good therapist. That therapist had
been preparing her for the worst. Actually, it was
Cece who always pushed the issue. She needed to
prepare herself for the chance that she'd never walk
again.

Her one bright spot each week was Lance's Monday visits. Blain's driver always made her laugh,
never failing to amuse her when he came by. She expected no different one sultry August night.

They were sitting on the back deck, a bug zapper
doing its thing behind them. The sun had just sunk
behind the lake so that the trees along the horizon
looked like jagged inkblots, the sky above a conch-
shell pink. It was Cece's favorite time of day, a time
when she could inhale the thick air and think about
how much her life had changed…and how much
she'd lost.

"You really need to get over your fear of coming to the racetrack," Lance said out of the blue. "Everyone keeps asking when you're dropping by."

And Cece, who just the day before had asked Blain to take her to that week's race in Michigan, had stared at Lance, dumbfounded.

"I mean, we all understand why you'd be a little afraid—it's not like garages have handicap access—but you gotta know how much the team wants you there."

Cece watched him take another bite of the chocolate chip cookies she'd made. Cooking. That's about all she had to entertain her anymore—that and physical therapy, because Cece was determined to walk.

"Did I say something wrong?" Lance asked, his boyish face filled with dismay.

"No, Lance," she said, her mind replaying her conversation with Blain. She'd been very clear about going. There was just no way he could have misinterpreted what she'd said.

"I'm tired," Cece explained, seeing Lance stare at her with concern. "Blain got home from the track so late last night."

"Did he?" Lance asked in obvious surprise. "Funny, we made good time from the racetrack."

Had they?

Cece looked away, and even though she told herself not to feel hurt that Blain had spent yet another late evening at the office in order to avoid her, she did. Lance must have seen that disappointment, because he quickly reassured her. "He must have gotten hung up at the shop. Never seen an owner work as hard as Blain."

Cece nodded blankly, Lance little realizing that that was the problem. More and more, Blain sought the shelter of his shop rather than her arms. But she couldn't really blame the man. How loverlike was it to lie down with a woman whose legs flopped around like a fish?

Lance stood up, bending down to place a kiss on her cheek. "Try to make it this weekend."

"I'll try," she told him, a part of her screaming inside. She inhaled deeply, hoping it would keep her from crying in front of Lance. It did, but only barely. The moment the door closed, Cece felt the pressure build, felt her chest expand as she tried not to lose control. But suddenly, it was all too much. For weeks she'd held herself together, forced herself to deal with her situation in as pragmatic a way as possible. Blain had been there for her, and for that she'd be forever grateful, because when she thought about it, he didn't have to be so nice. Yeah, he'd declared his love, but love could change, go in a different direction. To be honest, she didn't blame him for pulling back.

So when she heard his car turn into the circular drive, she wheeled herself outside. He'd made her a ramp off the back of the deck that led to a path she could take to the edge of the lake, and that was where she went. The moon that night was perfectly full, its shimmering white light turning the water quicksilver gray and the aluminum frame of her wheelchair chrome. It was near midnight, and Cinderella's slipper had finally fallen off. The fair prince had let her go. Time to ride the carriage back home.

CHAPTER TWENTY-SEVEN

BLAIN KNEW SOMETHING was wrong the moment he entered his house. Normally, Cece shut off the lights before she went to bed, leaving the house quiet as a tomb. But tonight the lamps in the family room still glowed, the kitchen lights reflected off the polished marble of the entryway. And for a second he had the same horrible fear he'd had the first few weeks after bringing Cece home. Had she taken her own life? Her therapist had warned him to watch for signs of depression.

He rushed to his converted dining room. The bed they'd placed in the corner was empty. He checked the bathroom off the kitchen next. Nothing. But a glance outside the window revealed the glowing surface of the lake—the waters completely still.

No, not still. Something moved out there. Cece. He saw her silhouette. Her blond hair glowed in the moonlight, and what looked to be a white sweater was thrown over her shoulders. He made his way toward her, wondering what she was still doing up. She should have been in bed hours ago. She needed her rest.

"Cece?" he said, the word a question.

She didn't look at him, just continued staring out at the lake.

Adrenaline caused by fear made his pulse leap. "Cece, what's wrong?"

"You mean other than being in a wheelchair?" she said. Then she huffed a bit, and Blain relaxed. Funny. She was trying to be funny.

"You should be in bed."

She shook her head. Blain squatted down next to her and for a moment was struck by how beautiful she looked in the moonlight. Her accident hadn't changed that. If anything, it had softened the angular edges of her face. A face that had been beautiful before looked even more stunning now, her blond hair longer and, more often than not, left hanging down her back, as it was now. Green eyes he'd once called the color of coolant seemed bigger, the lashes darker—or maybe that was the moonlight.

"Blain, why are we still pretending everything is normal?"

The words made him rock back. Those green eyes met his own. And for the first time he saw sadness in them, and resignation, and even a hint of fear.

"What do you mean, pretending?"

She looked away. He saw her straighten her shoulders. "I'm not a pet, Blain. You shouldn't keep me around because you feel obligated. I can take care of myself now. If being around me makes you uncomfortable to the point that you're trying to avoid me with late nights and long days at the racetrack, then I'll just go."

"Long nights—" He found himself incapable of words, but only for a moment. "Cece, that's not it at all."

She faced him again, a blond brow lifted. "Isn't it, Blain?"

"No," he said, trying to make her see the honesty in his eyes. "I'm not avoiding you because I feel guilty, or pity you, or can't stand to look at you, or any of the other reasons you might have come up with. I'm staying away because you're still just as beautiful to me as ever and I'm having a hell of a time keeping my hands off you."

That made her eyes widen. He could see the way her lashes flickered, even in the moonlight.

"What?" she asked.

"I want to make love to you, only I've been afraid to try. Afraid to ask. Afraid you might say no."

Those wide eyes of hers never blinked as she stared at him. And then she looked away, and he could see the disbelief in her face.

"I thought you were avoiding me."

"I am avoiding you," he admitted with a smile. "But not for the reasons you think."

"Geez-oh-peets," she said with a small huff of laughter.

He grabbed her hand, squeezing it. "Cece, I love

you. I want to be with you…in all the ways that a man and a woman can be together."

"Then why won't you take me to a race with you?"

"Because you're not ready for it," he said simply and honestly. "It's too much. Physically, you're not ready."

"Yes, I am, Blain. I'm a lot more ready than you think."

"No, you're not. Being out in public, the stress of being in a large crowd again."

She laughed. "Blain, I go out now, which, if you were around a little more often, you would see for yourself. Crowds don't bother me."

"Being in a garage is different."

"No it's not, Blain. So if that's the real reason, you're being ridiculous. And I'm putting my foot down. I'm going to Darlington with you."

"No," he said firmly.

"Why not?" she asked.

Why not? "I told you—you're too fragile."

"I'm not," she said. "I'm perfectly fine. Actually, I'm in better-than-average health for someone without the use of her legs."

"Don't say that," he said.

"Don't say what? That I'm paralyzed? I am, Blain. I'm a paraplegic. A 'D' classified, incomplete, lower extremity paraplegic, which means I have a better than average shot at walking again. And I *am* going to walk, Blain. I can promise you that."

"Of course you are," he said, shifting a bit so he could brush her face with his thumb.

"No. Don't look at me like that."

"Like what?" he said in exasperation.

"With pity. With commiseration. As if you're humoring me."

"That's not it at all—"

"Why are you with me, Blain?" she asked again. "Why have you stuck it out with me?"

"Because I love you," he said. "Because even though you're in a wheelchair, you're still the same woman who stole my heart."

"Bullshit."

He drew back.

"If that was true, you'd never want to leave my side."

"I told you, I'm worried about your health—"

"So worried that you take off first thing Friday morning with nothing more than a kiss?"

"You need your rest."

"So worried that you stay late at the office every night?"

"We're making a push to win the championship this year."

"So worried that you never take me out, not to dinner, not shopping, not anything?"

"Don't be ridiculous. I told you, I worry about you being around so many people. The doctor told us you'll be more prone to illnesses—"

"Bullshit," she said again, her left hand hitting the

edge of the wheel. "Don't kid yourself, Blain. You're not trying to protect me, you're trying to protect yourself."

"What?"

Suddenly there were tears in her eyes. Her hands clutched the wheels of her chair as if she were poised to take flight. "You're afraid if you start treating me like a normal person, I'll leave."

"What?" he said again.

"It's true," she accused. "And then where would you be? No way to assuage your guilt. No more taking care of Cece to make yourself feel better. No more treating me like a damn dog you accidentally ran over with that damn Hummer of yours, a dog you have to take care of now because you feel responsible."

"Cece, I don't feel responsible."

"Don't you, Blain? Didn't you tell Lance that this was all your fault? That if you hadn't gone to the track, I wouldn't be in a wheelchair?"

"I don't remember."

"You did. Just like you once told me you accepted how dangerous my job was. And that you loved me anyway. For better or for worse. Is this the 'for worse' part, Blain?"

"No, of course not."

"Then make love to me. Make love to me right now. Right this minute. Because while I'm flattered that you still find me attractive, I don't really believe it. Prove it to me."

So he tried to, rising up so he could bend over and kiss her, and to his relief the desire he felt for her sprang instantly and unmistakably to life. He loved her. He wanted to make love to her.

He did. He could feel his erection grow, could feel the way just tasting the familiar essence of her stirred his soul. He would lift her up, take her to the bedroom and do what he'd been wanting to do with her for weeks.

But he didn't.

She broke off the kiss, her chest heaving as she looked him in the eyes and said, "Go ahead, Blain. Take me inside."

He reached for her.

And just as quickly dropped his arms to his sides.

"Afraid you'll hurt me, or afraid you'll find out making love to me will be different?"

He didn't know. And, damn it, he should know. He should just pick her up. Carry her away. Do what she'd challenged him to do.

But he didn't.

And there were tears of sadness in her eyes when she looked up at him. "You can't do it, can you?"

He could. Yes, he could, damn it. He'd prove it to her.

But he didn't move. He couldn't move. Jesus, what the hell was wrong with him?

"And I don't blame you, Blain. I really don't. It takes a special man to overlook this." She patted her legs, a bitter, halfhearted smirk tipping up one side of her mouth, all the more poignant for the resignation it contained. "I prepared myself for the fact that you might not be that kind of man."

But he wasn't that type of man. He'd been wanting to make love to her for weeks.

Hadn't he? Or was the desire he felt only present during those moments when the wheelchair wasn't around, those moments when she sat on the couch or lay on the bed? Those moments when she looked like a normal person?

Oh, God, that couldn't be it, could it?

"Goodbye, Blain."

"What?"

She looked up at him, tears glittering on her lashes. "I'm going back to San Francisco."

"Don't be ridiculous," he said. "You're overreacting. Just give me some time to adjust. We can work this out."

"No, Blain, we can't."

She didn't move, not for a few seconds at least, and when she did drop her hands to the tires, he found himself saying, "Cece, wait."

"No, Blain. I'm not waiting. I'm tired of waiting. Life should always be lived to the fullest. You and I both know that hasn't happened in a while. And if you're honest with yourself, you'll admit I'm doing us both a favor."

She turned away, her wheels oddly soundless as she moved from the edge of the lake.

If you're honest, you'll admit I'm doing us both a favor.

The worst of it was, he was afraid she might be right.

CHAPTER TWENTY-EIGHT

IT SUCKED BEING OUT on her own. It sucked doing it all alone, because Cece flatly refused to take other people's charity—and there were plenty of offers. Bob volunteered to take her in, but Cece declined. He was her boss, after all, not family. She had no family—just a bunch of friends from the San Francisco office who tried to help her out, but whom Cece turned away. She couldn't take their pity.

So Cece paid someone to deliver the furniture she'd put in storage, then called a volunteer organization to help her set it up. And Blain never called. Well, he tried, a few times, but it had been so awkward and miserable, Cece had asked him not to call again. He had anyway. So she'd order caller ID. That took care of that.

She threw herself into her new life, trying desperately to keep the faith. But it was hard. She constantly found bruises on her legs from bumping into furniture, bruises she never felt happen. And then there were the battles with everyday living. Transportation. Shopping.

Breathing.

But she survived, although not without a few tears along the way. She ignored the looks of pity. Ignored the expressions of surprise that turned into embarrassment when people bumped into her chair. Ignored the bright, cheery smile people gave her—too bright, too solicitous. Children were the worst. They hadn't learned the art of duplicity. Their stares were brutal, honest and open. It was through their eyes that she saw herself: Cece, an object of pity. ·

But her lowest point came the day she got herself wedged in a doorway. It sounded funny, sure, but it wasn't when it happened. She'd been trying out a new grocery store, one of those small, neighborhood joints a few blocks from her apartment. Someone had come to her rescue. To be honest, it wasn't the first time she'd gotten herself in such a fix. But as two men helped her out, Cece had felt tears behind her self-deprecating laughter. And when she'd immediately turned to go home, she'd felt those tears fall free. Stupid. Stupid. Stupid. She'd swiped them away. And then she'd pushed herself home, groceries forgotten. Only, when she arrived she stubbed her toe on her way through the front door. Only, see, she couldn't feel it, and that started her laughing, laughter that turned almost hysterical.

She must have freaked out one of her neighbors, because she heard a knock on the door, someone asking, "Are you okay?" And Cece had wanted to yell at him, "No, you stupid idiot. I'm in a wheelchair. I'm *not* okay." Instead she'd called out, "Fine." And then added, "I just stubbed my toe." Which made her laugh all the more because her neighbors all knew she couldn't feel her legs, which made Cece laugh even harder, especially when she envisioned the look on his face.

She'd lost her mind, Cece admitted. Truly lost it.

She'd caught a glimpse of herself in the mirror, wheeled herself over to it without thought. And since she'd lost her mind she could stare at herself objectively.

Oval face. Long blond hair. Eyes red from her brief flirtation with tears. Pathetic.

Someone knocked. The face in the mirror didn't even flinch.

"Really, I'm okay," she called out, though a tear had started to fall down the woman's cheek.

"Cece," she heard from the other side, a woman's voice.

The eyes in the mirror blinked. Hands clenched the wheels of the chair.

"Cece, if you don't open up, I'll get the manager to do it for me."

Bob's wife, Lorna. It had to be. She was one of the few people Cece hadn't scared away yet. Terrific. Just what she needed.

Cece wrenched open the door.

Bill's widow stood there.

Cece's legs didn't work, but if they had, she

would have wilted to the floor. As it was, she sank farther into her wheelchair. "Kate," she said.

"You look like crap."

Cece wanted to laugh, but it would have been hysterical laughter again because she couldn't just couldn't believe the woman was here. After all these years. And at one of the worst possible moments of her life. *What was her dead partner's widow doing here?*

"You look…" Cece eyed her up and down. Nothing had changed about Bill Taylor's wife. Oh, she looked a bit older, maybe a bit worn, but that was it. The blond hair was still the same, as were the crystal-blue eyes. "Good," Cece finished. "You look good."

"May I come in?"

"Actually, this is a bad time." *I'm thinking of committing suicide. Well, not really, but it's tempting—*

"Good. Thanks," Kate said, pushing past her, which was quite a feat given Cece's wheelchair.

"Hey, I'm a little busy here," Cece said.

Kate stopped in the middle of her "family room." "Lord, Cece, if I'd known you were this bad off, I'd have come by sooner. Don't you have someone to clean up after you?"

Okay, so it was pretty bad. Dirty dishes in the kitchen off to her left. Clothes strewn around the floor. Covers and sheets tossed in a heap near the side of her bed, the edge of which was clearly visible from her spot near the door.

"Yeah, well, I can't afford a maid," Cece said, curling her hands in her lap.

"You could if you stopped sending me money."

Cece's gaze jerked to Kate's.

"Yeah, I know. Found out a few months ago, when you were in the hospital the checks stopped coming. I looked into it and *surprise*."

That must have been when her paychecks stopped and her disability kicked in. Cece had wondered if there'd been a lag time, but to be honest, she'd had bigger fish to fry.

"Why didn't you tell me?" asked Kate.

"What was there to tell?" she said with a shrug.

"That you've been supplementing my income for the past five years."

"So?" Cece said, pushing herself toward her kitchen. "Do you want a drink? I'm fresh out of sixty proof, but I might have some forty."

"Cece, don't," Kate said, and Cece could hear the hoarseness in her voice. "Don't."

"Don't what?" she asked, turning toward her with a spin of her chair. Actually, she'd gotten quite good at that. She could probably do pirouettes across the floor.

"Don't act as if it's no big deal. It *is* a big deal."

"Really, Kate, it's not—"

"Don't," she all but shouted, coming toward her. "Don't, Cece," she said, squatting down in front of her. And Cece saw the tears well up in her eyes. They'd been such good friends before Bill's death.

She'd missed her so much. But they'd never recovered from Bill's loss. And now here she was.

"It *is* a big deal," she said softly. "And I can't thank you enough."

The lump in Cece's throat felt as big as the world's largest ball of twine. "You're welcome," she said, wishing she could slip past her, move away, maybe show her to the door. Except that was kind of hard to do when one was in a wheelchair. Aside from mowing Kate down, she was stuck.

"Thank you," Kate said again. "And I'm so sorry," she implored, another tear escaping. "When Bill died I fell apart."

"I know the feeling," Cece said, because she knew where this was going and she wasn't really in the mood to bestow absolution.

"I bet you do," Kate said. "I bet you know exactly what it's like to lose something you'd always thought would be there. Bill was my world. My whole life. I loved him despite the fact that he managed to knock me up five times." She smiled wryly. "When he died, I fell apart. I was used to him going away for weeks at a time, but this was different. This was gone. And then you showed up at my door and I couldn't deal with the fact that you'd survived and he hadn't. I'll admit it, even though I'm not proud of it. You survived and my Bill was…" She looked away for a moment.

But when their gazes met again, all sign of tears had vanished. "I wanted him back, Cece, because despite the ups and downs of our marriage, despite the fact that I absolutely hated his job, in the end I wouldn't have changed a thing about Bill because he was my soul, my life, my love."

She straightened, Cece's head tipping back to follow her up. "And *he* would have hated seeing you like this."

"Like what?" Cece tried to brazen it out.

"Like this," Kate said, flicking a strand of Cece's lank and, all right, dirty hair out of her face.

"So I've let myself go."

"Bob tells me you've closed yourself off in here."

"That's not true. This morning I wedged myself in a grocery-store doorway."

"He said you never get out," Kate said, stepping behind her and grabbing the handles of Cece's wheelchair.

"Hey. Whaddaya think you're doing?"

"Taking you out."

"The hell you are."

"I've got a van waiting outside."

"I'm not going anywhere," Cece said, trying to stop her chair by putting her hands on the wheels.

"Too bad. You are."

"No, I'm—" The words died in her throat as she saw who stood out in the hall. Bob and his wife, Lorna, and two of her former co-workers, each staring down at her in determination, each unwilling to take no for an answer.

"Oh, damn," Cece murmured.

THEY TOOK HER to a riding academy. Cece balked the whole way. She even threatened to make Kate pay back all the money. Kate didn't listen. Neither did Bob and the rest of the gang. And so, against all her protests, Kate and company did what they called an "intervention," forcing Cece up on a damn horse.

Cece didn't want to do it. She hated horses, she told herself. They smelled.

And then the horse took a first step.

Cece felt instantly transformed.

It was like walking again, only...not. Like having her legs back. She felt free. And that was something Cece hadn't felt in a long, long time.

She'd been feeling useless. Somewhere along the way, she'd lost her self-worth. It returned the day she rode.

"Thank you," she later told them all as they wheeled her back to the van.

But it was Kate who leaned down and murmured in her ear, "Thank *you*."

And on that day a friendship was reborn. Kate came over whenever she could, which wasn't that often, what with work and the kids—one in college now. But it was enough.

Before long, Cece went back to work. It was just a desk job, but Cece didn't care. It got her out of the house.

It was the start of a new life. Yeah, it was hard to adapt to work in a wheelchair. But by God, she did it.

The pain began to fade. A little bit at first, but

enough that she began to feel things again. Disappointment, sadness, regret. She missed the physical intimacy with a man, was wise enough to admit she'd likely never have that again. And even though it had been weeks since she'd said goodbye to Blain, it still hurt. Lord, how it hurt.

Then one day she got a call from Lance.

It wasn't unusual to hear from him. They'd kept in touch. Actually, quite a few people from the track called her. Lance, Rebecca Newell, even Barry Bidwell had called to see how she was doing.

"You sitting down?" Lance asked.

That was the thing she liked best about him. He never ceased to make her smile, even when he was making fun of her.

"You know I am, you jerk," she answered with a laugh.

She expected another rude comment, but Lance didn't say a word. And that perplexed Cece enough that she sat up a bit straighter, something that'd gotten easier and easier to do in recent weeks.

"What's up?" she said when almost half a minute went by without Lance saying a word. That was also unusual. "Is everything all right? It's Saturday night. You never call me the night before a race."

"You got cable?" he asked.

"Satellite, actually." And then the oddness of the question struck her. "Why?"

"You need to watch *Raceday*."

"I need to watch—"

The phone disconnected. Cece just looked at the handset in shock. She dialed Lance's cell again, but got his voice mail.

What the heck was going on?

A check of the programming grid revealed the show would air in three hours. They must have done the show live back on the East Coast. Now she'd have to wait till six to watch.

But why did Lance want her to see it? She tried calling some of the other crew members, but none of them answered, something Cece found more and more suspicious.

Was Blain all right?

She shouldn't care, she told herself. If something had happened to him, it was none of her business. But the panic she felt as she checked the Internet for news of Blain Sanders made the thought a total lie. She did still care. Why else did her hands shake?

It was the longest three hours of Cece's life. She tried to fill the time with exercise. There was a special bike she used to exercise her legs and she'd ridden that thing all the way to China by the time six o'clock rolled around.

"Welcome to *Raceday.*"

The familiar words brought another twinge to Cece's gut. She used to watch the show all the time in her fan days. Now it was too painful to watch anything remotely connected to racing.

"I'm Rob Williams, and we're here today with Blain Sanders of Sanders Racing and his driver,

Lance Cooper," said the twenty-something host, a guy with a fake-bake tan and slicked-back hair. "Blain, let's start with you."

There he was. And the moment she saw him again, Cece knew she'd sold herself a pack of lies. She wasn't over him. She *couldn't* be over him. Not when it felt as if her whole body was hit by an electric shock when she saw him on the TV screen. Not when her breath caught in her throat as they zoomed in for a close-up. Not when just seeing him brought back every tender moment, every funny moment, every not-so-funny moment, just by looking into his blue eyes.

Oh, God.

"Blain," Rob Williams said. "It must be a bit surreal to find yourself leading the points race after the wild start your team got earlier in the year."

Blain gave the host an ironic half smile, nodding a bit as he said, "It wasn't the best."

"It was unreal," the host said. "Your license pulled, someone trying to kill you, that deal at Atlanta Motor Speedway."

She watched Blain closely, and so she saw perfectly when his face tightened, his smile freezing in place.

"How did you recover from all that and then get it together enough to start winning races?"

"Luck."

A cameraman focused on Rob Williams, showing the wry look he shot the viewers. "Bull," he said.

"All right then, hard work. After what happened

in Atlanta we put everything behind us and moved on," Blain said.

And for some reason, Cece didn't think Blain was talking about his race team.

"But how?" the host asked.

Blain shrugged. "When bad things happen, it makes you see life in a different light. Makes you change. I think our whole team changed after that."

The host nodded, then said, "Rumor has it that you loaned your home to one of the FBI agents injured in Atlanta, at least for a short while. Is that true?"

Cece's hands flexed. So did Blain's. She could see his knuckles whiten for a second as he rested his fists atop a checkerboard counter.

"It's true. She was there for nearly two months."

Rob Williams's blond brows rose. "That was a pretty cool thing to do."

"It was the least I could do, Rob. I was in love with the woman."

Silence. And though she had a feeling it wasn't easy to do, the host looked blown away.

"In love with her?" And then you could practically see the cogs of the host's mind turn. "What's this? Do I sense a story?"

Pain sliced into her palms. Her nails. She'd clenched her fists too hard.

"There's no story to tell except I was an ass and I let her go."

"You sure were an ass," Lance said. The camera zoomed in the driver's face. "Blain was a total jerk."

"I was."

"I almost quit driving for him," Lance said.

Because of her? Cece hadn't known about that.

"I would have understood," Blain said.

"Cece deserved better," Lance insisted.

"Cece—is that her name?" the host asked.

And Cece couldn't believe it. She was having one of those out-of-body experiences. It was some other Cece they were talking about on national television.

"That's her name," Lance was saying. "She was an old high school flame of Blain's."

"She was never a flame," Blain corrected. "But in hindsight, I would have been smart to snap her up."

"What's the story here, guys?"

Blain looked at Rob, and as calm as you please, relayed the details of how they'd met. Cece sat in her chair, dumbstruck, as he regaled the studio and the viewing audience with everything. The fact that they'd strayed completely off the topic of racing didn't seem to matter to anyone.

"And then she got hurt," the host said when Blain talked about Atlanta.

"And it was my fault," Blain admitted.

"That couldn't have been easy to deal with."

Blain shook his head. "It wasn't. She was so vibrant, so full of life—and then she wasn't anymore."

Vibrant? Full of life? She sounded like a shampoo commercial.

"But the worst of it was," Blain was saying, "I never told a soul about us. A few people guessed, but after Atlanta, I let everyone think we were strangers."

Was that true? Cece had been in such a void in the months following the accident, she hadn't paid a lick of attention to the press. Had he played their relationship off like it was nothing more than a friendship? Apparently so.

"And she deserved better than that. She's an amazing woman."

"Man," Rob said. "I feel like Jerry Springer."

"Can I be the one who hits him?" Lance asked, waving a fist at Blain. Laughter off-camera. Cece hardly heard it. Blain stared into the camera, stared at *her.*

"Well, Blain, since we've regressed to trash TV, I may as well ask. If Cece's watching, is there anything you want to say?"

It felt as if every organ in her body stopped working. She couldn't move—well, she couldn't really, anyway, but that was nothing compared to how she felt now.

"I'd tell her I was sorry," Blain said at last. "And that I love her. And that she's the sexiest woman in the world to me. I've always thought that, even when I was too scared to touch her. And that's why I let her go—fear. I was afraid things would be different, and I didn't want to face that." He blinked a few times as he stared into her eyes.

There was silence in the studio. Not even the host moved for a couple of seconds. Then he grabbed a stack of papers in front of him, tapped the edges and said, "Well, okay then. Cece, if you're watching, and you're in a position to call back the hit man you sent after Blain Sanders, you better get in touch with this guy."

"What about me?" Lance complained. "Don't I get to say something to her?"

"No one wants to hear what you've got to say," Rob quipped back.

The silence in the studio was once again broken by laughter. But Blain didn't laugh. He never once looked away, never once cracked a smile as he stared into the camera, into her eyes….

Will you forgive me?

God help her, Cece wanted to.

BLAIN FELT THE ODD LOOKS the whole way to the garage. It wasn't so much that people were laughing at him, it was more like they watched him.

Watching for what?

Granted, word had probably spread about his botched interview. The president of the Fortune 500 company that now sponsored his car even called to say he'd been watching. But to Blain's shock, instead of reading him the riot act, the man had wished him luck.

Maybe that's why everyone was looking at him so strangely, Blain thought as he headed toward his hauler parked along the edge of the garage. The race was scheduled to start in less than an hour. Race fans already swelled the stands, the pre-race entertainment already under way. Blain glimpsed some dignitary being driven around the mile oval.

He was late. Normally he liked to be at the track first thing on race day, but today his heart hadn't been in it.

She hadn't called.

Granted, he didn't even know if she'd been watching. It was ridiculous to assume she kept track of him. But there'd still been that hope.

"Gonna be a good day," his crew chief, Mike Johnson, said with an optimistic smile. Blain was surprised to see him at the hauler instead of at their pit stall. "I can feel it in me bones."

"Let's hope so," Blain said, looking down the long aisle of the big rig. "Lance at the driver's meeting?"

"Actually, he's in the lounge. Told me to tell you he needs to speak with you if you should happen to show up."

What now? The kid had been pretty easy to work with lately, but drivers were a fickle bunch, prone to drastic personality changes the higher their stars climbed. Lance's had been launched into deep space. Still, Blain liked the kid and appreciated the fact that he hadn't given him grief after yesterday's show.

But when he reached the step that led to the lounge, Blain happened to look to his right, and the sight of the wheelchair sitting there nearly brought him to his knees. It lay against the side door, the aluminum frame gouged with wear marks, the tires dotted with tiny pebbles and grains of sand.

Cece.

He shoved the door open, hardly daring to hope, hardly daring to believe....

And there she sat, her beautiful green eyes wide. The sight of her sitting at the black Formica table, her hands resting calmly on its surface, didn't seem real. How could it be, when the only times he'd seen her in recent months had been in his dreams? When the image of her face had been so overpowering at times that he'd had to physically restrain himself from picking up the phone and calling her?

Bob and Lorna had told him she was fine.

By the look of her, they hadn't been lying. She looked better than good. She looked fabulous. And as he took in her stunning green eyes, her long, blond hair loose over her shoulders, he realized he was on the verge of tears. Again.

"You came," he said.

"I came," she echoed.

"You look good," he said, because he didn't really know what to say to her. One of the drawbacks of having asked for absolution on national TV.

"You, too," she replied.

They stared. Neither of them moved. Of course, only one of them could.

"Jeesh," a disgusted voice said from behind him. "Do I have to kiss her *for* you?"

"Lance," Blain said over his shoulder, "get out of here."

"I will," his driver said. "But you better get a move on. We've got a race to run."

Blain reached behind him and closed the door in the kid's face.

Cece laughed that familiar, wonderful laugh of hers he'd fallen in love with, and suddenly everything was all right.

"Cece," he said, tears stinging his eyes. "Oh, God, Cece, I've missed you."

"I've missed you, too," she said, answering tears in her own eyes.

And then he went to her and pulled her gently into his arms, reached down and kissed her, and as he did, he wondered how the hell he could have ever been afraid to touch her. She was the miracle in his life. The woman who'd showed him the meaning of courage. Who'd fought for her independence in a way that filled him with awe. Who'd proved to him that love wasn't about physical intimacy, it was about the heart. She owned his heart, and he couldn't believe he'd let her go.

"I'm sorry," he said, his arms tightening around her so much that he worried he might hurt her. "I'm so sorry."

He felt her head move, but not away from him. No, she nestled closer, the smell of her hair a sweet essence that he'd missed in recent weeks.

"I don't know what happened."

"You behaved like a jerk," she said in her forthright way.

"I did," he admitted, drawing back. "I did, and I'm sorry." He swiped a lock of hair away from her face. "I'm so, so sorry."

"But I behaved like a coward long before you behaved like a jerk."

"Nah," he said, suddenly feeling magnanimous.

"Yes, Blain, I did. I was afraid of falling in love with you. Afraid of laying it all on the line. But someone recently told me that she never regretted marrying the man she loved, even though she lost him. He was an FBI agent, and she knew that going in, but she wasn't afraid to love him like I was afraid to love you. I'm sorry for that."

"You don't have to be sorry. You're here now."

He waited for her to acknowledge his words. But she didn't move, and for a second fear rose in his throat.

"Cece?" he asked.

"I need to know that this isn't about guilt, Blain. I need to know you aren't saying this stuff out of pity."

"Pity," he said, touching her face, dragging a thumb down her cheek. "You think this is pity?"

And then he kissed her, kissed her in a way that only a man who desired a woman could kiss, touched her as he touched her in his fantasies. Only this fantasy woman was real, breathed her essence into him, sighed when their tongues met.

"If this is pity, Cece," he said against her lips, "than I hope I go on feeling sorry for you the rest of our lives."

And that was the moment Cece lost control. God, she'd told herself she wouldn't cry. But when she looked up and saw the passion in Blain's eyes, when she felt the echo of his rapid heartbeat against her chest, when she saw that his hands shook as he swiped at a lock of her hair, she did so, anyway. But it was a good kind of crying, the kind that erased old wounds, that brought peace, and contentment.

Blain held her.

The world was all right.

"Will you marry me, Cece?" he asked, his own voice hoarse, as if he'd been silently crying along with her in that odd way men had, as if by making noise they would be considered less masculine.

Will you marry me?

"Before I answer, I have something to show you."

And watching how his expression turned from curiosity to sudden concern as she shifted her legs off the edge of the couch, to a look of unmistakable hope, nearly made Cece cry all over again.

"Watch," she said, pushing him away.

Blain stood up and Cece scooted to the edge. Using the table and the back of the couch, she pushed herself up just as she'd practiced a hundred times before. Slowly, ever so slowly, she straightened, then gently let go.

There were tears in her eyes again as she said, "A

month ago I started to get some feeling back in my legs. At first I was afraid to hope. But the doctors, they confirmed...."

And they were both crying as she swayed there. But she didn't stand by herself for long. She swayed toward Blain, who looked only too happy to pull her into the shelter of his arms.

"So, yes, I'll marry you, Blain Sanders," she said, tears making her vision blur. "But not before I can walk down the aisle on my own."

He smiled, sheltering in her in his arms. "I have no doubt that you will, Cece. No doubt at all."

And one year later...she did.

EPILOGUE

ONE HUNDRED THOUSAND FANS came to their feet at
Phoenix International Raceway as the thirty-five car
field made the final lap.

Actually, they watched only the front two cars.

Lance Cooper, Cup racing's brightest star, raced
side by side with the number thirty-two car, Lance's
brightly painted red-and-orange front bumper barely
in front of the other.

"Careful," the spotter's voice said in his ear.

I am, I am, Lance thought as he gripped the steering wheel, trying hard to maintain control. Tires
were old. Too much scuff on the top line. Might
have been a bad move…

His back end pitched.

"Son of a bitch."

The crowd roared. Odd as it seemed, Lance could
hear them, could feel their energy and excitement as
he fought to maintain control.

He let his car drift down…in front of the thirty-
two car.

The flagman waved the checker.

Quarter mile to go.

An eighth.

A tenth.

Finish line.

"Whoo whoo!" AllenMike said, the sound of his crew yelling in the background. "We *did* it!"

Yeah, they had.

He'd just won his first championship.

"Blain there?" Lance asked, the track in front of him suddenly shimmering.

"Here," came his boss's familiar voice.

"This is for you and Cece," he said, feeling the tears hit the edge of his asbestos fire mask. The bitch of it was, he couldn't wipe them away. But, hell, he didn't care.

"We know, Lance," Blain said. "We know."

And in the pits, Blain looked over at Cece, who stared out at the track in between hugs from his crew, awe on her face as she looked up at the screaming fans.

"We did it," he telegraphed to her.

Oddly, she seemed to hear him. She met his gaze and mouthed back. "We did it."

And never, not once, had Blain believed this could happen. Two years ago he'd been struggling to put his team back together after Randy's murder, with no sponsor, a new driver and a fiancée who refused to marry him until she could walk. And then this year... Blain swallowed as he looked up at the sky. Cece had married him. She'd walked down the aisle, smiled into his eyes and said, "I do," in front of racing's finest and half the FBI, people who had become good friends.

He felt her arms wrap around him, arms that just a year before wouldn't have been able to reach him without the help of her wheelchair. Now she was walking again, working, even undercover...although she'd been recently offered a job heading up the stock car association's security, a job he was pretty certain she was going to take.

"Cece," he murmured. And even though they both wore headsets, even though she probably couldn't hear him, he heard her answer back, felt the rumble of her voice against his chest.

"Blain..."

Just then a reporter came up to them and a TV camera was shoved in their faces. Blain removed his headset, though he kept one arm firmly around Cece.

"Blain Sanders, what an incredible year," the commentator said.

"Got that right, Dick."

"Did you ever think at the beginning of the season that this is where you'd end up?"

"It was always a possibility," Blain said, looking down at Cece, who'd removed her own headset. They caught each other's eyes and smiled.

"This is a pretty neat wedding present," Dick said to Cece. "Wouldn't you say?"

"Oh, I don't know," she replied, giving the reporter a mysterious smile. "I might have a wedding present that's even better."

"Oh, yeah? What's that?" he asked.

But Cece didn't answer. Instead, she looked into Blain's eyes.

And he knew.

"Cece?" he asked, in front of a million viewers.

"If it's a boy, I think we'll name him Randy," she said softly, the tears that had been in her eyes since Lance crossed the finish line rolling down her cheeks.

"Am I understanding this right?" Dick asked. "Are you two expecting?"

Cece's smile was suddenly blinding as she answered, "We are."

Blain barely heard the reporter; he was too busy pulling his wife toward him.

"Why didn't you tell me sooner?"

"Maybe I'm not the only Sanders who likes to announce things on television."

He hugged her as tightly as he dared without crushing her, and then he laughed. His crew slapped him on the back, word having spread of their good news. Someone showered them with something— water, champagne, Blain didn't know. He didn't care. He was too busy kissing his wife, too busy getting lost in the taste of her.

"Happy?" she asked when they drew apart.

"Happy," he answered back with a soft smile.

"Good," she said, snuggling into his arms.

And then he turned her to face their crew, face the people they loved…face their future.

* * * * *

CENTURIES AGO existed a silver ore so pure, so unique, that the skills of three noble families were needed to forge it. "The Lords of Silverton," they were called, their wealth and power surpassed by none.

But greed, as it often does, plays a part in this tale—for the glittering silver ore would prove to be their ruin. A Celtic priestess came to them, demanding some of the magnificent metal in tribute. But the lords would give none away, for they considered their silver too precious for mere pagans. Furious, the witch called down a curse upon their heads. Each lord would lose something invaluable to him, something personal and far more costly than the cold, lifeless ore. Honor, faith, courage—these things would they lose, not only in their own lives, but in succeeding generations, never to be recovered again unless they sought and gained the help of a woman who, like the priestess, came from a far-away land.

And thus the curse came to pass. The mine they

so coveted became flooded, the silver ore covered by a layer of water as cold as their hearts. And as foretold, the families lost the things most precious to them—their fortunes, their power, their prestige—all because they had lost honor, courage and faith in each other.

For centuries the curse would hold, and would likely have continued but for a trio of devilish lords on the brink of ruin. Their adventures set to swirling the ancient tendrils of the curse, and as luck would have it, they would find redemption and love in the arms of three daring women from distant America. Women as untamed and wild as the place they called home...women fated to tame the Lords of Silverton.

London, 1818

THROUGHOUT HISTORY, some men have been gifted scholars. Others have gone on to make great discoveries. Some have virtually changed the world.

The Duke of Lynford would do none of these things. Marcus Lucas Sutherton was, however, a *fabulous* lover...or so his reputation claimed him to be.

Which was how, Marcus reasoned, he found himself in bed with Lady Parkmoore. How he found himself looking up at her as she straddled him—an occurrence for which he was rather grateful, given the woman's rather wide girth—the velvet-smooth white linens that covered his bed, thankfully, between her legs and his. And how he found himself asking in a wry voice, "You would like me to cup you *where?*"

Giving him a tight smile, her ladyship reached out and clasped first one of his hands and then the other, indicating that he should place them over those breasts that had nurtured a trio of Parkmoore heirs— and had the size to prove it.

"Are you certain?" he asked with an arch of his brows. Gads, he might have trouble lifting the things.

Lady Parkmoore's matronly face pulled into a grimace of determination. "Quite."

"Very well," he sighed, doing as instructed. But when he looked up at her, he tried not to laugh at the way she stiffened when his hands cupped her breasts. Granted, those breasts were covered by her frilly, rather frumpy night rail, but he could still feel her warmth seeping through the material, which meant *she* could feel the coolness of his hands.

She gritted her teeth…he could hear them. Having second thoughts, was she?

"My lady, we do not have to go through with this."

She frowned, and the expression—combined with middling brown hair ravaged by static electricity—contrived to give her a somewhat Medusa-like appearance. "Indeed we do, Your Grace, for I expect my husband to arrive at any moment, as I had someone tell him—"

"*Felicia,*" a masculine voice roared, the bedroom door thrust open with enough force to fan the flames in the grate like a miniature circle of hell.

Ah, the husband. Right on cue. And thank God. Marcus's legs were growing numb.

Marcus regarded his bed partner, a woman who was not, nor would ever be, his lover. She was far too mature to suit his jaded tastes. Still, he'd not minded complying with her wish to be caught in a compromising situation. Games of revenge were ever entertaining, especially when they involved a woman with three children, a sterling reputation and a husband old enough to be Marcus's father.

"Dickie!" she gasped, flicking her loose hair over her shoulder as she swiveled to face her outraged lord.

"Why, you little harlot," Dickie cried, swinging his walking stick through the air with a *whap-whap-whap* of fury. Gray hair mussed, he planted both stick and feet on the blue-and-white carpet with such force that Marcus felt certain the servants below stairs were now staring at the ceiling. "And with Lynford! Of all the disreputable young pups. Felicia, how *could* you?"

Felicia lurched off of the young pup in question, who sighed with relief.

"How could I?" she asked, as Marcus shuffled back on the pillows to watch the show. Damme, but his toes tingled.

"*You* were the first in this marriage to take a lover," she said, her hands clenched. "And rumor has it there may be more."

"Lovers? What nonsense is this?"

To give the man credit, Lord Parkmoore looked stunned by the accusation. Marcus leaned over and plucked an apple from a bowl.

"Lady Catharine," Felicia said with a toss of her head. "*And* the Countess of Lockford."

"At the same time?" Marcus asked, apple poised before his mouth. Neither of them heard, which was a pity because he was rather curious. Lady Catharine had bedded men other than the effeminate Lord Chalmers, to be sure—but he'd never heard of her bedding a woman before. If he had, it might have made his own tryst with her last week more interesting.

But Lord Parkmoore didn't look the least bit mortified. Indeed, he looked rather disgusted, his black jacket all but popping open under the force of his puffed-out chest. Marcus worried that his buttons might launch themselves from the fabric like tiny cannonballs.

"Why, the woman is young enough to be my daughter."

"Does that matter?" Lady Parkmoore asked. "It has never stopped a man before. What is more, I saw your carriage before the woman's home with mine own two eyes."

Tsk-tsk, Marcus thought, taking a bite of his apple. Parkmoore should learn the art of subterfuge.

"When did you see this?" asked Dickie.

"Tuesday last, the night you were supposed to be at your club."

Marcus lifted the apple again. Tuesday. Why, that was the very night he himself had been with the lady in quest—

The fruit froze between his teeth.

"I *was* at my club that night," Parkmoore said.

Was that the night? Marcus wondered. Truth be told, most evenings blended into the next. Still, he was almost certain....

"Liar," Felicia accused again.

"Do not call me that," his lordship huffed. "Half a dozen of my chums saw me at White's."

White's? Marcus thought. It would have to be White's. What an ironic twist of fate.

"You think I would believe your friends?" Lady Parkmoore asked with a sniff of disdain.

"Perhaps you should," Marcus interjected.

Both Felicia and Parkmoore looked his way, his lordship's face taking on a sudden, evangelical glow of fire and brimstone. "You," he hissed, brandishing his walking stick. "You, sir, shall meet me at Potter's Field!"

"Do not be ridiculous," Marcus said, slipping from the bedsheets.

"Lynford," Lady Parkmoore gasped, and not because of his lack of attire. No, she cried out because she knew well and good that "Dickie" would see that Marcus was fully dressed.

"What the devil?" Dickie's gaze slipped downward. "Why, you wear boots!"

"I was concerned I might have to run," Marcus said, "in the event you held a pistol."

Lord Parkmoore looked even more aghast—and confused. "Felicia, what in blazes is the meaning of this?"

Felicia crossed her arms. "I set it up," she admitted with a lift of her chin, her night rail rising a bit to expose puffy ankles. "I approached the duke at the Sotherbys' ball. When he learned what I had planned, he was only too happy to pretend a tryst with me."

Her husband again swung his gaze toward Marcus. "Pretend? Why, you—"

Marcus held out a hand, his signet ring catching the firelight. "Do not attack me, Lord Parkmoore, for I am half your age and I will take great delight in snapping that stick in two." He turned toward Lady Parkmoore. "Madam, it appears as if I owe you an apology."

"You?" she said with a confused fluttering of her lashes. "I should think—"

He held up a hand again. "It was *I* who visited Lady Catharine Tuesday last."

Now it was Lady Parkmoore's turn to look flummoxed.

"I took your husband's carriage."

"You *what?*" Parkmoore bellowed.

"Took it. Well, borrowed it, at any rate. 'Tis a trick of mine. I bribe coachmen to let me use their masters' carriages while they are otherwise occupied— for example, at their clubs." He smiled widely. "Goodness knows Lady Catharine is a harlot, but she *is* unmarried."

Felicia gave him a wide-eyed stare. Dickie did, too.

"Let me see if I understand," Lord Parkmoore said. "You borrow gentlemen's carriages in order to have assignations with unmarried women?"

"I do."

Parkmoore appeared ready to box him in the ears, and the look was especially convincing given the man's age.

"Then 'twas *you* at Lady Catharine's?" Lady Parkmoore asked.

"It was."

Her ladyship stepped forward. Marcus wondered if she would thank him for saving her marriage with his confession, not that that might have been a favor. Most marriages were tedious affairs. Witness this couple—

The lady slugged him.

"I say," Lynford said, clutching his ringing left ear. "What the devil did you do that for?"

Lady Parkmoore shook her hand in pain, but she didn't look away as she said, "Because you, duke, are the most disgusting, disreputable debaucher it has ever been my misfortune to meet."

Marcus lifted his brows. "That's not what you thought the other night when you asked for my help."

"How many marriages have you destroyed because of your machinations?" she demanded, ignoring his question.

Truth be told, Marcus had never given that much thought.

"I know for certain Wakeford was accused of an affair he swears he did not have," Parkmoore said.

Marcus looked from husband to wife, wondering when his situation had gone from mildly amusing to rather precarious.

"Lord and Lady Wakeford are now living in separate homes," her ladyship pronounced. "In separate *countries.*"

Marcus's brows lifted at that. "Really?"

"I wonder how many more would come to light

if we were to begin probing?" Lady Parkmoore mused, her face turning rather angrier than before, which was saying quite a lot. "You very nearly ruined *my* marriage." She turned to her husband. "Marriage to the man I love."

"*Felicia,*" Lord Parkmoore muttered fervently, taking her hand and lifting it to his mouth.

"Lovely," Marcus said. "Now that we've kissed and made up, I wonder if I might have my room back?"

The couple drew apart. Lady Parkmoore's eyes narrowed. "I think not. You, sir, have much to answer for."

A chill crawled down Marcus's spine, as if a thousand condemned men danced upon his back. *Uh-oh.* "I do?"

She nodded her head. "Indeed, and I am thinking it will be my pleasure to make you pay for the trouble you've caused."

"*I* caused?"

"I would never have had the courage to approach you were it not for your disreputable reputation."

"And so this is now my fault?" he asked. Lord, how women befuddled him.

"No more assignations using other people's carriages," she said.

"I beg your pardon?"

"No more trysts," she added. "If I hear of one more woman associated with your name, *one more,* I shall tell people far and wide what game it is you've been playing at."

"Absurd," he said, looking to her husband for support. The man merely gave him a stony glare, crossing his arms for good measure.

"Not absurd at all," Lady Parkmoore said. "For I am determined to stop your philandering ways before you destroy someone else's marriage."

"And how do you intend to do that?" he asked in disbelief.

"Blackmail, my lord."

"Blackmail?" he repeated.

"Indeed. If you do not behave, I will tell Lady Catharine's father what you have been up to."

Marcus gave a snort. "Half the male population of London has been with Lady Catharine. Gads, her own *footman* has been with her."

"Her father will not care," Lady Parkmoore replied. "He's been looking to foist her off. You will do nicely. Only think, duke, you need to marry, and marry well. All of society knows of your desperate financial straits, of what you've risked trying to develop your silly silver mine. Should your mining venture fail, you will need to marry well…but how will you do that if no one will have you?"

Her eyes narrowed as she delivered the final blow. "You will behave, my lord, because if you do not, I will see you ruined."

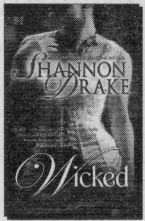